Shoe Burnin' Season:
A Womanifesto

9-21-19

Judy – for a "woman of a certain age" – I hope you enjoy – Suzanne

Shoe Burnin' Season:
A Womanifesto

By R. P. Saffire

R.P. Saffire

With an introduction by Suzanne Hudson

Suzanne Hudson

Front cover art, *Pizazz* by Fidelis/Linda Perry-Ledet

Back cover art, wine glass, by Kevin D'Amico

Tech support, Taylor Michael D'Amico

Introduction
By Suzanne Hudson

This has to be one of the more bizarre tales in literary lore. And I am sincerely honored to have been asked to write an introduction for it, for my dear, dear friend and fellow author, Ruby Pearl Saffire. I would be remiss if I did not make you aware that the substance of this remarkable tale consists of the grotesquely aberrant—yet it is exquisitely relatable. It is both hilarious and heartbreaking. I am tasked, in introducing *Shoe Burnin' Season: A Womanifesto*, with making you want to read about, well . . . a laugh-out-loud, side-splitting train wreck.

But first . . . about a shoe burnin' . . . it is a tradition that we (my friends and I) launched back in the 1970s, out in a cow field, in a ramshackle farm house, on a frigid night. When the host began throwing shoes in the fireplace (rather than braving the cold to fetch wood), those of us in attendance (yes, I was an original shoe burner) began making up stories about the shoes, the symbolism, the poignancy of letting them go. Fast forward to the 21st century when we revived the tradition out at Waterhole Branch, near Fairhope, Alabama, holding shoe burnin's whenever the mood strikes us, and we have declared shoe burnin' season to be anytime between Halloween and Fat Tuesday. And yes, R.P. Saffire took her title from that tradition, symbolically I believe, which is to say that shoe burnin' season really *is* a season of "letting go," which in reality can be anytime it is needed to be.

For her, though, the "letting go" has been pretty much excruciating. Let me explain:

Ruby Pearl Sapphire's first manuscript began in whimsy and free-spiritedness, ferried along by her carefree soul, wholeheartedly engaged in the written word and the pursuit of publication. She was genuine, still is, and earnest and bawdy and politically incorrect and god-awful funny. Our paths first crossed back in 2007, re-crossing many times over the next couple of years, a sure sign of some kind of sublime energy in the ether. I adored her immediately. She was slightly my elder, thus I refer to her as "my little old lady friend, Miss Ruby." She exuded such a light, a playfulness, along with an enviable stubbornness, the sheer will to find her niche in the ever-changing writing biz. I tried to warn her, about the buzzards and such, but she would not be deterred. As a result, unfortunately, her world became a trifle darker, when the hammer dropped, in 2009.

It is now nine years since then. It has been quite a lengthy recovery for Miss Ruby, but she has grown into her art—one either grows from trauma or retreats into it. You will see for yourself, within these pages, a slight contrast from then until now, the gestating transformation of her phrasings. And with her next book, *The Fall of the Nixon Administration*, a comic novel that I'm salivating over, as a co-author, due out within the year, you'll see an obvious change of attitude and a seriously new-found gravitas. And all because of a toxic waste dump of a woman, whom she names flat-out in the book but to whom I will merely refer as "Annie Wilkes."

We've all know an Annie Wilkes, an emotional arsonist with an affinity for drama, a woman whose energy screams, like that *Lost in Space* robot, "Danger! Danger!" Your gut roils, your neck hairs rise, and you *almost* know you should be running like hell, like a politician on steroids, to escape that pull, that lure, that unthinkable part of the human psyche we are loathe to acknowledge: evil.

But is there really any such thing as "evil"? Yes, it's a loaded word, and some folks think it is nothing beyond that. But I say it's sort of like really good art—hard to define, but you know it when you see it. Or, like Miss Ruby, sometimes you have to hang it on the wall and get used to the lines, textures, and colors, before you can really decide if it's for you or not. Yet art can't *really* betray you, give you a proper back-stabbing, like an Annie Wilkes, who exhales on the blade, huffing thrice, and gives it a good and proper shining, on her sleeved forearm, before finding her mark, right between your shoulder blades. Evil enough for you?

Here's the thing: one really does want to look for the good, in everyone, and I'm optimistic enough that I can find it, the vast and overwhelming majority of the time. For example, maybe Annie is truly ill, mentally; that would be "forgiven," would it not? Problem is, Annie Wilkes fits so many pages in the DSM-V that it's hard to know which "diagnoses" to apply—that is the frustration that moves me to use the "e" word. Can one really be a walking, talking, example of so many mental disorders, all at once? She absolutely, bullet point for bullet point, meets just about every descriptor of the "Cluster B" personality disorders: borderline (one of the toughest nuts to crack), histrionic, and narcissistic personality disorder. Or is she just your garden variety sociopath? All of the above? Does it even really matter, given the scorched-earth rendering of a perfectly lovely little old lady's life? Who cares what lies behind such a vindictive soul? And I just referenced a soul, which, in Annie's case, is either nonexistent or is as wretched as her heart of darkness. Which brings me back around to that "e" word again.

At any rate the damage was done, so you decide. Take a look at Miss Ruby's life, pre- and post- Annie. Look at the original manuscript, which was embraced and subsequently sabotaged by the machinations of said sociopath. It was a gem—an unlikely mish-mash of memoir, poetry, social commentary, and self-help, a "sure thing" according to Annie, before she did the deed. Yet here is the bittersweet irony: Annie might have temporarily succeeded in wreaking havoc in a sweet little old lady's life, but she ultimately succeeded in making our dear Ruby a markedly better writer. You see, Miss Ruby knew her original book was a lot of fluff—ingenious and funny as it was—destined to do well at the box office. That is, commercially. And it was on track to do just that, when the rug was snatched, which was the beginning of a very long, sometimes lonely shoe burnin' season for Miss Ruby—nine winters' worth.

Context matters. 2009 was a lifetime ago, in our country, in our culture. With the election of the first African-American president came an infusion of optimism in the face of an economic crash, almost defiantly so. Back then, the female experience was subverted enough that Ruby's play on the word "slut" would have been seen as caustically funny. The #metoo movement was gestating and would be carried for years before its birthing, not long ago. The harassment called "slut shaming" was nonexistent. Miss Ruby will, indeed, address these two worlds-apart zeitgeists, but asks that you read the words of her original manuscript in the context of the time—2009. What a difference nearly a decade makes, politically, socially, in every way. I have pointed out that this is an aberrant tale; do we live in aberrant times? These days feel uncertain at best, with our darker angels circling like birds of prey, while we seem to be waiting . . . does history tell us to wait? What will the outrageous R.P. Saffire have to say about these outrageous times?

I hope I have not painted too depressing a picture here—this tale is the flip side of depressing; it is uplifting, joyful. Because ultimately, Miss Ruby did what most of us do—got up, dusted herself off, and began to let it go, word by word, phrase by phrase, a la shoe burnin' season. Then, because she is talented and highlarious, she did what most of us cannot do, via her mighty pen, proceeded to dish up serving after serving of sweet, sweet revenge—not in a mean-spirited way (well, not much), but in a coming-back-from-the-betrayed, tongue-kind-of-in-cheek, in-your-face-funny kind of way, which is on much higher moral ground that any high ground an Annie Wilkes could ever reach (and she'd better be wearing her rock climbing gear). If one has no insight, one cannot really have a sense of humor about oneself—and if we can't laugh at our flaws, our inadequacies, or, as Miss Ruby says, "our big ol' hairy warts," then where is the humanity? R.P. Saffire knows that laughter brings warmth, nourishes insight, feeds the spirit. She knows that giggles grow the soul in ways exponential. Miss Ruby, who loves Jesus and Buddha and all things spiritual, knows that, in the end, it is humor that sustains us—in fact, humor is our ultimate salvation.

Prepare to be saved.

And if you want to cut to the chase, flip on over to Chapter 1.

SECOND SLUTHOOD;

BEING A MANIFESTO FOR THE POST-MENOPAUSAL, PRE-SENILIC MATRIARCH

by Ruby Pearl Saffire. Copyright @ 2009.

Cover and interior illustrations (in the first edition paperback) by Nancy Raia
Cover art for the second edition by Linda Perry Ledet/Fidelis and Kevin D'Amico
Cover layout: Jamie, at PostNet
http://www.postnet.com/al108

A Disclaimer of Sorts:

A Romantic Dedication:

For my favorite author and someday to-be lover (once I have run my course with the current one), A. J. Waters

A Brassy Epigraph:

"If you are offended by anything in this book then you are in *dire* need of being offended. Trust me. You have one foot in the grave. Let's extricate that sucker!"

—R.P.S.

Addendum to Disclaimer: Please be ever-aware that the first paperback edition of this manifesto was **not self-published**, so you can rest assured it had skillful editing (unfortunately an unedited version went to the printer, by mistake, or was it sabotage? Welcome to the cutthroat world of publishing)—BUT, my editor does not speak French. Therefore, you will find a tiny smattering of French that is spelled not so much correctly as it is spelled as I imagine it to be (you see, once upon a time my bizarro bipolar mother would go weeks and weeks speaking nothing but French, so some of that language lodged deep down in my emotionally bruised brain; those manic times of hers were so traumatic to me that I cannot bear the idea of wading into the world of Parisian words long enough to research spellings—but I digress, as my warped and whacked-out childhood shall be covered within the covers of my next book, a novel). Also in the area of spellage, I tend to play with these words we humans sometimes take a bit seriously, so be aware that I do, indeed, know the difference between a tenet and a tenant. *You* decide why I might have chosen which-a-one of the aforementioned spellage. Yes, this book is the real deal (as in, R.P. Saffire is not some egomaniacal hack who knows a little bit about a lot of things and thinks the world is salivating after her words). It was published in 2009; however, due to our homeland's economic woes, and more exclusively due to the aforementioned sabotage, was never officially "debuted" or promoted or reviewed (much) or shipped to many bookstores. Such is the biz. *The Bestseller That Never Was*, by me.

Yours,
Ruby

Preface

I do so love these prefaces and forewords and such! They are bibliophilic accessories, if you will—librarial augmentations that accentuate the body of work proper. As you come to know me within these literary leaves, you will see that my sense of appreciation is all about living large—not monetarily/wastefully, but a taking in of all of living. Ergo, my book was not about to be without any and every piece of every vivisection of said book.

That said, the anticipation of writing a Conclusion, an Afterword, a Post Script, and Acknowledgements is nothing short of an approaching Climax.

(But if you want to cut to the chase, as my authoresse friend and introduction writer, Suzanne Hudson suggested, flip on over to Chapter 1; after all, you are driving this train. And yes, it will be wrecking, post haste . . .)

R. P. S.

A Dazzling Foreword

Red, White, and Blue

In the years since 9-11 there has been a lot of shouting, name-calling, and grappling for the high moral ground of being "patriotic." Name-calling and grappling, however, in no way make one a patriot; I, with my jewel of a patriotic *nomme*, Ruby (red) Pearl (white) Saffire (blue—even though I did alter the spelling) should know.

My name is only that which *signifies* me; it is not who I *am*.

Likewise, cheap insults and hypocrisy are not patriotic in the least; they are empty words and gestures. Nor is it automatically "patriotic" to fly a flag from one's front porch, wear a flag lapel pin, or in any like manner advertise, via bumper sticker or car magnet, one's "patriotism." Symbolism and substance are two entirely different creatures.

Genuine patriotism of the good, red-blooded variety consists of fulfilling three basic duties. First, one must **inform** oneself, for a stupid populace is easily fooled and likely to enable despots or dictators (and it's bye-bye, democracy). Secondly, one must **engage** in the political process, i.e., vote, on all levels. Finally, it is imperative that one be willing to make sacrifices for one's country. When one poses the question to oneself: How have I **served** the good old U. S. of A? then one must be able to rattle off an impressive list.

This book allows you, the reader, to participate in the doing of all three: **inform, engage, serve**. As

20

there is a good bit of information, along with lively political and social commentary within these pages, well—no-brainer on the first two, eh? I would wager it's that "**serve**" thing that might be giving you a mini-pause. You are asking yourself: In what universe does the purchase of this book embody my service to my country? But think about it. As these pages first went to press, times were uncertain—downright hard for many. The economy was in tatters, continues to struggle, and has been a bit of a wobbly roller coaster for quite a while. So it is incumbent upon all good, red-blooded Americans—if not already serving in a branch of the military or the government or in the community or in the diplomatic corps, etc. (or, heck—even if you *are*)—to infuse the economy with good old U. S. dollars. Open up that purse or wallet and spend! And, if you have already purchased this book and find yourself reading it now, then, by golly, thank you for your service! You are doing your part to economically maintain the nation. God bless America!

—R.P.S.

Introduction

In southwest Georgia—where, before melting into the humid mists of moss-laced swampland, the soil of the Velvet Corridor offers up peanuts and soybeans and corn and pecans—there is a very presciently named little town called Climax. I am certain that it is named for some high point in someone's life or travels or spirituality and has nothing to do with the Summit of Sexuality. However, since for most of my life I have wrestled with *le climax*—with its comings and goings into and out of my quintessentially bizarre, sex-and-secret-ridden life—I find it deliciously ironic that I was born there.

And now, after a dubious raising from Bizarro Ozzie and Harriet; several thousand dollars' worth of psychotherapy; visit upon visit to my physician Dr. Jimmy; hours of anguished telephone conversations with my semi-senile-on-top-of-being-already-crazy mama and my prissy-ass, pity-pot-sitting sister Deborah; and the demise of a twenty-plus year marriage to an unfaithful, erectily dysfunctional political hack, I have no other option than to be re-born into honesty, tell it like it is, feel it like it was, make it what it's gonna be, and just have a good goddamn time, as I traverse the decade that will carry me into my (gasp) sixtieth year, and fully engage in my **Second Sluthood**. Enough moaning, dissecting, ranting and berating; enough looking for a reason or an explanation or an excuse. Death looms ahead, in the second half-century of my life—I hereby vow not to lie upon my inevitable bed of demise regretting that I did not get it on with that acutely cute NYC publishing assistant half my age; that I did not slither beneath the sheets of the nationally reviewed author I closed down the bar with in Chicago; that I did not conduct a naked reading session with the rugged Tennessean, a genius of a writer, who drawled his words into the damp flesh of my neck; or that I did not pursue my undying love of the written word.

My *nomme* and its attendant plumage come directly from my word lust. I was born Ruby Pearl Rutledge, namesake of my grandmother Ruby and great-grandmother Pearl. My daddy, like any good Southern daddy, used to call me his "little ear bob" or his "twinkly sparkly" or his "jewel of the Orient," so I suppose that has fed the Electra in me, giving rise to a lifelong need to add a few more carats here and there. I adore baubles and brooches and stones of the semi-precious variety. Hell, I feel naked if I'm wearing fewer than five or six rings at once. I have always been a sucker (in more than a few ways) for a man bearing jewelry, but it was during my second marriage that I met Lucky Safire, the man who would forever infuse jewelry into my name (yes, I added another "f" to make it my very own). I loved him—a stranger, brimming with kindness (yes, I had a Blanche DuBois moment), turned acquaintance-soon-to-be-husband—and his name immediately. I left my frat-boy of a then-spouse just that fast, so I could string Lucky's last name onto mine, creating the most exquisitely eye-catching name imaginable for an author-to-be.

I came of age during the 1960s, my musings somewhat steeped in the hippie juice of the 'shroom, the fired zigzag, the fluidity of the acid trace. But after a seminal burst of youthful, free-spirited creativity, I faded into subconscious obscurity, lost (post Lucky) in a bland, upper middle class life with the aforementioned, impotent paramour-cum-husband, my fourth, with whom I learned bushels about lovemaking, but that is for a later chapter. I was a mere carcass, having given up on the feminist ideal of self-actualization in order to pay the bills, participate in the daily grind of workaday life in the USA, molding little minds in a middle school by day and selling moldy little houses by night, accumulating credit cards and rut-dom. I lost my Self and my artistic ambitions. It was only after the trauma of my dissolving lie of a marriage that I plunged into a despair born of befuddlement, then re-emerged on the other side and took up that which is mightier than the sword: the laptop. I began attending writers' conferences, chitchatting with the famous, the infamous, and the never-to-be famous because they can't write worth a shit (as opposed to those who *are* famous in spite of not bothering to write worth a shit). At the dawn of the new millennium came my own rosy dawn, my resurrection, the desire to wax poetic rising like a Phoenix in my spirit.

Much of what motivates me now is my impending mortality, the urge to continue feasting at the banquet hall for as long as I can in my waning years. My best friend Opal White says I am too dramatical (she actually says that—"dramatical"), reassuring me I have decades left to my feeble-yet-faintly-plumpish physique, the dew on the lower curlicues not yet steel-dried (just a bit of rust causing a mimicry of petrifaction that, like the Tin Man's joints, requires occasional lubrication in order to render them both productive and receptive to motion). And maybe she is right. Maybe I *am* being dramatical. Maybe I do go over the top with the grandiose phrasings of my mental meanderings. Maybe I am not at death's door. But when one has already lived a couple of decades as a dead person, then it does not behoove that person to squander even a millisecond of the short eon remaining. And I sure as hell don't intend to squander anything, any opportunity—ergo, my **Second Sluthood**.

My Second Sluthood: Being a Manifesto for the Post-menopausal, Pre-senilic Matriarch. That is this self-help treatise, with its **Twenty-Seven Tenets (or Tenants,** maybe?) woven throughout, an unfolding blow-by-blow account of my own revelations and counter-revelations, a validation of the carnal incarnations of the soon-to-be (*gasp*) elderly. For if there is such a thing as a "second childhood" then why not a "**second sluthood**" to keep it all in perspective? And if one never had a *first* Sluthood, then that person would be duly due. And I use the term "Slut" very (pun intended) loosely. I realize that in some rather humorless circles of folks who consider themselves

26

morally/intellectually superior—say a group of anal-retentive reverends or a covey of prim little c*#ts who take themselves oh-so-very-seriously— the term "Slut" is considered, at best, politically incorrect and, at worst, crude, repulsive, and the mark of a stupid, unimaginative writer. I care not. Perhaps I shall take on a sociological examination of the term at some point in my Manifesto, but, for now, suffice it to say the term works. Period.

I use it as a synonym for *joi d'vivre*, *carpe diem*, *la dolce vida*, *la vida loca*, just plain fun. Sluthood, particularly the freedom of a second one (i.e., not looking at men as potential life partners but as the temporary little thrillers they are wont to be; and more particularly after a priestly but pathetic life of semi-celibatic withering), is pure delight, whimsy, joy, exhilaration, just look in a thesaurus for more. Furthermore, folks have a soft spot in their hearts for Sluts—perhaps tied up, somehow, in the Slut's more humanitarian persona, the hooker with a heart of gold (think Dolly Parton in *Whorehouse* or Jamie Lee Curtis in *Trading Places* or *Pretty Woman* Julia Roberts, or, back in the day, good old Mary Magdalene). People are inevitably drawn to those who enjoy rule-breaking, nose-thumbing fun, convention-be-damned—because she, the Slut, gets to act out all the things they keep hidden in their inhibited little bosoms.

I do believe my **Second Sluthood** was seeded by an event—or, rather, a procedure—done unto me twenty years ago, my hysterectomy. My mother's generation saw this as the close of one's feminine functionality, the loss of womanhood, the tip of the scales into heat-flashing declining years of pudgy thighs, leaky bladders, low libidos, pinched-in labia, and random chin whiskers. My generation sees it (rightly so) as the casting off of the chains of menstrual swamps and bloated obsessions over birth control, and the beginning of a new era, free of ovulatory hubbub and pernicious, cycling hormones. "Free at last, free at last, great God Almighty," etc. I even sang the praises of the procedure in a couple of poems written for friends' "coming out" parties, meant to celebrate this new era of an unencumbered c*#t (there's that *c-word* again, used here for alliterative purposes; do forgive me this little indulgence).

One Less Uterus

It's coming out!
No more procrastination!
No more swinging moods, bad attitudes,
Or yucky menstruation!

No ranting fits, no tender tits,
Hey, chick, you're gonna rule!
No more attacks of bitchiness
To make you lose your cool!

You used to think hormonal law
Was bound to rule your life,
But once you chunk that uterus
There'll be no menstrual strife.

There'll be no more potential birth
When you crawl into the sack.
And where your family's concerned,
You'll cut them way more slack . . .

Because that monthly visitor (Aunt Minnie)
Is bound for her final tomb,
And if anybody gives you shit,
You're chillin'—cause you ain't got no womb!

* * * * *

Eulogy for a Uterus

It ruled your moods,
Your attitude
It made you act so mean and rude!
You knew it had to go one day,
And take your life's vicissitudes.

And besides . . .

You cramped and thought you'd float away,
No good reason for that womb to stay,
When all it did was give you grief,
When all you needed was relief.

As for your man . . .

He bought up all the Tampax stock

29

He could get his hands on; that man knew
What the curse of Eve had put you through;
Might as well take a little profit home
To help get through those nights alone,
When you spent most of a month all—you
know, "disabled"
While he began to believe that sex was a fable . .
.

The poor man.

And so . . .

You've finally, finally had enough!
And yeah, yeah, sure, we know you're tough,
But . . . DUH! It's time to lose that menstrual
stuff!

It's time to raise your fist and give a shout
Of Jubilee . . .
It's coming out!!!

I think it not a coincidence but perhaps a part of
the Divine's Plan for R.P. Saffire that the casting out
of my womb occurred at a time in the history of
undergarments when the thong was at the height
of its popularity. Yes, that slender little elasticized
g-string had wriggled its way into the gluteal gorges
of society, prompting not only mega-millions in
sales but also the inspiration for a Top Forty tune
or two. I was initially horrified by the notion of
under-drawers meant not to be worn as a covering

but to be instead inserted in and among certain meetings of flesh. Yet, I felt compelled to find out for myself how it would look on a budding little old lady, and also how it would feel—an experience that only fueled the aversion, as I was at a low point in the self-esteem department.

The Pro and Cons of Thongs

If your glutes are round and firm and bronzed and well-defined,
It might be cool to place a thong upon your fine behind;
But rampant cellulite and age can shrivel up a butt . . .
To put a thong on flaccid flesh, you'd have to be a *Slut*.

Sure, a skinny super-model's arse can give a thong appeal,
But put it on a big chick's ASS, if you want to get it Real.
The sight of it might give your love a killer heart attack,
Cause a thong is really something else if "Baby Got Some Back."

It creeps into the Great Unknown with most determined stealth,
The crevice seems to masticate, take on a life unto itself;

This monumental wedgie makes me bitchy, mean, and cross
(Though it clears out any lint and such, that silky anal floss!)

I even heard of one poor soul, whose thong was so dug in,
It worked and wandered deep inside—and was never seen again!
This disappearing act, you know, a thong can't help but do . . .
That's all I need to know—to baggy drawers I'm true.

No! Of such slivered step-ins I do vow to keep my quiv'ring buttocks free!
I'll spare my man the sorry sight of that disappearing "v"
Of lacy nylon crawling up into my big old ass . . .
I'll stick with baggy grandmaw panties—to prove
(along with this refined poem) I still have class!

The point being, I *am* wearing thongs these days—all colors and textures and laces and frills and thrilling potential adventures—because, hey, my butt's not all *that* big. And it's pretty damn firm, kind of like a thumpishly ripe acorn squash. And with the thongs came the pen and my desire to be the bearer of a Clarion Call to all the wrinkled warriors out there who wish to flame out like a meteor as they cross over to the Other Side.

Opal told me the only way I would ever break into writing was to go digital, venture into "cyberspace", that invisible, electrical, no-tell motel where she has had so many online affairs and netgasms that I have lost count. Opal and I tell each other everything, like good girlfriends should; especially everything about men and desires (the two being pretty much mutually exclusive; I like men and I like sex, but what I have always *desired* is to be a real writer, as in, *author*). So Opal convinced me to put my life on out there, into the bloggy ether that drives this mind-*bloggling* Internet stuff, which I don't begin to understand; I was just following the advice of a friend who also happens to be a longtime cyber-Slut. I have always been much more of an in-the-flesh kind of Slut, but Opal assured me that if I put my richly weird life experiences out there, then anonymous browsers would actually read it. "Build it and they will come," she said, perhaps meaning it a little too literally, whereas I am all about the literarily angle (as opposed to such carnal declensions).

So I started a blog—but I only managed five entries over a period of a year—2005, maybe. Here is the first one:

July 17
I put my heart here before you, kind strangers, in the hope that you will nurture it, tend to the chambers and valves of its creative spirit, resist the

urge to bypass it or shun(t) it or inject it with the purple dye of your disdain, and simply respond with tenderness. Just Try a Little.

You see, I am a writer.

I am over fifty.

Of late I have been wanting to be "published"—validated, as it were, by the minions of the mega-millionaires who decide what you beings out there ingest into your cerebral cortexes. Ah, you might say that you alone select what you read, and well you should, yet it is all predetermined by those business men and women who study the bottom line, who package their book writers in Back Street Boys cynicality, and who purchase real estate along the Boardwalks and Park Places in every bookstore chain in the land. Yet and still, I have sought out said book writers.

And lo, I say unto you, I have followed the wisdom handed down by those anointed ones who have the advantage of corporate validation, having had their egos salved with the ointment of ad men and publicists (whose own egos were most certainly primed with greased palms, so to speak). They are called "authors." A distinctive word, since the world is filled with writers and wanna-be writers. My manicurist is writing a book, as is my neighbor, my florist, and the cashier at the corner Mini-Mart. Everyone else *wants* to write a book, because, however unremarkable, dull, and boorish they are, they really do believe they have something like a shot at being entertaining. And with the increasing incidences of unpolished self-publishing, there is a tidal wave of written trash trending in ripples from your second cousin once removed to big, profitable splashes of poorly written, hollow character-inhabited jaw droppers of excuses for real literature. Them folks ain't authors.

An *author*, at least for a tiny while longer, is a writer who has been **published**, designated "legit" by the industry, **edited** and **promoted**, thus becoming akin to something like a holy one, larger than life—like Gandhi, say, or the Pope, or Oprah. I have listened to these gods, demigods, and semi-gods at conferences, seen them in person, out of person (as in on Book TV and the like), via magazines and National Public Radio. I have gone through demoralizing, failed attempts at making those oh so very critical "connections" the Holy Ones discuss, "connections" which actually involve puckering up one's Revloned lips and connecting them to someone's divine derriere. I have kissed perfumed asses, pimply asses, hairy asses, and flaccid asses—all figuratively, of course. I have sent the odometer on my Mustang convertible spinning like the window-paned panel of a Gulf Coast slot machine, handsomely boosting the profits of the oil industry as I drive from conference to conference all around the Southeast, even venturing forth to Chicago, New York, Washington, D.C., and . . . nothing. What was once a heaving hunger within my voluptuous bosom has become a deflated implant, leaking a poisonous, siliconic sap into my sagging spirits.

I chose to use the second entry (note entry dates; I understand that blogs are supposed to be posted pretty much daily; Opal was not impressed) to explain the over-arching story that seeded the **Second Sluthood**:

August 2

I have come back to writing in the midst of a second life that, combined with the afterglow of menopause, gives me the attitude of nothing short of an *uber*-heroine, a mouthpiece for those females among us who have arisen from such ashes, such incineration as we never in a million years expected or even suspected, in our wide-eyed youth, might be awaiting our fragile frames. I have returned to my core, my self, after a lifetime of being in the dead zone of a charade of a marriage and, as a meaningless moonlit (to subsidize my daylight job as a teacher with the pittance-paying public school system, yet another nightmare scenario) career as a real estate agent on the coast. A question you might be wont to ask comes to mind: "Which coast?"

I did not pimp for the rocky shoreline of Northern California, nor the drab brown beaches of that state's lower half; the Eastern Seaboard, too, pales in comparison to the sugary white dunes of the Redneck Riviera, which is where I plied my trade. Gulf Shores, Alabama; no longer a secret, the last bit of Caribbean Island-colored sand before the coastline meanders around the Mobile Bay, then dwindles across Mississippi, to be swallowed up into the Louisiana Delta and regurgitated alongside the not-so-great state of Texas.

I have been told by my guardian angel that I should keep my eyes open for a man of the "uncomplicated" variety—one not addicted to anger or guilt or terror or any emotionally destructive impulse. I hope that is not too tall an order. Intellectually I demand satisfaction, banter, humor, and an utter lack of drama. Physical appearance is not nearly as important as character. A brilliant mind would be nice as well.

Sigh.

A good man is, indeed, hard to find.

In the next, my third blog entry, came a bit of social commentary along with the chumming of the waters—the throwing of the bait promising poetic phrasings in the form of, um, poems:

August 30

In my travels across the literary circuitry of the Southeast I have gotten an up-close look at the unwashed masses, and it gives me a mini-pause. America the Gluttonous. Big fat men and their big fat wives and their roly-poly kids (while I do admit to being somewhat butterballish about the edges I will not, ever, enter the realm of orbed and lobed

37

obesity, Big Gulps be damned). Herds of gastro-intestinal trough-feeders at the byways and buffets of Shoney's ("Home of the Big Boy") clones and Cracker Barrel country chic knick-knack collectors. These folks are deadpan-serious in their attention to death pans chock full of greased and gravied goods, to such monumental tasks as selecting limp vegetables and slathered chicken parts and blistered bread. In fact, the overall lack of humor in Americans across the board is beyond disturbing to me. As determined as they are to ingest and force digest, they seem as much determined not to express—afraid even to laugh, in a genuine way, to just let it roll up their throats and through their pudgy lips. Hell, I certainly could have never survived the bizarre set of circumstances of my life (such as the time I read a newspaper article about two women of the evening having a catfight in the rotunda of the state house in Montgomery over *my* husband; patience, dear reader—I shall relate it later) up until this moment without the ability to laugh at anything, everything, and even inappropriate things, so I fail to understand those who hold on to their flat affects until their spirits resemble squashed road kill.

Road kill. Cracked armadillo shells splintered against glittering black tar; the popped blot of a busted vessel on concrete and kudzu; an antlered head contorted into its own gut, gaze fixed on its very own disemboweled entrails.

But I digress, as I am wont to do.

I suppose my aversion to gluttony (over-kill) and my fixation on flattened possums and such (road kill) are what have fed my first forays into writing. I do fancy myself something of a poet, although I hear tell, at all these conferences and such, poetry is impossible to sell. So I gave up on the idea of selling it. Instead I shall set about posting it on this rather bizarre, webbed piece of real estate and hope to be appreciated, just a little bit, by some segment of the unwashed masses venturing into cyberature.

And so in my next installment I shall offer up my "Road-kill Trilogy," three poems inspired by the great ones. Borrowing a bit of their (Dickenson, Frost, and Noyes) rhyme and meter, I decided to craft a metaphorical medley of my worldview—a warning, if you will, about those who would smash the delight out of us if we wander into their paths (okay, not really, but it's poetry, so it's supposed to be all deep and all). Anyway, it's a frightening thing, putting one's words out there. What if you don't like them? What if you think me inadequate? What if I become the flattened bug on your windshield?

And speaking of road kill, there's this scruffy guy I've been seeing at a conference here, a book fest there (here a fest, there a fest, everywhere a fest-fest) a rumpled, downward-looking kind of guy who could certainly fit into that category. The man is a train wreck, I'm thinking. And what a nifty project would such a train wreck be for a soon-to-be failed poet and turned-into self-help guru like yours truly. Mega-pause. Maybe a make-over, to fit with the current American obsession with making all things over: bland, cave-mannish spouses enlightened by their homosexual brethren, less than attractive portly chicks being lipo-suctioned and derma-brazed into princess-hood, or swapped houses repainted shades like "honeyed shrimp" or "frosted avocado" or "misty pimento." America the Gluttonous. America the made-over. America in disguise. Will the real America please stand up? Please stand up? Please stand up?

But, once again, I do digress.

There you have it—the tenor and infrequency of the thing. And yes, the scruffy man shall reappear in this, my narrative.

Opal was as frustrated with me as I was frustrated with the traversing of the nets. Clearly I was not cut out for techno-world (until now, as I prepare the first edition for its second edition incarnation as an e-book; who knew?) Ergo, a book. A real life, hold-it-in-your-hands, smell-the-pages book, aimed at ladies of an age and even ladies just coming of age—validation for the former, and wisdom/warning/guidance for the latter. A Matriarchal Manifesto of twenty-seven rules for living the Slutty life, along with poetry, self-help, and a bit of social commentary. From the tattered tapestry of my experiences I offer an alternative path back to desire. From the dull frost of frigid goals, I offer the shine of creativity, like the facets of an indigo sapphire against vulval verbosity, the most cunning of linguistical conclusions. I have built it, and hope that you have come.

(Or that you will, and soon.)

TABLE OF CONTENTS

Chapter 1: Home page/Formatting: My Bizarro Family

I DID not grow up in the aforementioned Climax, Georgia. My parents were only passing through when my monster—I mean, mother went so serendipitously into labor. My actual hometown was the steamy, tiny timber town of Anyplace, Alabama.

I grew up (much to my own credit) a player in a patriarchal parody within a consanguineous satire surrounded by an inherently black comedic drama that was peopled by beings quite unlike oh, pick any black and white family show of the squeaky-clean, pre-clitoral Cold War era—*Father Knows Best* or *Ozzie and Harriet*. Such halcyon days were lived out by "Kitten," "the Beave," and "Princess," and all the other happy, fresh-faced, milk-drinking, cookie-eating (mom made them from scratch!) white children I watched every week on the boob tube. Their dads had it all figured out, by gum, and their moms had the cleanest starched aprons imaginable. Meanwhile, my dad barked crazy prayers over crappy meals, and my mom was a chaotic mess. Their dads read the newspaper as their moms looked up from darning socks to occasionally beam adoringly at their buttoned-down spouses. My parents hardly noticed one another and when they did, it was not necessarily pretty.

I present my certifiably crazy family to illustrate **Tenant (or, hereinafter, "Tenet," for all the word**

Nazis out there) Number One of my Manifesto: **Thou shalt not have children, whether it be via biology or adoption or test tube or commerce or whatever, unless it is an endeavour that is well thought-out, meticulously studied, and the product of a healthy relationship, a healthy singularity, or a pure love of any kind;** and once children have been birthed or otherwise acquired, **Tenet Number Two: thou shalt not brainwash or otherwise mentally cripple thy children.**

(As one who has dealt professionally with children, seen the decomposition of their compositions, the gradual degradation of their thought processes, the dumbed-down tenor of their discussions, and the overbearance of their parents, I can safely say our society is in grave jeopardy. We need creative, inquisitive minds to take hold, not inhibited little robots, threatened by ideas that are different from what they have been force-fed. The situation is grim; the gravity of the situation seems to demand an entire book . . .)

My dear dysfunctional family's days, far from halcyon (more like hallucinations) seemed laid out like a schizoid teleplay; I felt that I had been dropped into a sitcom Bizarro World. In the Rutledge household the perverse script had these two parent *creatures*, whose behavior was diametrically in opposition to that of the gray-grained images on the old Zenith on any given evening.

For example: my father, Bizarro Ozzie, decked out in white short-sleeved shirt and tie like some

44

Kennedy-era NASA geek, would come in from a day at the Anytown Insurance Agency, begin opening via church-key a series of Falstaff or Pabst Blue Ribbon beers, and by the time he hit number four an hour or so later, he and Bizarro Harriett would be engaged in two one-sided conversations that might go something like this:

BH: (whirling dervishly through the kitchen, a clatter of cutlery, the sharpening of knives—not for use, mind you, but because she liked to sharpen them—the chew of an electric can-opener) How was your day, Dear?

[Yes, she really did use that TV line, only she did not really want an answer.]

BO: It's a goddamn jungle out there.

[Which it wasn't; as noted, we lived in a very small town.]

BH: I have the biggest pile of dust bunnies you ever saw that I swept out from under our bed. It was criminal, what I swept out from under there.

BO: (turns the pages of his newspaper) Me Tarzan.

BH: You could stuff a mattress with what I swept out from under there. I think I'll collect all the dust bunnies from under all the furniture and put them to some kind of use.

BO: Where are my cigars?

BH: I mean, surely *something* needs stuffing, wouldn't one think?

BO: Did they just walk off?

45

BH: And I'm almost finished with Deborah's dress for Vicky Watson's party. It's so sweet—the dress, I mean, not Vicky. That child is a horror. And it was so hard to cut—the pattern was so complicated. And it's Simplicity, too, not McCall's. If they are going to call it "Simplicity" it should be simple. There could be grounds for a lawsuit.

BO: (gets up, rifles through the drawers of the end tables).

BH: (opening another can) I think we'll have some peas with our Spam tonight.

BO: Since when can cigars walk?

BH: I wish they would come out with Spam gravy.

BO: Where are my goddamn cigars?

BH: You silly man. Tarzan doesn't smoke cigars. I wonder if they have rabbit tobacco in Africa.

You get the idea. Ping-ping-ping, the words would go, like ricocheting rounds from a couple of Tommy-guns. BH usually took the conversation around the world and back, all the while fixing meals from boxes and cans. I don't think I ever saw her make anything from scratch, but that could be my tendency to exaggerate her flaws, which I am wont to do. After all, she was my very own "Mommy Dearest," who overshadowed, stage-directed, attention-grabbed, and badgered until my true Self could only later finally erupt in shudders, seizuring the day from whence Ruby Pearl could emerge.

At any rate, once the canned veggies were set out on the table with the main course (frozen fish sticks, say, or chicken pot pies, or the aforementioned Spam), we were expected to sit around the table like the Nelson boys (but within the Bizarro alternate reality), chatting amiably about our day—after asking the blessing, of course. This honor, of raising the blessing, usually fell to BO. One holy riff went, "Let us pray. Sounds like *lettuce spray*. We are grateful for the pesticides that keep the goddamn bugs off our lettuce. Amen."

Another heartfelt prayer went, "Let the food we enjoy at this table, surrounded by our loved ones, be taken in to our bodies without repercussions to the yards of intestines through which it shall surely pass. Amen."

Sometimes he lampooned one of the classics: "If God's so great and God's so good, then why we got to eat this food? Amen."

During the Watergate fiasco he offered up this emphatic plea: "Dear Lord, I pray with all my might that you strike Martha Mitchell lame and mute. Amen and amen." BO was a big Nixon fan.

Yes, this was the same "daddy" who bounced me on his knee when I was small, calling me his "jewel of the Orient," his "twinkly-sparkly," "bubbly bauble," "errant ear bob," and "multifaceted moonstone." My theory is that, over the years, as my mother became crazier and crazier, his own nascent mental illness kicked in, transforming him into the scrappy disengager he ultimately became. Sounds good, anyway.

For her part, my mother, who (as earlier revealed in the Addendum to the Disclaimer) was a bona-fide, certifiable, card-carrying "manic-depressive" (the psychiatric lexicon had not yet evolved to the velvet-gloved "bipolar disorder"), never failed to "amen" him at the dinner prayer and insisted that we girls do so as well.

"You did not 'amen' your father, Ruby Pearl. And everyone knows that if you do not 'amen' the prayer, it will not go through to Heaven. End of connection. Finito. *Ex libris*."

"Where does it go if it doesn't go to Heaven?" I remember asking at four or five.

"It goes straight to the New York City dump and gets bulldozed under all the filth."

My dear Bizarro mother had such a lovely way of putting things, especially when she went off her lithium, which she did regularly, wreaking havoc during the occasional social event, church supper, or bridge club soiree.

"I just love the ride too much. I miss it."

The ride was her euphemism for the manic "high" she claimed to be pharmaceutically lobotomized right out of her brain chemistry. BO never batted an eye when she announced that she would be off the lithium for a while. He would simply grin at Deborah and me and say, "Fasten your seatbelts, girls."

I never recall being embarrassed by my parents' behavior as a child, but, when adolescence

It is amazing, upon reflection, that my parents actually *had* a social life—but they did, when BH was in relatively sane mode. It was all very white-collar, the occasional cocktail party or steak dinner (BH could usually manage potato baking or a salad)—the cranking up of the hi-fi, the breaking out of the silverware, the good china. BH would chat with other Stepford Wives, all perfumed and coiffed and decked out in high heels, cinched waists, and pearls. BO did the honors at the grill, talking business and football and hunting with the men, who had also cleaned up for the occasion. After dinner there would be drinks and dancing, cigarette smoke coiling about the living room, furniture pulled back so the grown-ups could jitterbug and cha-cha the evening into midnight. I watched from the hallway, sometimes dozing until the slide and slap of another 33rpm record revived me. Other evenings, even after I had hunkered down beneath the blankets in my bedroom, the laughter that grew louder as the hours went by and the drinks went down brought me back to the show.

So there was a semblance of normalcy, but even that seemed surreal when contrasted with our usual atmosphere: the barrage of criticisms, the lack of genuine engagement, the disjointed ramblings, and the cyclical darkness, when BH's "ride" inevitably crashed and she drew the shades, sucking any remnants of joy into the black hole of her bedroom.

My goodness, this is taking a most disturbing turn. Enough!

I lived with Bizarro Ozzie and Bizarro Harriet for as long as I legally had to do so, which was for much longer than I could take it. Which is why I married as soon as I could after being handed a high school diploma.

My most delicious and warm-fuzziest memory from my Wasteland of a growing-up era? Easy: it was my very first look at a color television program. It was at our obviously more well off neighbor's house, on a Sunday evening, and the sense of wonder that blanketed the entire experience was unlike anything I had ever known. There was that NBC peacock, its feathers spreading like playing cards in my mother's bridge-playing hands, vibrant colors overlapping, changing hues by degree, dancing to the magical accompaniment of the notes of the network's logo tune. I wanted to BE that bird, resplendent, new, the very best next thing. It made no difference that the peacock was a boy, that the girl pea hen was plain, unremarkable, drab, destined for plain Jane world and a grainy gray future. I was going to be extraordinary; I decided that would be the course of my life at that very moment. And, in a most remarkable roundabout way, I feel in my marrow that it shall come to pass.

The end.

(Note how short this chapter about family has been. If I can ever bring myself to purge my childhood from my crippled inner tyke, it will no doubt be in the form of an entire book—as revealed, my next book, a novel. 'Nough said.)

Chapter 2: Cut and paste: My Love Life in No Telling How Many Pages

I HAVE participated in a preponderance of dysfunctionally-charged heterosexual liaisons, the longest of which was the one that broke me down, and for which I am most grateful. If I had not been broken in twain, I daresay I would never have put myself back together again, in grand Humpty Dumpty tradition, to sally forth into the revered **Second Sluthood** in which I now revel.

I got married the first time right out of high school and for the most inconsequential reason in the world—because it was there. Marriage. The Big Wedding. The Big Enchilada. I had not fully risen up in revolt yet, and Bizarro Harriet wanted me to be the Bride of the Universe. A wedding was just the thing to show all her country club friends that she could, indeed, rise to their occasion and plan a day any Emily Post zombie would pronounce a smashing success. She not only wanted to put on the dog, she wanted to show a Great Dane.

Mayhaps you have noticed there has been no mention of a groom to this point. It could be that you find that strange, given the ceremony—love and commitment before God and all. My high school boyfriend, a quiet, laid-back kind of football player to whom my precious virginity was given, (not in a bedroom bed—how many teenage de-flowerings are conducted on an actual mattress?—but on a horse blanket in the galvanized steel bed of a royal blue Ford pickup truck), was, at the time, the love of my life. What did I know? I wanted out of the Bizarro world. I was young and I had a mother who was dying to throw a wedding and I had a boyfriend who was so blown away by a semblance of real sex (even though the two of us clearly had no idea what we were doing or how to better do it) that he would do anything to hang on to a willing partner.

There it is. The crux of all cruxes: *sex*. In *Cat on a Hot Tin Roof* there is a scene in which Big Mama tells Maggie the Cat, "When a marriage goes on the rocks, the rocks are there—right there!" and she slaps the bed for emphasis: a golden nugget—no, a golden *boulder*—of wisdom from an older woman who has learned the truth. The Truth. And yet so many women want, neurotically, to keep and hold a man over the long term while precious few of these women are willing to do the one simple thing it takes to make that happen: participate (preferably enthusiastically) in coital maneuverings. Have relations (preferably rollicking). Or, to put it in distasteful yet exquisitely direct street language: just fuckin' *fuck*, you dumb fuck. More than once every six months. Once or twice a week is a failsafe measure any woman can take to keep whatever man she is so dogged and determined to keep (well, it might *not* work if he is a repressed, alcoholic homosexual, like Maggie the Cat's Brick, but other than that . . .) It doesn't even have to be fancy fucking, no special costumes or props, nothing requiring personal lubricants, candle wax, chocolate syrup, Tic-Tacs, frankincense, incense, or myrrh. Just plain old, all-American, moaning and sweating, eyeball to eyeball, Hard Shell Baptist, missionary-style fucking. The occasional oral gift as well, that keeps on giving—let's face facts, ladies: with blowjobs come beaucoup benefits. I know, I know, the simplicity of it is stunning and seemingly beyond belief—but there you are: The Ultimate and Unadulterated Truth.

And with this Truth comes **Tenant Number Three: Thou shalt enjoy sex until the undertaker arrives.**

Whatever your age or proclivity, do not procrastinate the plying of the cleft. The Grim Reaper can be swift, so waste not a millisecond in the quest for orgasmic success. Do this cuntinually, with pussnaciousness, either alone or with whom or whatever, battery- or fossil fuel-powered (or do the right thing and go green with a little something that is solar- or even wind-powered) and dare death to come before you do. Women who do not enjoy said activity already have one foot in the grave (or they tend to put all their energy into things like extreme shopping, plastic surgery, fad diets, Holy Roller crusades to stamp out sex toys, or—the worst of the worst—living through their children and grandchildren).

It took a few decades, several marriages, and many "relationships" fraught with heartache, *ennui*, bad theatre, and retaliation before I myself came to this Ultimate and Unadulterated Truth. And it all began with that poor, horny halfback from my tenth grade civics class, a Testosterone

Drone who passed me notes during the anti-communism reel-to-reels, which warned us all about the Evil Empire of the USSR. I played it coy for a while, then the Cold War escalated as we began to date, building to a summit of heat during which, at last, I shed the Bobbie Brooks dress, and the heels of my Weejuns pounded the Ford tailgate like an angry Khrushchev. We were both hooked, so we forged ahead until graduation.

Which brings me right straight up to the wedding. As I said before, my nut-covered cheese ball of a mother was tickled senseless, flinging herself into the planning, the picking out of the silverware, the winnowing of the Wedgewood, the registrations at select gift shops for the avariciously desired accoutrements, the teas with little old blue-haired ladies, the showers with giggling girlfriends, the luncheons, dinners, barbecues, receptions, soirees, fetes, *ad nauseum*. I yielded to her in *toto*; she seemed to be having such a grand time with it, the most fun I had ever witnessed her enjoying. Besides, I resisted taking it too very seriously, already enough of a budding feminist to see it as an archaic little minuet, the purpose of which was to transfer ownership of the non-existent maidenhead from the father to the husband.

I did not, however, want to wear white, having already concluded that virginity was nothing to bother about guarding, sensitive as I was to the old double standard of boys-will-(read: **are allowed to**)-do-it-whenever-they-can/girls-should-(read:

must)-save-themselves-for-marriage. I considered red or black or even the spermatazoanesque psychedelic paisley that was all the rage at the time. Of course, Bizarro Harriet would have none of that, and I ultimately did not take a stand, figuring that, when it came to the wedding production, I certainly had no dog in that fight.

But as the day of Pachabel, *petite forts*, and the passing of the property (me, with Opal at my side) unfolded, it dawned on me that I was nothing more than an actor on an elaborate stage, my adoring fans flinging rice and rose petals, my reviews due out in Sunday's society section of the *Mobile Press Register*. And my co-star was not even my soon-to-be spouse; it was my mother. She was beaming and curtseying, bathed in the glow of the footlights, my prissy little sister Deborah (by now sixteen and insisting that her name be pronounced De-*BO*-rah) basking, in turn, in our dear mother's glory.

About DeBOrah. Certainly you have observed my lack of inclination to say much about her. I do apologize, dear, dahlin' reader. It's just that my sister has been the fly in the ointment of my entire life—demanding, sashaying, manipulating, denigrating, very much her mother's daughter. The "mean girls" of today have nothing on Miss DeBOrah. If there is such a thing as a "bad seed" in the human genome, then surely it can manifest itself as shallowness and narcissism, dooming its carrier to a life of perpetual frustration born of attempting to make the universe revolve around one's own, teeny-tiny, itty-bitty reality. That would be DeBOrah's role in life: to tug and yank and lean on and badger reality into admitting that she is the only one who matters.

I know what you are thinking: RP Saffire, you have quite the ego yourself. Are you not being a bit hypocritical? A bit hard on your sister?

Um, no. Admittedly, I do have a dash of the diva in my bloodstream. But at the same time I avoid excessive gossip, constant endeavors at triangulation, and outright mean-spiritedness, three of DeBOrah's primary endeavours. She is a dumb, mean, dour diva. I at least have a bit of wit, verve, and interesting friends (whom you shall, indeed, meet!), *n'est-ce pas*? Of course, I love my sister, wish her well, adore her three children (well, two out of the three anyway, and only as much adoration as I can manage as I am not a big fan of children), and gather the where-with-all to abide her hairball of a husband during the requisite holiday visits. I simply do not *like* her. She inherited a goodly chunk of the Bizarro genes—the worst of the already toxic pair of double helixes of our parentally-challenged progenitors.

And so it was that DeBOrah managed, via a tantrum over a hair crisis (one quarter inch of one of her waves did not "wiggle right") and another tirade over a run in her stocking (above the knee; the bridesmaids' dresses were full length, but "*I* know it's there—I can *feel* it," she wailed), to make the wedding at least as much about her as about me—I mean, about our mother. By the time the reception was in full swing, DeBOrah (having

59

sneaked several flutes of champagne into the empty manager's office, where she conducted a serial make-out session with several pimply tenth graders) was dancing on the diving board at the country club pool (and, yes, of course she eventually ended up drenched and sobbing) a veritable tsunami of disgust rolled over me, washing up the primal urge to flee the scene, take a do-over, and elope with my true love.

Which he wasn't. My true love, that is. He did have a name, which I have not yet mentioned, a conscious literary device intended to symbolize his presence in the wedding/marriage as a sort of prop in the pageant, as it were. We had not spent much time conversing, sharing life goals, swapping opinions or philosophies or desires (or lack thereof) for offspring.

My dear husband's name was "Doodoo."

Okay, it was a nickname. All the jocks had nicknames; it was some kind of requirement. His real name was *Daniel*, but I recall wishing the preacher had used his nickname in the nuptials: "Do you, Doodoo, take" etc. It would have revealed our marriage ceremony for *what* it was: manurage. At any rate, Doodoo and I found ourselves wedded strangers for whom the novelty of sex wore off post haste and for whom the bell tolled with due certainty. The reality of morning breath, dirty underwear, bodily functions, and a mother-in-law who had instilled in her only son a learned helplessness that made an infant look self-sufficient ensured that it was annulled in well under three months.

I flung myself into college, that academic collage of high ideas, illegal substances, and random sexual encounters. When I enrolled, the University of South Alabama in Mobile was a relatively young school, with modern buildings constantly sprouting across the piney hills. Opal and I shared a dorm room but went our socially separate ways, she to assorted Christian groups and I to an assortment of groping Christians (and Jews, Buddhists, atheists, etc.) Her love affair with Jesus took hold whilst I pursued an affair with love, or what I wrong-headedly *assumed* to be love, damaged and youthful as I was.

Without the first notion of pedigree, I treated the institution as a Whitman's Sampler of disciplines, beginning with Psychology 101. I was determined to be renowned as a female B.F. Skinner, navigating the maze-like minds of my fellows. Or I would come up with my own theories about the behavings of the brain, winning prizes, winnowing my way up the Hierarchy of my Needs. But alas, I could not pass statistics; after failing it for the third time, I moved on. (But not before getting id-ish with a professor who taught me the value of delayed gratification. What a gynecological gestalt that was! With Doodoo it had been all about frantic friction, so a whole new world was now my Carnal Oyster, over which I salivated with Pavlovian glee.)

61

My love of semi-precious stones led me to geology, but precious little time was spent discussing gems. It was all about crusts and rocks and such, so I again moved on. (But not before a graduate student fractured another barrier to my sexual elation, excavating and spelunking his way to my Pacific rim. Maybe it was all those discussions of the hardness of specimens, or rings of fire, erupting volcanoes, shuddering earthquakes. That particular department was simply bathed in heat and steam and fissures and rumblings and boilings and spewing, glowing lava flows; "Stoney" and I utilized lab tables, broom closets, and empty classrooms and offices, swept up by tidal surges of lust born of deep oceanic quiverings that would build into furious, demanding, sweat-glistening explosions. "Rocks" took on a whole new meaning for me.)

Since my wedding had been a bit of bad theater, I decided to experiment with good theater, and declared that to be my new major. As I have always taken a goodly amount of pleasure in performing—sweeping into a room, say; or storming out of one—I was certain I would be a natural. After all, the many dramas of Bizarro Harriett and psycho-spawn DeBOrah had provided foundation enough for what might end up being for me a red-carpeted walk, all decked out in haute couture and drippings from Tiffany's, to collect an Oscar or two.

By now I was sporting hairy underarms, bouncing breasts, and eschewing make-up: the hippie chic style of the day. And the theatre department was literally crawling with free spirits eager to guide me on various odysseys of experimentation: chemical, political, thespial, lesbial and heterosexual. I did dabble in the psychedelic realm and made Mary Jane an occasional acquaintance, but my chemical inclination tended toward the vine. And, surprise-surprise, I was attracted to the one male who stood out as completely different from all the rest: a frat boy named Bobby. Whom I married.

I know, I know. It all seems silly and shallow and flighty, but I assure you that I, like so many of the walking wounded, was only attempting to make my way—somewhere. I tend to flavor my words with the herb of humor; consequently, dear reader, you might forget from time to time that R.P. Saffire was mightily shell shocked, coming off an extended tour of duty in Bizarro Land, the line of demarcation between the sane and the insane one of fluctuating borders, subterfuge, and downright mentally bloody fraggings.

And yes, it was a "mixed" marriage. He was a wholesome, Pat-Boonish (though he, like my father, could damn sure put away some PBR) kind of a Kappa Alpha. I was a wild, Janis Jopliny kind of a GDI, having much earlier in my college life briefly put my toe in the Greek waters at the urging of Bizarro Harriet.

"It's all about making useful social connections," my socially inappropriate *mater* advised.

"You know I am not a joiner of things."

"Yes, alas," she sighed, martyred at the holy blissful shrine of her Disappointment In Me.

"Please don't do that."

"Prithee, what?"

"Make me feel guilty."

She gave me her eyes-brimming-with-tears look. "If the guilt fits," she said.

So I became a Chi Omega during my freshman year, and for exactly seven months was immersed in everything Chi-O, from propagandizement in pledge world to the official acceptance (initiation) to songs to rituals and candles and frat boys, whom I found too familiar, too home-townish, when I was sensing a yen for the exotic. This was about the time I began to size up the geology department, so I was already riled, steeped in the cyclic heat of the estrul ether. Those frat boys just were not ramping up the heat, determined as they were to impress one another with their ability to win drinking games. I began to skip the Greek parties in favor of more artistic groups, began to gain a little knowledge of myself, began to feel creative stirrings within my soon-to-be unbound bosom.

And as I came into my own, sprouting golden hairs upon my tanned (via basting in Johnson's Baby Oil) legs; casting off my padded and be-hooked Maidenform brassiere and girdle, my sisters of the sorority became sore confounded. At first they let out little bleats of disapproval.

"Ruby Pearl, you're starting to look like one of those hippie people." Sissy Somebody said.

"Must you label others?" I replied, bosoms bobbing beneath my "Chi Omega" t-shirt.

"There *have* to be labels," SS (and no, the significance of her initials is not lost upon moi) said, going through a list of Pan Hellenic Council groups and their respective traits—such as which sorority was known for serious, brainy girls, which for unattractive and downright ugly "dogs," which for party girls and sluts, always winding up with, "but the Chi-O's are known for being the best looking."

"Have you not read *The Feminine Mystique* or *The Female Eunuch*?" I retorted. Blank stares. "In which such terms as *dog* and *slut* are explicated and revealed as the objectifying slurs they are?"

Even blanker stares.

(Hmm. Perhaps my then-adamant attention to the S-word was a feministical foreshadowing, albeit ironical, of my embracement of the term in recent years.)

They finally grew desperate enough to stage something like an intervention, gathering in my dorm room, speaking in hushed tones, wearing looks of exaggerated concern.

"We love you," Buffy Somebody said in that sweet, fake-Christian tone so rampant in the South. "We're your sisters."

Now, I am not one who is fond of being gushed over, told I am loved, or given advice—particularly from fake Christians, and especially when I have not, in any way, shape, or form, sought said advice. Granted, these "sisters" were much more bearable than DeBOrah. Or were they? What was the source of all the concern? After much and mighty buildup, it came out.

Not only did they object to the body hair, I was dating "hippie guys" and "everybody knows that Chi Omegas go out with Kappa Alphas—at least on this campus."

"The least you could do," Tootie Somebody sighed, "is date a few Greeks."

I left their ranks. That day.

(That was the seed for what has become **Tenet Number Four** of this Matriarchal Manifesto: **Thou shalt not join clubs, churches, associations, philanthropical cadres, cooperatives, political parties, communes, covens, revolutionary armies, etc., for any reason that smacks of rising in social status, making the "right" connections—i.e., using others—or excluding others.** It is not only shallow, it is mean-spirited and always shows you for the opportunistic whore you inevitably become.)

Yet there I was, nearly two years later, dating—lo, marrying, a KA. Such are the twists and turns and lovely little ironies of life.

He was all laughter and banter, and the butting of our respective heads made for lively discussions. He was athletic, taught me a good game of tennis, and berated me (good naturedly) for my burgeoning tobacco use. Somewhat more maritally sophisticated than I had been the first time, I queried him about children, and he, like me, was fairly certain he would never want a child but allowed that there was always a chance he would change his mind. *Yes!*

My little psyche whipped into overdrive, mapping out the perfect life we were bound to enjoy, desperate as I was for a shot at something on the cusp of "normalcy." And most verily and mightily, I became one with the thoughts and the lure of security took hold. We made a beeline to Justice O. Peace.

Your fingernails are likely scratching your noggin, as you wonder why we did not simply keep it simple and live together in sinful non-commitment. Alas, that was my desire, but Bobby was old fashioned and did not want my reputation sullied by such an arrangement (obviously he was not aware of my sexual tour of the arts and sciences). Ironically, I found this quaint, lost in the newness, the blinders of bliss still blocking my budding blush of feminism, preventing me from connecting the dots. A young man who links female sex with a sullied reputation? I know, I know.

I am certain that you, dear reader, already see the perfect penmanship on the wall, and you are supremely correct. Our differences were much too different. Our initial attraction was much too intense. Our ideas ultimately clashed. We fell into a disturbing routine, a grind, the kind of marital rut that does not set in for a decade or two and is usually accompanied by the scent of carrion. We went to classes, he worked, and the PBR cans began to mount. I even considered bearing a child, just to liven things up and give him something to do besides drink beer.

I made gains on fronts other than the personal/marital, however. I immersed myself in literature, got acquainted with Faulkner and O'Connor and Eliot and Wright, found voices and inspiration. I wallowed in poetry, steeped my soul in stanzas and sonnets and all manner of pentameter. And I took up the pen, in fact garnered praise for my verse and prose. I completed a degree in English, followed by a teaching certification, and ultimately fled into the arms of Lucky Saffire, from whom I gleaned my plumme of a nomme and who was sent by God Almighty, the One True, unto me.

He was, I later discovered, six years my senior, free spirit, Peace Corps volunteer, professional student, Castaneda devotee. He had the presence of an old soul, the most steadying aura of calm, not a whisper of materialism or ego. In fact, he was a trust fund baby who refused ambition, eschewed capitalism, and had decided to use his inheritance to travel, to help, to learn, and to do a spiritual internship with LSD, along with a goodly amount of pot and the occasional peyote. On top of that he was beautiful—not handsome, but flat-out beautiful—blonde hair to his shoulders, Newman-blue eyes, surfer-boy skin, white teeth framed in a deep tan. I was crossing the pine-treed lawn behind the Administration Building and came upon him in the midst of a group of other, younger students. A glint of sunlight caught his hair, as if the Life Forces were grabbing me by the lapels—um, straps of my halter top—to force my gaze upon him. As I drew closer the brightness grew, then receded, and the full force of his beauty struck me.

"You are just too goddamn pretty to be a guy," I said.

He laughed, as did the others.

"You've never met Doc Lucky?" someone asked.

"You're kidding—that's your name?"

"Yeah," he said. "And no, it's not a nickname. I'm for real."

"You're a professor?"

"No," someone said. "He's just attended so many schools he should qualify as honorary."

"Yeah," someone else said, "an honorary Leary."

"No shit," went another.

But I was responding to no one else. My eyes locked on his. "Names are important. I mean, the symbolism. I am a lover of words."

"Words are just words, if they even exist. We freight them with too much history. That can be a downer."

The fact that he was so pretty *and* so easily engaged in talk that did not bore me (see: Bobby) *and* had such a luscious name took my heart just that quickly. And, to be accurately honest, he was quite obviously taken with me as well. Although looks are superficial to me now, in my youth I valued my physical appearance—and it valued me. In a word, I was *fine*. And bra-less. But I also had enough charisma and intelligence to grab his attention. The other Doc Lucky devotees peeled away, one or two at a time, surely aware of their sudden irrelevance.

69

"True, but therein lies the delicious symbolism—in my history. You are Lucky. I once had a dog named Lucky Strike. I don't suppose your last name is Strike? That would strike *me* as too much of a symbolic coincidence."

He laughed, "No, not Strike. Safire."

I do not have to tell you that God's fingerprints were all over this. From the heavens came a chorus of hallelujahs raining down beneath clouds fluffed and buffeted by the downy wings of holy angels.

"Well, I have news for you, Mr. Lucky—oh! I just realized you are also a long-past TV program! Even more symbolism. I think it was some kind of crime show? Or a detective thing?"

"I'm a seeker, that's for sure."

"Seeking what, pray tell?"

"Oh, you know, the usual—God, the meaning of life, how to make a difference in the world, that's all. And you were about to give me some news?"

"Oh—I was just going to say we should get married. Okay?"

He laughed again. "Are you crazy?"

"Quite probably. My gene pool is marinated in crazy."

"Look—marriage is what's crazy. It's just an empty institution. A piece of paper. I would need a real reason." But he was smiling, dimples deepening.

"There's a perfectly good reason to."

"Besides, you don't seem like the type."

"To—"

"Care about marriage."

70

"Well, I don't, really. I've done it twice, and badly, a fact which I attribute to my crazy childhood. This time I simply need to use you briefly."

"That's cool. I love being used by sexy chicks who have an enigmatic edge." His calm was remarkable. This man was not taken aback, not offended, not deriding me. He was flirting with me.

"So you're willing to hear me out?"

"Of course."

"And if I give you a good, edgy reason to marry me—temporarily, of course, and without residing together or any sort of consummation, unless, in the course of our short-lived union we decide, *what the hell?* and go for it—then would you do it? Marry me?"

Again, absolutely no eye-battage. "Sure. You seem genuine. Life's an adventure. I'm up for it."

I explained my desire to go about authoressing, my revelation from on high at the gift of his name, and offered a brief, encapsulated version of my life story in two hundred words or less. "And what is your life story?" I asked.

"No story. Apparently I was just put on this earth to get high, build huts, and be used by sexy, freaky chicks."

"Yes, I believe you were."

Surely, sweet reader, you doubt the veracity of this little vignette but it is the gospel truth. So just go with the strangeness of it; or, if you are a spiritual being, then give me the fact that miracles happen. Or just go with a willing suspension of disbelief.

He took my hand and kneeled. "So we are betrothed. When do you want to get married, beloved?"

"Oh, get up. You are *not* to step out of character like that. Besides, there is paperwork, is there not? Does the system not require us to certify that we do not have syphilis? As I told you, I have been married twice, and I seem to remember some such business."

"For somebody who doesn't care that much about marriage, you're pretty young to have been married twice."

"True."

And, of course, it was *very* true—for one who had already been lost for a life, who was only now embarking on a journey, a tour of the world of words, to add to the words, with a deliciously authorly name—for one who was coming into her own. A name chosen, selected in the context of an act of the gods.

"Well," Lucky said, "let's make it a condition of our agreement—that if you ever decide to marry again, you'll do it for every good reason there is. Or better yet, just give marriage up altogether. It really is a part of an artificial America." And he smiled again, as I began to more deeply understand that he was, truly, my spiritual guardian, sent to put me right. Years later, as I crossed the half-century mark, I became even more solidly convinced that he indeed was that sort of force.

"Why don't you just go to a judge and change your name? Re-name yourself on your own? Why marry for a name?"

"No. You don't get it."

"Lay it on me then."

"I was made aware of this name, *Safire*, when the light of Helios glanced, god-like, from your hair, signaling you as my protective spirit, a guiding force, or some such. And this makes so much the better story, which well suits one whose destiny in life is to write stories. I mean, anyone can go down to the courthouse and change a name. How many writers have a tailor-made name delivered by the deities? How many have a celestial protector, in the flesh?"

"Ah, so in this instance you have a hand at writing your own story." His old-soul eyes were kind, his generosity genteel, his heart in empathetic harmony with my dream.

"*Exactly*."

"I get it," he said. "Cool."

Maybe he was half kidding throughout the conversation. I, however, was not. We spent subsequent time together, discussing Life, God, and Love.

"I've never been a fan of monogamy. Never," he offered as we lazed among the blue satin sheets on his waterbed one afternoon, bathed in the glow of black lights, lava lamps in a constant flux of amoeba shapes re-making themselves, notes of King Crimson in the background.

"I'm a serial monogamist, clearly—but now I'm an adulterer, technically."

"Adultery. There's another meaningless word."

"I just think monogamy is the *intended* way."

"Intended by whom? God?"

"No, by society. No—I take that back. By me, within my life. Well, except for now."

"That's cool." He drizzled some leafy shreds into rolling paper. "But within *my* life I've got no use for some kind of possession that calls itself *monogamy*."

"But haven't you ever been in love?"

"I don't know what that means—*in love*. I feel love—intensely. I love love. But 'in love' is just an expression that doesn't work for me. If you're *in* something, especially an emotion, it can be difficult to get out. My emotions are in me; I'm not in them."

"So you've never had an exclusive girlfriend?"

"Of course not. I don't think that's even in the nature of, say, a quarter of humanity."

"You have studied this?"

"It's just a gut thing. From watching."

"It bears researching I think. You want to have the facts on your side."

He lit the joint. "Seriously, will my habits upset you?"

"My dear golden angel," I said, "this is to be a brief marriage of convenience. I do not intend to be a clingy wifey. Jesus. And what are your 'habits,' anyway?"

He blew a cannabis cloud. "I didn't mean to sound negative. It's just that I've seen a lot of miserable shit in the world, and so I'm pretty determined to live in the moment. Trite, I know, but, as it turns out, spiritually correct."

"And a slice of trite I'd love to eat."

He handed me the joint. "Far out. Let's do it."

Being that I had been lacking the motivation to end a marriage that was already over, and certain that I was hurtling, full speed, toward my literary destiny, to join the chorus of great and varied verbal vocalists with whom my spirit had been singing via the turning of the page lo these many months, I wasted not a nanosecond. Nor did Bobby the Kappa Alpha. It's funny how easy it is to motivate the miserable. The face of my dear second husband lit up when I broke the news, obviously to his unbroken heart, that divorce was imminent. And our domestic domain was thus sundered, amicably and with no muss and no fuss. In BH parlance: Finito. *Ex libris.*

Mayhaps you are wondering about my parents' reaction to my flurry of marriages and my foray into the feminism (such as it was in southern Alabama) of the day. I had moved beyond needing their approval (my *inner* tyke, however, had other things in mind). I discovered, during these youthful years, that I had the power of being an adult, no matter if I were right or wrong. When BO or, much more often, BH offered disapproval or advice, I would either point out that said advice had not been sought, that disapproval was essentially rude, or I would change the subject. Eventually they ceased their (her) yammering. I recommend you use this approach for all sorts of folks who insinuate their opinions into your life—from politicians to Jehovah's witnesses; it works every time.

For Lucky's part, not only was he a quintessentially heavenly arbiter of my spirit, he was also the best of sports. How many other beautiful strangers *cum* guardian angels would go so far as to marry another perfect stranger simply to honor her with a name? We carried on fluently in the boudoir, romping and talking, sensualizing and fornicating, confiding and cavorting; and, over a period of weeks (and to my chagrin), I found myself falling full-bore *in* love—for the first time in my life, I figured.

It's a funny, tragic thing. When love enters the picture, the paradigm shifts—or attempts to, when it is one-sided. Not that Lucky did not *care* for me. Clearly he did. And he had been up-front honest, was a man who shared himself freely with women, made no bones about it. So, when the feces hit the oscillator, I had not one leg upon which to stand.

"We agreed it was a lark," he said.

"I know."

"I've always been honest. I make a point of being honest."

"I know."

"It kills me that you're hurt."

"I know."

76

"You really do feel like some kind of piece of my spirit."

"I know."

"To say 'soul' would be trite."

"I know"

"I'm so sorry."

"I know."

I mean, what the hell else can one say when one falls in love with a deity who is shared by the masses?

Maybe, if only I could have been as polygamous or as pure as he—as free from jealousy—then maybe it would have lasted, but I doubt it. I'm not made that way; my polygamy (like my aforementioned monogamy) is serial in nature, never (well, mostly never) concurrent. He had clearly transcended something that shall probably take me a few more lifetimes to "get."

Of course I was devastated, and Lucky was gentle with my feelings, and, in spite of the emotional messiness, he became a consistent presence in my life, in an uncommon way. He never did marry (surprise), never wanted children (I know, the irony is never lost on moi), believing the world needed rehab more than it needed more people in it. He continued his travels and his work with humanitarian causes, but throughout my post-Lucky life, he never allowed me to lose touch, always made certain I had a current address and phone number, as if he had the prescience of mind to know I would surely need him one day.

And he was righter than right.

Which brings me to the apple's core of a life in Eden, **Tenet Number Five: Thou shalt not ignore the voice of God.** Whether it be a capital "G" God or a lower case "g" god; or a Jesus, Confucius, Mohammed, Krishna, Zeus, Diana, Gaia; or a sunset, a mountain, a gentle rain, a flower, or a star; or a poem or a dance or a work of visual art; or a Force, or a Higher Power; or a word or a breath or a whisper. Do not tune it out, thereby emptying the spirit of truth, honesty, and hope. If you need a guardian angel like Lucky Safire to keep you tuned in, then by all means keep in touch with that soul better than I did over the years. I lost my way for lack of listening to the inner thrum of my own spirit.

Furthermore comes **Tenet Number Six: Thou shalt not be consumed by dogma, indoctrination, petty judgments, boo-hoo-ing preachers begging forgiveness, nor any of the myriad trappings of organized religion (particularly the fringe nut-jobs).** Sadly, many folk are so god-deprived they are too knocked down by spiritual famine to even consider this. And I speak here of many who go to church regularly, believe themselves to be good Christians, Jews, whatever—when they are merely spewing the tapes programmed into their pea brains as children. And yes, this is an echo of **Tenet Number Two**, for that tenet is near and dear to me. Brainwashing, especially of innocent children, is diabolical. If one cannot trust in the purity of the Little Ones to hear the voice of G(g)od, then one is wedded to the darkness. If children, 'tweens, teens, and even some older folk are taught *how* to think as opposed to *what* to think; and, further, if they are exposed to the world of ideas and spiritual thought that is out there, they will find their way. They will listen to the G(g)od in which/whom they come to believe, just as I have.

Of course, I totally respect atheists as well. And agnostics are tres entertaining.

Chapter 3: Hacked: Into Pieces, My Heart

JUST as **Tenet Five** is the heart of the manifesto, Chapter 3 is the heart of my darkness—darkness and depression, which I do not take lightly, particularly since these were two important elements of my life for something like two decades plus; however, I do not mind *making* light of them. In fact, making light of things, as in Humor, I have discovered, is a wonderful coping mechanism. And that is why I shall, in the context of this tome, refer to my fourth ex-husband as "Hand Job," the meaning of which shall become apparent in the telling of the tale.

At the urging of my dear friend Opal, I found myself employed by the Baldwin County Board of Education, teaching at a school near the Gulf Coast, which is what ensnared me into real estate a half dozen years later (upon the hitting of the first crap on the ceiling fan). My job sufficed, was not a grind, as long as on weekends I could venture out to the screened porch of my little cottage and tap upon the typewriter, endeavouring to create an illustrious work of literature. I was making acquaintances of some of the artists, writers, and other such creative folk as were found in abundance in this small, superficially serene little place, and counted myself fortunate to have finally found my niche, my people, my center, my life. My World.

Which then collided with that of Hand Job.

The collision: I had joined an insignificant acquaintance for a soiree at one of the mansions along Belleville Avenue, in Brewton, Alabama. As a budding poet/great-American-novel writer at the time, I was looking for a patron, which translates to courting wealth, which irked me no end (I was of the "you do what you gotta do" school of thought, an attitude which thrust me in a tenuous but temporary direction upon the entering of the **Second Sluthood**). Outside of my beknownst was the presence of one Hand Job—engaging, intelligent, seemingly principled, witty, attractive, courteous, and kind-hearted.

I met his date before I met him, a woman who for later-to-be-revealed reasons shall hereinafter be referred to as Miss Clitopatra Denial. Although a beneficiary of oil and timber, most certainly rolling in the old dough and therefore quite lowered in my estimation, she seemed pleasant enough—dark hair, nice smile, but oddly wholesome in appearance (this was the sexually charged 1970s, after all), wearing a button-down oxford cloth shirt and Weejun penny loafers. I, on the other hand, was resplendent in my black jeans, flowing peasant blouse and bangles, big floppy hat, all bedecked in garb *d' artiste*. We chitted. We chatted. The earth did not move. It did, however, move when Hand Job approached. You ladies know the feeling. Strains of "As Time Goes By" swell in the background, the lens zooms in, the eyes connect, the pheromones frolic, and eventual bodice-ripping sex is guaranteed. I left not with the commitment of a wealthy patron, but with Hand Job assuring me that he and Miss Denial were nothing more than "very good friends," promising to come down to Fairhope and visit sometime.

Which he did, took me for coffee and then to bed, along with his recalcitrant organ.

I attempted to assuage his ego. After all, this was the male's all-time nightmare scenario. "You know, I was with a man once—we were quite attracted to one another and ended up rolling around on the floor of his apartment, and I reached down at one point—we had not disrobed—and latched on to what I thought was his thigh, only it very slowly dawned on me that it was *not* a thigh."

"Uh, that's not very comforting."

"No—the point is I was shocked. I completely froze up. Could not move. Absolutely could not deal with that—appendage. Not in a million years. And I felt bad about rolling around on the floor, getting him all—you know. But he was very sweet about it. I guess it had happened to him a lot. He said, 'You don't have to'."

"That's the moral of the story—'you don't have to'?"

"Correct. We don't have to."

He narrowed his eyes at me. "Three things you need to know."

"Do tell."

"One: this happens to me a lot—kind of like Thigh Boy. Two: I ain't a quitter. And three: there are a lot of ways to skin a cat."

"Certainly."

82

And he proceeded to skin mine. In an alternative manner.

Which solidified for me the notion of sex being all about the bean, as in *brain*. For he more than compensated, taking me to Everests of ecstasy that pooled snows and ice, mixing with the moist breaths of the Gulf Stream that wafted through my core. And lo, I was transformed, rebirthed into a Nirvanic level on the carnal hierarchy. I had seen the face of God. Just as Doc Lucky had transcended jealousy, I had transcended intercourse.

He had not been completely truthful, however, about his wayward member. Its noncompliance did not happen "a lot;" it happened **all the time**. And, like a trooper, I sought out said organ on occasion, attempting to lure it into stiffage with anything in my repertoire that seemed to fit the bill at the time, experiencing bouts of inadequacy when all was for naught. Was I not sensual enough? Attractive enough? (Fill in the blank) enough? What terrible words to utter to oneself, the flagellation, the verbal flogging, the self-esteemed carnage! Still, he had it all, it seemed, including a most pleasing style of love-making, albeit alternative. And if we continued to fail at intercourse, well, at least I would never have to be concerned about any buns in the oven.

A juvenile dance ensued when he admitted there was a little more to his previous relationship than he had initially declared, and as a result he was unable to completely disengage from Miss Denial, latching on to the fear of retribution, wallowing in the guilt. I failed, unfortunately or not, to pick up on that glaring clue. I was in the middle of transcending intercourse and was a mite distracted. "Alright," I said, still silly enough to be seeking a mate as opposed to a thrill, "I can offer the ultimatum you obviously seek. Consider it done."

This was a man who responded best to crises and therefore tended to create them. Faced with the choice between the crisis of losing me (to whom he had by now declared love, kinship, and a pristine respect for my talent with words), and the crisis of getting shed of Clitopatra, he chose the latter. Ardor swelled, although without the swellage of his troubled member, and we embarked upon a period of fierce romance, each with an ideal of the other, heady with the nectar of an emotional cocktail that knocked us into an almost junkie to dealer connection, in both directions.

Which is certainly not a healthy thing for anyone, but especially for him, as another very large clue to which I paid never-mind was the fact that Hand Job was a recovering addict, having saturated himself in alcohol in the years preceding our coupling, having hit the bottom of the rocks in his highballs, having gone into rehab, and having finally been pronounced clean and sober, pre-moi. I was thrilled to have a man who could be counted upon to drive us home safely after an evening of wining and dining. I was thrilled not to have a clumsy drunk slobbering over me in the boudoir (as had been the case with a couple of the children I married too early in life). I did not, though, consider that an addict is an addict is an addict; that is, an addiction to one thing may be the only presentation one sees, and there could be many other monkeys, not just on the back, but under the surface—addictions to anything. What I have come to realize is that Hand Job and I were emotionally addicted to one another. We glommed together at warp speed in a covalent bond of bondage.

Mayhaps you are querying yourself along the line of: How did such a scintillatingly brilliant woman get all embedded with such a dysfunctional delusionary?

Initially it was one of those instant, chemical reactions. What it became was my undertaking of the discovery of who he was, my abandonment of who I was, and what is now an occasional source of conversation for my current posse, as we try to get to the bottom of Mr. Hand Job and my disappearance into him.

"Honey, that closet is *huge*," my gay friend Micah often opines when the topic raises its ugly, flaccid head.

"Oh, come on," I counter. "Not every screwed up male is stuck in a closet."

"You think?" he says. "Because the state parks and rest stops and airport bathrooms are sincerely full of them, doing their Cold War signals at each other like kids playing 007. Just ask Larry Craig. Or any televangelist."

"What I think," my token rich friend Marble Gotrocks offers, "is that he is a study in classic sociopathology,"

"Sorry," I tell her. "There is a conscience in there. He's no sociopath. None of the therapists over the years—his, mine, or ours—ever saw that."

"I don't know," she says, skeptical.

"It's true," Opal says. "I knew him, after all. He's not a con artist—more of a tortured artist."

"I was the only artist in that relationship," I say. "He was all about logic and science and social consciousness and the repetition of history, which we repeated into the ground."

"They are very smooth liars, sociopaths," Marble insists.

Here friend Diamond Jones, a bona fide psychologist, interjects, "Nothing R.P. has ever described about him makes those bells and buzzers go off for me, and I dissect crazies for a living. Anyway, the bigger question is, why were you drawn there? And why did you stay there?"

"I can't add any more to what I've already explained. Sometimes the neuroses are a perfect fit. Sometimes the endorphin kick is too fierce to fight. It was what it was."

And on it goes, this investigation into my psyche, my heart, oft times even my inner tyke, all the aspects of me that, a la *Sybil*, could possibly merge together into some kind of explanatory on-ramp. Sometimes we spin our wheels, skidding against the traffic, but occasionally we grab traction, and insight is not far behind, there in the rearview, with 20/20 clarity.

On one seminal (sweet irony) occasion, however, sipping lemonade-laced vodka in the twilight on Waterhole Branch, Opal leaned forward and said, "I think you were avoiding writing. You know, that 'impostor syndrome' and all?" She tends to go with whatever is fresh in her mind, and I think she had heard about that topic on *Dr. Phil*.

"I think you're on to something," Diamond said.

I laughed my lemonade cocktail out of my nostrils, then, "Opal? *On* to something?" But then I remembered the weeks and months after the breakup, when Opal, along with dear Angel Lucky, was so critical in helping me get perspective—to get back to authoressing.

"Sad to say, I thought I could change Patrick," Micah said in a flat tone. "You know, make him over, like a penthouse I was decorating for some rich bitch, but on his inside. Did you think Hand Job could be revised, like one of your glorious poems or one of your sundry tales?"

Hmm. Maybe they *were* on to something.

"Which is it?" friend Emerald Gray demanded. "A sociopath, a just plain cheater, or a project for you?"

Diamond gave me a knowing look deep into my heart of darkness, eyes brimming with liquidation. "None of the above," she sighed, oozing the empathetic engagement I so love about her.

She has been there, in one of those embalmed states of settling, knowing the settling is inevitable, having erred in her choice of terms, and mourned a dead marriage. For verily I say unto you, and with a perfectly straight face, Hand Job was at heart a good, well-meaning entity, as most of us are. A pestilence upon those (including moi) who pound the stings and errors of humanity with the clenched fist of judgment! That is the trouble with our sick, sick society. One cannot examine a life without appreciating the throws, flashes, and spectrum-shaded glimmerings tossed about that mysterious prism. To borrow a cliché, very little, if that, is black or white. Just ask Diamond, who "gets" it.

"We all weigh everything out, take the good, see what bad we can tolerate or even ignore. There were aspects of his intellect and humor and nature that I found so far above the mundane that they were worth any complication," I tried to explain.

Emerald spoke up right away. "Complication? *Complication*? Now don't get me wrong," she said, cocking her head, left eyebrow punctuating her expression, "but if Charles Terrel Gray ever was to cheat on me he would be one left-in-the-dust Negro."

"So that's a thing you won't trade," Diamond said. "Each woman has a different hierarchy of trade-offs. Is C.T. perfect?"

"Of course he isn't. He's not a patient man, and his temper pops off like the bubble on a bad tire. He goes to cussing and kicking and slamming and sweating sometimes so bad he reminds me of a brat that's never been swatted, and I blame his mama for putting that in him, but don't get me started on *her*. The point is that I know after about ten minutes of that shit he's going to cool down and be reasonable. Else I'll tell him his time is by god up. It goes all over me, though."

"But that's hardly equitable with cheating." Marble said.

"It depends on what you're willing to trade off," I offered. "You know, like favoring money over true love."

Marble, gold-digger that she is, giggled. "Touché." God love her.

Emerald leaned forward. "I already said I couldn't take a straying man."

"You wouldn't look at the circumstances?" Diamond asked. "Maybe forgive him once?"

"No damn way. Hell, R. P.'s fool couldn't even give her a proper fucking! Why would I keep a cheating man who can't even do me proper?"

Opal's eyes took on that faraway glaze I recognize as a precursor to some kind of inane observation. "He would have been perfect for me," she sighed. "Imagine. Never having to worry with one of those—'things'."

"Imagine all the people, living life in peace," I mumbled, thinking, *damn if she does not have something of a point, a rare occurrence in Opal World.*

But unless one believes in the perfect mate, which I have never observed in the world (well, okay, I can count soul-mated couples I have witnessed on one hand) there is always going to be a compromise in one's expectations—unless, of course, one is doomed to be one of those oh-so-particular, icky-picky inventoriers, male or female, who end up at the Door of Death alone. They have driven their few friends away, friends who grew weary of listening to their thin criticisms of the latest flawed potential life partner. And they wanted a life partner ever so much, even as they crossed possibility after possibility off the list, for the least egregious of offenses: "doesn't like Hemingway"; "parts hair on left"; "chews funny"; "bites fingernails"; or "talks like a hick." No. Back in the day, when I desired a life partner, I was happy to compromise a little thing like a bendy boner in order to enjoy the other multis in his faceted personality.

Ah, Hand Job. I did so admire his politics, his altruism, his championing of the underdog, his deep brown eyes, his strong, steadying, sensuous hands that, in the absence of a productive member, could do ever so much to please. He was intelligent, funny, and at the core, guilt-ridden and self-wounding. He revealed layers of himself like unto the proverbial onion, layers of fear and vulnerability that were in stark contrast to the self-assured advocate who advanced causes on television with a level gaze and a steady voice, standing up ramrod straight to the powers that be here in the good old once-upon-a-time Confederacy. He had gone to jail during the Civil Rights era. He had organized workers. He had fought injustice. There was much there that was truly righteous that I did not allow myself to see into the other compartments of his existence.

Which fed into my own need for the veneer of security as I studied this human, about whom I might one day write. The writing, I constantly told myself, was a noble endeavour, and I seemed to be in a steady state of pre-writing, making ready. As he fed me morsel after morsel after morsel, our dysfunctions locked into place like a stuck gear on a motorboat. The winds rose, the eye wall formed. We were, indeed, a most perfect storm.

And so we passed through the 1980s with the flush of hot sexy love, minds that engaged one another, and a deep emotional investment in purpose. We bedded and wedded (I did not take his name as I continued to have writerly aspirations, albeit muted) and rutted (after a fashion), the falling into the rut being the Novocain that allowed us to go through the motions. There were good times had, laughter laughed, and intimacy imitated; but his job as a sometime political consultant took him on the road a good bit, and by around 1990 he resided in Montgomery a goodly portion of the week, making nice with senators and such, old white men he never would have ass-kissed back in his day. And yea, my solitude grew in upon me, took me easily into isolation; I rarely saw Opal and encountered Emerald only at our mutual work place at Sandy Dunes Real Estate offices anymore, though they both made attempts to say "hello in there."

"You have to come eat dinner with me," Opal would say. "You're like an old musty rug. You need to be aired out."

"I'm afraid it is you who have erred," I would retort punnishly, "for I care not to be aired."

Emerald would press me to go out for drinks after work of a Saturday, but I always made some feeble, transparent excuse, drawing in to the flicker of the old Phillips television screen, red wine and chains of smoke.

Of course, over the long term I slid ever further from my Self, as did he. I systematically clicked off the edges of my own personality that threatened to look into his other lives, those I knew were out there and those I sensed were out there in the ever-dimming ether. My blockage in the writing department certainly eroded his respect for me, as that was a large part of his attraction to me. And he? For his part, he gradually let his ideology slide from fighting for lost causes, reviving them, even winning some, to pimping for smarmy political candidates, crossing over to the Dark Side of "victory at all costs." My respect, in turn, was sore eroded. But of course, as I told myself—I am no naïf—that is the ecosystem of the American Experiment. It's a dirty job, as they say, but somebody's got to do it.

I suppose.

The catfight in the statehouse around ten years into our estranged coupling, of course, could not be denied. It made the *Montgomery Advertiser* for god's sake. I trembled for a time that it would be picked up by the corporate media and garner huge ratings and put me in a scandalous spotlight that I was ill-prepared to navigate. If it had happened this century it certainly would have been fodder for the 24-hour news cycle, with empty-eyed anchors and breathless panels raking it over and over and over the coals in a never ending loop of mindless voyeurism. Luckily, the single newspaper story here recounted was the beginning, middle and end of the public drama:

POLITICAL PUSSYFOOTING LEADS TO PUGILISTIC POONTANG!
Call Girls Tussle over Hand Job
Two capitol security officers were summoned to the state house rotunda last Tuesday to break up a brawl between two Montgomery call girls who were apparently fighting over Democratic campaign manager and former union lobbyist Hand Job, whose twenty-five-year career in state and regional politics has been one of distinction.

Christie Anne Dawson and Tashanna Ember Crook disrupted a routine day when a group of state senators found them fully engaged in a fury of fingernails, wigs, and hair weave at around 8:30 a.m. Officers Big Boy and Bad Ass were able to quash the altercation promptly, and neither woman was seriously hurt.

Hand Job, who has been associated with many prominent Democrats over the years, had no comment on the pugilistic display. Charges against all involved are being considered.

Of course, charges were never filed, most likely because so many in the legislative branch of Alabama the Beautiful are tres familiar with the seedy side of Monkeytown. Republican or Democrat, they have their own little subculture in the city that gave us Zelda Fitzgerald and Hank Williams. They have their favorite bars and their favorite women. Yes, these good old white boys—for it is still, even in the twenty-first century, a predominance of (old) white boys who run my fair state—many of whom were nerds who never scored with girls in their former lives and discovered that power, however limited, is quite the aphrodisiac for a good percentage of the shallow chicks out there in the world. And the rest of the white boys, former jocks who demeaned the aforementioned nerds in high school and who learned about shallow chicks much earlier in life ("Oh, Johnny, let me keep your chin strap as a memento of your winning touchdown!" swoon, swoon) continue to live those glory days on into perpetuity—or at least until voted out of office.

Ah do love me some politics.

Of course, I did not have the entire posse to buffet me at that time, but Opal and Emerald stuck by my forlorn side, commiserating in the humiliation, urging me to ditch Hand Job, growing more and more frustrated at my lack of anger, my preponderance of tears. This was at the height of a mountainous spike in my depression. I simply did not have the energy to be wrathful. It was my

94

mentally deranged parental units, unfortunately, who were energized. Bizarro Ozzie and Bizarro Harriett came running to shore me up, which only plunged me deeper into the black hole, as ancient muscle memory kicked in and splayed open even more old wounds from which to run.

"Nobody's going to treat *my* twinkly sparkly that way," BO attempted to snarl as I pondered the notion of "belonging" to another.

"My God, prostitutes! Can you imagine where they have been?" BH offered up as a reassuring balm for my emotional fragmentation.

"Call girls," I replied, attempting, I knew not why, to clean them up a bit for my crazy mother. "Apparently there is a difference."

BH sniffed. "Well I am most assuredly certain that they are breaching some kind of professional ethical standard that disallows them from becoming enamored of their clientele. At the very least one would hope that such a public display would be verboten."

"My poor little twinkly sparkly." BO soothed, or attempted to. Keep in mind I was well over forty when this precursor event to the Big Break Up gave me a preliminary shatter.

Preliminary? Precursor? I can hear you now, eyes wide, in solidarity with Opal and Emerald, uttering an amazed, "You did not divorce him then, at that moment?" Alas, only one who has been in shut-down mode as I was could ever understand the desperation to re-make, self-justify, re-structure the only house of cards I knew, hearkening back, in BO fashion, to my own psych-ward style Childhood in the Land of Denial, having lost the me I so briefly found in the Glory Days of my twenties, unable to even attempt to get her back.

I forgave him. Was that not the "divine" course of action?

I told myself they were whores, paid for hire.

And it was not deep, emotional quality time for him.

After all, he is a male. A myriad of studies has been done verifying the high percentage of what supposedly monogamous men will do when presented with their "act" of choice. How different was he from the average run-of-the-mill Joe, whose wife routinely withheld sex for weeks and months on end, blowjobs a statistical impossibility?

Okay, so these women of the evening had become inappropriately attached, apparently got sucked into Hand Job's darkness, found his sexuality a challenge, just as I did, then got wrapped up in rivalry, then lost their heads over his lack of interest in their contest. He did not have a ho in that fight. Poor girls. Their presence was a function of his unfulfilled carnal desires, which, I surmised at the time, surely resided out there on the fringes of heterosexual sex. Obviously they were not hired to engage in anything like a missionary position, so there had to be a catch.

As previously noted, I have never shied away from a bit of happy sexual fun—until my collapse into clinical apathy, that is. And lo, I began to turn a bit of our old friend Guilt back upon myself, mustering only enough energy to realize that Hand Job's and my descent into rut-dom had created a culture of not rutting (after a fashion) in our boudoir. Perhaps I could try to turn that sad fact around. Perhaps I could take on the prostitutorial role and convince him to share his fantasy of choice and method of satiation.

And lo, with tremendous wherewithal and something remotely akin to gathering glee, I pumped myself up. And more and more did the pumpage produce results prolific. And yea, I pounded the imaginary shoulder pads, throttled the air with a defiant fist (*Whoop! Whoop! Whoop! Whoop!*) I could do this! I was woman enough to take the challenge! I could peel back another layer of the onion and engage his rotten core, bring him through the darkness, into the light, and we would live happily ever after while bluebirds sang and gauzy, pastel butterflies laced the emerald trees in my sunny little fairytale land.

I coaxed him—rather forcefully, after the tears and the screamed curses (all right, I did manage a modicum of fury) and the glasses I hurled, one by one—to reveal all. What the hell did he need with high paid hookers (okay, "call girls," but really what's the difference unless you are framing a retort for your crazy mother)?

And he did reveal, slowly, that the kind of interplay required to resurrect his wayward wang involved a harmless bit of theatre along with momentum of the autoerotic genre. It was all so un-unnatural—white-bread common, even—to the point that I was a bit disappointed. No perversion, not even any light bondage? A leather riding crop? A tutu? Something? And yet he agonized so over the verbalization of it. Do you now begin to understand how full of guilt this spouse of mine was? Think engorged. Like a blood-bloated tick or the full-blown throat of a tree frog or a three-weeks-overdue Octo-Mom.

I suspected even then that there was much, much more to the traumatized terrain of his *id*, though I am a bit embarrassed to say I had never considered, even in the context of his other addictions—to booze, to work, to chaos—that there might be a sex addiction at play, or worse. Bill Clinton had not yet ascended and reached his own seminal moment and raised our awareness of such—had not yet soiled the infamous blue dress getting what every man in America wants but rarely, as afore-noted, receives from his spouse. And I was not even being asked for said oral gift— the one Willie J.'s detractors apparently never got or they would not have been so damn angry about all the language parsing. What I was being asked for was something that just happened to be right down the *alley* of my former self: drama, whimsy, a grand performance, the telling of a story! This had potential, not to mention the fact that he would do most of the heavy lifting. Thus his moniker: Hand Job.

My dear, dear, friends ask, from time to time, whether I have any regret about that decision, the one which led to my murdered heart, my disemboweled trust. And the short answer is: no.

You see, I believe if I were supposed to rebound at that point in my life, I would have mustered the wherewithal to do so. Call it hokey pop psychological gibberish if you like. I care not. It's true. So deeply dug into my own gruesome grave of unawareness, I had to be totally obliterated before I could even think to begin to tunnel my way to the Upper World. Look at Jesus, whom I adore. He was all about death before resurrection—not that I in any way put myself in the category of the Son of God (or, at least one of them). It is one of the great Truths of Life that we all struggle through unique personal adversities, and some of us actually learn from them, on our own individual learning curves. Show me a person who says otherwise, or worse, someone who claims a charmed and perfect life, and I will show you one of two things: a liar or a bore.

At any rate, the beat, as it were, picked up and went on, as did Hand Job and moi. We laughed and dined and were intimate and socialized, and it was with this last exterior behavior that yet another of his compartments was laid at my feet, that of the long-time "other" woman, who, I discovered, apparently considered *me* said "other" woman.

She was from a former life of his, the one he apparently only temporarily discarded when we married. And, as lives are wont to do, our former ones had briefly intersected once upon a time, as recounted earlier, so that there were a handful of

99

mutual acquaintances—a few barely on the cusp of her life, a few more barely on the cusp of mine. Yes, you are correct—Miss Clitopatra Denial.

It was the turn of the century, Y2K, when the maidenhead of the new millennium reared up like an asp. Hand Job and I had slogged on for another decade in our dance of dysfunction, and of course I find the historic timing of my downfall deliciously symbolic. The world was ruminating over whether global computer systems would crash the planet into a modern Dark Ages, as world markets crumbled and hospital patients expired in numbers that heralded a digito-viral plague. A blank screen, and—poof!—one no longer existed. Surely the End Times were upon us. Talking heads yammered. Alarmists shrieked. Hoarders scrambled to ensure that they would have theirs, everyone else be damned.

It was in the midst of this apocalyptic frenzy that I ran into X, a vague and distant acquaintance of mine but also an old friend of Miss Denial. X was in Fairhope to browse the trendy little shops that are all the rage with moneyed out-of-towners. How she recognized me is beyond comprehension, unless I capitulate to vanity and boast that I have aged quite nicely, in spite of sun and cigarettes, having embraced fish oil, melatonin, and gallons of water per day. And, like Old Faithful's waters, she commenced doing this annoying Southern thing that seems to be required of the preciouser sex, spewing overly expressive, overly religious enthusiasm upon me. (Florence King called it "the pert plague" in her high-larious book, *Southern Ladies and Gentlemen*; if you have not read it you simply MUST)"Oh, my Lord!" X gaspy-shrilled. "If it isn't Ruby Pearl! It's so heavenly to see you again, precious! Sweet Jesus Lord! I never would have thought for a second—what in the name of the Mardi Gras have you been up to? Isn't it a small world?"

(As opposed to a simple "Hi, R.P. How have you been?").

I thought it was not such a small world, what with Fairhope being my hometown and hers being ninety miles up the road, but one should always (attempt) to be polite, so I commenced a more restrained gushing in return, exchanging the requisite queries, wearing the expression of overstated sincerity which is expected during such encounters.

Three minutes in, her expression ramped up a notch on the sincerity meter as she forged into the "Have You Heard About?" realm. I was attempting to revise my body language to insinuate a Most Important Engagement Elsewhere and it was so nice to see you and you tell everyone hello and be sure to keep in touch, none of which was sincere but part of the script we Southerners know inside out, when she hissed, "Did you hear about Hand Job and Miss Denial?"

The pairing of the two names set in me a paralysis beyond what is found in petrified artifacts from an archaeological dig, along with a chilled gut that went quickly to nausea. I maintained my composure, though, and managed a very weak little, "What's that?"

"It was absolutely horrific! They were mugged. They're both in the hospital in New Orleans."

"Really?" Was my level of shock-induced underwhelment tipping her off to the fact that I was flashing forward to the pulverization of everything I thought to be true?

"Yes! They go there a couple of times a year. They were in the wrong place late at night and a group of colored boys flat out attacked them. Hand Job was stabbed in the shoulder and beaten really badly. And they hit Miss Denial so hard in the face that she is going to lose her left eye. Can you believe it?"

Well, I was too shocked to believe anything, though at the moment I noticed two things that stand out to this day. The first was that despite definite shock, I did not feel much surprise. Had I been aware, on a deeper level, of this betrayal all along? The second thing I noticed was being repelled by her use of the phrase "colored boys," though, again, not surprised. There is a certain class of folks in my redneck of the woods who, while certainly not looked upon as "rednecks"—more like aristocrats and their hangers-on—still use that label in spite of its being altogether pre-mid-twentieth century. Was it odd that the term stood out? Maybe it went back to my lack of surprise that I could even process the particulars of what she was saying.

The remainder of the exchange, however, became a muted, fuzzed and garbled jumble of words that had no form. It was as if I were under water, she above, and after nodding and inching away from her, bit by itty bit, I was finally relieved to be, as the country folk say, "shed of her."

I called him, to get it from the horse's mouth. I knew not which hospital to call, so I tried the usual suspect numbers. There was no answer at his Montgomery apartment or his cell phone. I left messages in the usual tone, laying the groundwork for what I hoped would be either a successful entrapment or, pathetically, the exposure of a simple rumor or a bad joke.

He called back, later in the day, and, unable to restrain myself, I set upon him. "Which hospital?"

"What are you talking about?"

"Look, I know, okay. Just for once, be honest. You know how I feel about honesty."

Silence.

"I already know. Why are you so terrified of just telling me the truth?"

More silence.

"Are you going to survive the attack?"

"Yeah. I'm fine. I'm out already."

"For the moment, anyway," I retorted. "What about Miss Denial?"

Yet more silence.

This was a familiar theme in our relationship— knowing that he did indeed have compartments and layers of insanity, just as I did; he, frozen like soon-to-be roadkill in the headlights of exposure. I often made the case that if he did not come clean and integrate all the compartments, the day would come when a small event would spill one into the next, into the next, into the next, and, like Lollipop licked, like the good ship Titanic, Hand Job would surely go down. And now here it was: our relationship was officially a shipwreck.

The following days were a jumble of tirades, tears, soft words, solid embraces, and vindictive vitriol. I truly did want the truth from him but discovered a man addicted to guilt, which can only be created by lies, and also addicted to terror, which can only be created by confrontation that is the inevitable result of dishonesty. For the time being, the pull of guilt was much stronger coming from Miss Denial's quarters; he could feel responsible for letting her down, being unable to protect her—hell, he had a one-eyed, half blind dependent on his hands.

"How do you manage sex with her?" I asked, ever the inquisitive writer, studier of human motivations and flaws.

"Sex isn't an issue."

"What?" I was overtaken at once by a fury as I have never known, unable to appreciate the fact that said fury was reviving me as it had failed to do following the Call Girl Incident. "Your penis has no issues with her?" This was beyond the pale. I prepared to pummel him with follow-ups, unleash the green-eyed whatchamacallit upon him.

"I didn't mean that."

Yet he did not elucidate.

"How the hell is it not an issue?"

"Not everyone has to have sex."

And, yea, it dawned upon me, the symmetry in neon within my understanding. Impotence meets Frigidity. Opal had, indeed, been correct. Everybody wins.

Would that it was so exquisitely simple.

Seems he had never thoroughly broken it off with her, and he saw her sporadically and sometimes not for months at a time. He never told her we were married, and he effectively kept the fringes of the worlds from colliding. He's a man who wants to save the world, remember—wants to do good deeds, make everybody happy. So, of course, he is a lousy breaker-upperer. Although he did accept my demand for a divorce—reluctantly— here it gets even crazier: he fastidiously maintained that it would be temporary, that he did, indeed, feel an obligation to get Miss Denial through recovery, that we would ultimately remarry. "You're it. You know me. I've told you things that I never—you just have to trust me. This arrangement isn't going to last forever."

That was the moment when the reality of his madness, and mine, set in. I had heard of a temporary separation, but a temporary *divorce*? Work out—what?

I, who had fallen into an appallingly familial need for security, now had to, as they say, deal. So I spent several days sobbing; the fetal position was *de rigueur*; the thought of sustenance repulsive. I grieved myself hollow and fifteen pounds lighter, which, I had to admit, gave me back a very youthful, flat stomach. "Every cloud . . ." etc.

Yes, I was in grave need of nourishment during the grief storm. But I needed spiritual help even more, so that I could get back to the food. My guardian angel and I had maintained a correspondence in letters, and, with the advent of the cell phone, every six months or so I would call Lucky (he never called, but I knew he would always answer) and unburden or regale or complain or dissect. Of course, as the years grew darker, I called less. But, as the fourth marriage dissolved, I found myself on the phone with Lucky for the first time in a long time, pouring out my grief, sobbing, bemoaning my stupidity and the wasted life I had lived, the shadow life, the emptiness, the deceit.

"All those times you said you were fine, I knew. I knew things weren't cool."

"Yes," I said. "I lied to you."

"Only because you were lying to yourself. It's not a betrayal."

"Why do I keep dancing with the devil I know?"

"Because you want to make life complex when it's way simpler than you can fuckin' imagine."

"But—"

"Look. Are you still determined to attempt this strange thing you call monogamy?"

"Probably so—if I ever get to that place again."

"You will," he said. "And here's what I want you to do, if you've got to latch on to someone."

"I've wasted so many years by not being honest. I'm not about to *not* probe you about any advice you have to offer."

"Latch on to someone uncomplicated, someone who's easy in his skin."

"But how boring would that be?"

"I didn't say unintelligent. Uncomplicated doesn't equal unintelligent."

"But where would the mystery be? The intrigue?"

"I think you'll be surprised. There's a lot of mystery in the uncomplicated."

"How is that?"

"Well, if you observe yourself interacting with the uncomplicated, then you can more fully understand why you ever needed to plug into the complicated."

"My life's been a total waste."

And he, being the touchstone, the center, the anchor of my spirit, said the kindest words I ever heard. "No. You didn't waste those years."

That did it. I disintegrated. In a bit I managed to breathe out, "How can you say that?"

"I just can, unequivocally. He was worth it. Worth trying."

"Trying what?"

"To save him, understand him. Ultimately, to get to your self."

I sniffled and hiccupped as it settled into my mind.

He let a few beats go by, which I recognized as his usual signal for some big-ass revelation.

"Nothing happens in a vacuum; it all leads to this moment. You're a writer. It's time to get to it. And all that you've lived will make you an even better writer, this time around."

He was telling me it was okay, that I was not worthless, that I could still do something that mattered. Yes, my friends said the same thing, but it's always different coming from a holy angel with a glittering voice full of Celestial Truth. "This time around? A second chance?" I needed to hear it just a time or two more, in spite of his holiness.

"There's always a second chance," he said.

"Always?"

"Absolutely. And I shouldn't even call it a chance. There's always everything, all at once. You just step into the reality you want."

"So I can still write my own story." It was stated as a plea.

"Of course," came the no-big-deal answer. "It's your reality to choose. Get to work."

And herein lies the soul (I already gave you the heart) of this thy post-menopausal Manifesto, **Tenet Number Seven: Thou shalt cut bait and fish.**

No bitching and moaning allowed (well, keep it within reason). God knows there are enough pathological whiners in the world; no need to unnecessarily taint it further. This tenet is always a good one in a crisis or a time of emotional upheaval. "Wash your dishes," in divine Buddhistic, taking-care-of business fashion. Adhere to Morgan Freeman's *Shawshank* line, "Get busy living, or get busy dying," or, as my grandmother put it, "Blow your nose and pull up your socks." Or, as I am wont to put it: "Color your hair and love your wrinkles." Misery and self-pity are two of the most unattractive things in the universe, certainly and especially in the sexual realm. Whether male, female, he-male, or she-male, victims are notoriously lousy lovers. Enough said.

It was Opal who let me lay my head on her lap and wail, God love her. She stroked my hair in as maternal a mode as she could muster, soothing, showing a valiant level of tenderness and friendship.

"You know," she said, as my tears abated some time later, "you were happiest when we were in college, when you decided to write, when you were a poet."

"You aren't telling me to write poems are you? Because they are likely to be self-flagellating, man-hating pieces of adolescent trash."

"So what?"

"Jesus, at this point in my life I certainly do not wish to become clichéd."

"Sweetie, you've already been that."

"When?"

"These past two decades."

It takes a truly, truly good friend to say something that harsh to you at the lowest moment in your life. Do you begin to understand exactly why I love Opal? I *had* been a cliché, and the realization flooded into my bloodstream, down into my cells. I had not even been on automatic, but rather, stuck in "park." My hand had not been pristinely poised above a virginal, white sheet of writing paper for lo the preceding twenty years. I had invested my tattered faith in a man who initially appeared to be intriguingly complicated only to find that he was disappointingly unsalvageable, in a viable relationship kind of way. I had invested my soul in uncovering an utter mess and subsequently become a mere hull of my former self. If there had been a Miss Flat Affect America Contest, I would have won it handily.

So it was that Lord Lucky's words, followed by those of Miss Opal, led me to a genuine moment of clarity.

There was nothing to do but rise to the occasion, nowhere to go but up. **Cut bait and fish**, by god. So I retired from my twenty-something years of teaching, and not a moment too soon, as the last thing I wanted to be around as an "adolescent" author/poet was a cadre of real life adolescents, with their pimply dramas and whispered judgments of one another. As the digital age was dawning in full, and the school library converting away from Mr. Dewy Decimal, I requested and received, in appreciation of my years of service, a free standing card catalogue, rows of drawers at the ready, as my own personal nod to my love affair with books. It was the most divine memento I ever could have imagined, the perfect keepsake of my decades in public education, a true personal treasure.

I continued part-time hours at real estating, scaling back each year, through early 2007, when I closed the book on that as well—again, not a moment too soon, as the housing bubble was building up to its bursting point. And, lo, I say unto you, I hurled every free moment of my waking energy into the written word, and, yes, the first drippings of my Schaeffer fountain pen were saturated in juvenile *angst*, followed by the anger and bitterness of a spurned woman, until, finally, after months and months and more months, the fanciful began to bleed onto the page. And while the early indigo etchings are embarrassingly trite and will never see the light of publication for every right reason, I here offer one of the first breakthroughs, when I began to find a touch of lightness, the acknowledgment of the absurdity of life with Hand Job. I did this by simply listing rhyming words such as:

after shock
cold cock

and:

turncoat
cutthroat
footnote

and:

Mr. Cheater

maltreat-her
Masterbeater
Mis-skeeter
secretor

Which I would then spin into very bad, aforementioned adolescently purging little ditties that, regardless of their lack of literary merit, most assuredly put me on the poetical path back from perdition.

I had found my way to **Tenet Number Seven**; I was **cut**ting **bait and** preparing to **fish**. And what I had learned from my travail actually does involve cutting and the balance needed when making the cuts. Therefore, I proclaim unto you **Tenet Number Eight: Thou shalt cut slack**. In other words, be in possession of a critical lack of criticism—which goes to the heart of kindness (thank you to Lucky), the creation of an atmosphere in which blunders, *faux pas*, even mega-screw-ups are (gasp!) allowed, lawsuits are discouraged, and the belief in the goodness of humanity encouraged. Quaint, I know, but do-able; HOWEVER, it does have a corollary, which is: **Tenet Number Nine: Thou shalt recognize that slack is not always well-deserved and should not be cut in such cases**—i.e., have a backbone (thank you to Hand Job). No need to cut slack for slackers, bruisers (literal or figurative), losers (unless they are loveable ones), or users (of people, that is; I care not one whittled sliver of wood about one's drug of choice). Bottom line: Sluts are nobody's doormats and so should have a low threshold for disrespect, should show their brass knockers when necessary, and should speak up for themselves and those who need such advocacy.

As for Hand Job, he continues to contact me to, as my countrified old grandmaw used to say, "beg me back."

"Have you come clean in your other lives?" I ask each time he begs.

Silence.

"Then how can I possibly even take it under consideration?"

"Because it's me. It's us. You're *it* for me."

"Can you lay out for me how exactly you have been managing all your lives until now and give detailed descriptions of each?"

Silence. Then, "I'll tell her. I'll just do it."

"Today?"

Silence.

"Alright then, do you object if I ask Miss Denial to lay out some answers for me?"

He sighed. "You do what you have to do."

It was just like him to allow me to do the dirty work, and I saw him more and more as the worst kind of coward. Brave in political battles, yes. But self-acknowledgement? Infinitely easier to attempt to save the world than himself. The irony was quite painfully beautiful.

And here is another surprise: I found the possibility of having a sit-down with Miss Clitopatra Denial stirringly intriguing. Perhaps we could compare notes and get a true picture of our overlapping lives. Perhaps we could even bond, become fast friends. Stranger things have happened. No doubt Dear Abby would not approve of my inclination to make contact. Miss Denial had a right to her privacy, after all. Then I thought about a short list of acquaintances who had surely known about this charade and kept quiet. More cowardice, although none of my bosom buddies were in that number. These days I tell my posse that sisterhood trumps any unworthy man, and we are all in agreement. If any of us sees a wandering spouse or temporary boyfriend in a compromising situation, we shall speak the truth.

Miss Denial was not in my posse, though. I did not know her as more than a blip in my life, a shallow conversation at an afternoon garden party. What if she were emotionally fragile? What if this sent her over some devastating edge? Wait a minute, I told myself. You are not asking her to hand over her charade of a boyfriend. You are not threatening a Goat Hill catfight. You are not asking for anything but the truth, and it's possible that she wants the truth as well. I found myself becoming more and more selfish. If she had answers that could offer me this so-called "closure" that was/is all the rage, why not simply ask? I took a deep breath. What the hell. Being the quintessential poetess/authoress, I would write Miss Denial a letter—a very grand letter.

My Dear Miss Denial,

I do hope this missive finds you recovering from your brutal injuries, and this is quite a sincere statement, as I do not lie, at least not consciously. Therefore, I shall get immediately to the point.

I have been married for twenty years to your (sometime?) boyfriend, Hand Job, whom I have recently divorced. As Hand Job has been unable to provide details about the nature of his relationship with you, other than characterizing it as "platonic" and "asexual," I was wondering if we might meet and share details with one another. I assure you, I am no lunatic set upon revenge against you as you no doubt have been as clueless as I; nor am I some sort of stalker to my ex-husband. *Au contraire*, it is he who continues to call me, professing love and the promise of *rapprochement* once his duty to you is fulfilled.

My intention is not to cause you upset, as I believe we are two sisters sitting in the same canoe on Shit Creek, as it were, and as a re-forming feminist I believe it would be to both our advantages to lay cards upon the table in the interest of surmising exactly what the hell just happened.

What do you say, kiddo?

With Surprising Sincerity,
Ruby Pearl Saffire

I congratulated myself for being direct, friendly, and lighthearted and was certain that she would be a woman of enough substance to seize upon the opportunity to get reality aligned to something like an honest one. But, alas, it was not to be. Miss Denial offered no response whatsoever.

So I confronted Hand Job, demanding to know if he had, in adolescent-pre-empting-bad-report-card-fallout style, intercepted my pink envelope from her mailbox.

"No," he said, irony in his tone. "She got it all right," and proceeded to tell me that she ripped him a new one over it all.

"So you must have convinced her that I am some kind of Bizarro Harriett nut job or else she would have contacted me by now."

He did not deny that accusation but only said, "She's probably not the type to respond."

"I don't wonder. Unresponsive sexually. Unresponsive honestly. She sounds like a spineless, idiotic, anti-feminist, dry puff."

Of course, my own words were rubber and I was glue (well, not the "dry puff" part).

Still, I had to give her a third strike. Had I received such a letter, ever—something as tangible as pink stationary bearing critical information—I would have been there in a broken heartbeat. Wouldn't I?

"Damn right," Emerald said. "I would've taken you my own self."

"Forget it," Opal chimed in. "You have all the sisters you need in me and Emerald."

And that was the moment I promised myself to accumulate a wider circle of friends, interesting ones, who would always respond to a damsel in distress, a sister sundered into subterranean sadness, befuddled bewilderment over a rent reality. This is by no means a slam against Opal and certainly not Emerald; I simply had an insight about there being more strength in higher numbers—but numbers of quality. And lo, I opened myself up unto it.

And into the void rode the Magnificent Three, giving rise to the Dirty Half-dozen: Opal, Emerald, Marble, Diamond, Micah, and moi; and the quality of my existence and my tapping of the keyboard of life burgeoned into a love of the moment that many never, ever find. That is why I truly consider myself supremely fortunate and steadfastly refuse to ever fall back into bitterness, despair, guilt, or any dark, counterproductive emotion out there in the universe of heart, soul, and mind.

Chapter 4: Buddy List: The Dirty Half Dozen

MY posse is unique, well-rounded, and engaging. Already established as my best friend is <u>Opal White</u>; she is accorded that status only because of longevity—seniority, as it were. She is much like family, is certainly more of a sister than my biological one, and just as we tend to put up with more of the fecal matter from our own families, so we do with those friends who last us a lifetime. My fellow Slutswomen tolerate Opal for that reason as well (just as I tolerate the occasional childhood buddy of theirs whom they bring into the fold), but not without a great deal of eye-rolling and subversive glances at one another. They, and I, refer to Opal as my "token childhood friend." Actually, the fact that they do suffer Opal's insensitive quirks and remarks quite well goes to their willingness to cut slack of their own (Reminder: **Thou shalt cut slack**). A variety of age groups and interests are well represented, and you can be certain that I, Ruby Pearl Saffire, do not surround myself, in this my **Second Sluthood**, with dullards. Those who are not the brightest of the beams are at least eccentric or downright crazy enough to be entertaining (witness Opal). So allow me now to more thoroughly introduce you to my tight-knit group of token friends, my posse, my set, my peeps, mis amigas, for, as everyone knows, women travel in packs, and at the core of mine are five, plus me—the Dirty Half-Dozen.

As with any pack, there is a hierarchy, and, as the sluttiest and most vocal of the group, not to mention the fact that I came up with the entire notion of a **Second Sluthood**, yours truly serves as the alpha female. The ranks of the others are sometimes in flux, but I can give you a quick bio, role within the group, personality traits, and, most importantly, what I give and what I take from the relationship, for verily I say unto you, without both the give and the take there is toxicity and/or doom.

Marble Gotrocks is my token wealthy friend. True, Opal has plenty of cabbage, but, after a brief marriage based on idealism (followed by a dose of reality in the form of a vicious, retaliatorial divorce) Marble remarried, quite by design, into a boatload of it. Her new husband, a lovely gentleman now in his seventies (Marble is forty-three and is drop-dead gorgeous, which is pretty much required if one intends to marry into caverns of capital— *hmm*—"Marble's Caverns"—sounds touristy), is simply rich for a living, managing trusts and giving orders to attorneys and accountants and whatnot. Timber and oil. In this part of the piney woods those are the two mother lodes, one literally right on top of the other. Old Gotrocks could live off the interest into perpetuity.

Marble lives in a stately manse, high on a bluff overlooking the Mobile Bay. Mr. Moneybags also owns a beach house in Destin, Florida, and a Mountain house in Steamboat Springs, Colorado. She calls them "homes," but I maintain that you must live in a structure for the majority of the year before you can call it a "home." Besides, the word "home," as in, "my beach home," sounds utterly and completely pretentious, and I do not hesitate to call Marble on her attempts at snootiness. She is not snooty by nature but sometimes allows it to rub off on her when she spends too much time with the Arts League or the Junior League or some Mardi Gras society that fancies itself the ultimate in exclusivity. Those of us who know her background have no truck with her faux-aristocratic posturings. Her daddy drove an eighteen wheeler when he wasn't drunk and her mamma was a clerk at Bill's Dollar Store.

To be perfectly honest, I have a very intense prejudice against wealthy people, so I was surprised that I got to like Marble so easily. She's smart, reads books, loves to discuss things and talk through points of contention, often with a very quick wit. Politically, she is to my right and Opal's left, which fills out the dialogue a bit. She is honest about her life choices. Furthermore, I give Marble what Opal gives me: needed comeuppance. And, to pro quo the quid, *from* Marble I get the chance to at least think about keeping a check on this admitted prejudice of mine. While I have always (well, of late) admitted to my tendency to make generalizations in general, Marble has helped me to subdue my determination to generalize about wealth in particular. Still, the fact remains that I simply have not met many (in particular) rich-via-inheritance folks I can abide. Marble (rich via gold-digging) I love. Therefore, I can assuage my failure at completely overcoming prejudice by having her as a friend. Of course, this does not mean we fail to challenge one another.

"Have you ever considered that you are covetous of what other people have?" Marble might ask me. "That you are *jealous*?"

"Jealous of what? Of those among us who have the ability, the connections, lo the monetary means, to lift others up from the mire of poverty or disease but fail to do so because it would cut into their time with their personal trainers?"

"You know good and well that my husband has his charities."

"I was not speaking of you personally. You are the Mother Teresa of rich bitches."

To Marble's credit, she usually laughs before she insists "Lots of people keep their charity work private. And everybody wants the American dream."

"And which dream is that?"

"To not have to worry about money. To make a million dollars."

"Or to marry it?"

"That, too."

Here I should interject that my bias is not focused on a specific amount of cash. To be sure, the unbridled greed and wealth that qualifies one to be profiled on some sleazy television hand job about the rich and famous puts one immediately, in my mind, in league with the Devil. However, there are at least fifty shades of gray in the worthiness of any given individual who inherited a dumpster of money, having not toiled a moment in his or her luxury-lapped life. Perhaps we could come up with a sliding scale or something, an evaluative process through which one's charitable deeds are calculated against one's net worth, with an algorithmic formula to determine one's decency level and his or her rank within the realm of the Moneyed Ones (Bill and Melinda Gates, for example, would definitely get a pass, as would Oprah). Unfortunately, I don't do math and so am left with only my gut reaction, which is not always one hundred per cent. Just so you know.

I can't resist a tiny jab at Marble. "You went a little beyond a million, didn't you? What does old Gotrocks make, a million a month? Besides, a million is yesterday's thousand, just like today's size six is yesterday's size ten."*

"That's more of an inverse, don't you think?"

"You know what I mean."

"I wanted to never worry about money," she will say, tossing her very expensive blonde hair, flashing a very expensive pearly-white smile (she was contemplating some very expensive breasts until the posse staged an intervention; as a Slut such a surgery is verboten).** "My parents were always worried about money and I was always scared we would be living in the car. Do you know what that does to a kid over time?"

Which is pure obfuscation, but what the hell. I am patently true to **Tenet Eight** when well deserved.

I did not, however, **cut** Marble any **slack** when she was fighting a speeding ticket because she claimed the officer who stopped her was prejudiced against rich people.

"I was driving the Jaguar near our neighborhood at the beach, and—well, there really are people who are jealous and who want to get even for things," she whined.

"What things? Was Officer Porcine traumatized by a sports car when he was a child?"

"Just *things*. Who knows what things? Things like maybe they believe my wealth comes at their expense. Or some kind of perverse jealousy. Or maybe they're closet communists."

"That is certainly a scary word! I remember the Red Menace films in high school. You think they've infiltrated the police force?"

"Well," she says, aiming a below-the-belt jab at the President, "if socialists can infiltrate the White House . . .

This was early in 2009, so my response was rather raw. "I shall resist the urge to launch here into a discussion of taxation and fair shares and socialism and such silliness as that. I shall not go into how Teddy Roosevelt, Republican, came up with the notion that the rich should pay their share in order to benefit from the wealth garnered as a result of the privilege of *living* in this democracy. I won't go into how that selfsame Repub said that the working folk *building* this nation deserved three things: a living wage, affordable health care, and retirement with dignity. Jesus, he must have been, what—a terrorist? an Islamofascist? What about another scary word that means nothing but the ability to manipulate stupid, non-critical thinkers by scaring them to death? He must have been a—dare I say it? It's so goddamn scary. But here goes: he was a Republican socialist. I shall resist that urge. "

"Thank you, because the point is, *I was not speeding*!"

"It's not as if the Destin police force is not very *literal* when it comes to the speed limit," I pointed out. Which is a fact. And which, by the way, I believe is the correct way to proceed. Why bother calling it a "limit" if you are going to allow five or ten miles per hour over that "limit," at which time it ceases to be a "limit" and then there are no "limits." Then what kind of system for the orderly movement of vehicular sojourners do you have? Well, you have "anarchy," that's what you have. Marble disagrees, of course, as the vast majority surely does as well, careening through the streets in NASCAR mode, like the multiple ghosts of Dale Earnhardt, oblivious to any line of demarcation on the speedometer, which brings them, ultimately, to the point of running afoul of the law, as did Marble.

"I was *not* speeding. And he was very rude, calling me 'lady' and all. 'Where you going in such a hurry, *lady*'? and, 'Didn't you see the speed limit sign, *lady*'?"

"But you do consider yourself a lady, right?" When Marble has been in Junior League world for too long she clutches onto those quaint old Southern customs and archaic niceties, chief among them being considered a "lady." I chalk it up to Stockholm Syndrome and continue to **cut** more **slack** until she comes around to her genuine self.

"Don't be disingenuous, R.P. You know very well that addressing a female as 'lady' is crass and low class. Unless it's in the context of 'Lord and Lady' I mean."

"Mostly it sounds as if you're addressing a pet collie."

"That would be Laddie."

I told you she was quick. "For god's sake, Marble, he did *not* know your name."

"It's on the license, isn't it?"

"It's just cop talk," I tried again. "They do love their lingo. How does it feel to be a 'perp'?"

"God! It's not like I ran over an old lady and fled the scene. You have to do something more violent than speeding to get that designation."

"Aha! So you *were* speeding." A true Perry Mason moment washed over me in a shimmering wave of self-satisfaction.

She narrowed her green-as-new-money eyes at me. "No. I was not."

I tried a new tack. "Okay, you're right. You are one hundred per cent right. You have convinced me and I agree. You are one of a group of oppressed and abused citizens, an American secret and an American tragedy. Go ahead and fight this evil speeding ticket and fight the rude, rude policeman, and I will stand by you."

"Damn right I plan to fight it."

"With a legion of lawyers and advisors—a real Simpsonian legal team."

"Whatever it takes."

"Yes! Yes! In the name of all who have gone before, you fight it. We cannot have this oppression of the wealthy. In fact, we should organize, start a real movement. Or—what about a revolution? We can call ourselves the Rich Americans' Liberation Front."

"Oh, good lord."

"Acronym RALF. Perfect! Motto: *We gag the maggots who are the haters of privilege.* What do you think?

"I think you are twisted and sick." But she was smiling as she said it.

"And we can unite to get the law off the collective back of the wealthy man, he who has toiled and suffered long enough, the last of the misused minorities."

"Blah, blah, blah."

"We'll have a Rich Man's March on Washington. We'll call it the Million Dollar March."

Marble finally burst out laughing, having "come to," as she generally does. And as for her regular forays into the teas and polo tournaments and exclusive clubs, I appreciate her offering vignettes about the vestiges of the Old South that cling like cockleburs to the underbelly of the region. They are often humorous until examined more closely, for truer meanings. Sometimes they are downright disturbing, less like cockleburs on the underbelly and more like the rubbery dingleberries on the derriere of what passes for decency.

It has verily amused me, however, since the 2008 election, and yet again in 2012, now that there is more color about the house at 1600 Pennsylvania Avenue, that the cockroaches have been scurrying out into the light of day, revealing themselves as the fecund little-minded racists they are. Their heads are now officially on fire, and my fervent hope all along has been realized: that they keep on screaming, keep on revealing their ignorance, keep on trying the same, tired tactics over and over, which amounts to (1) BOO! Or (2) Smear! And if there is a god, they will continue to paint themselves into a corner with the 2016 smack-down looming as I tap out these words.

Okay. Time out. Let's calm ourselves with a lengthy aside: mayhaps you noticed my asterisks, a few pages back. One looked like this: * and one looked like this: ** Take a moment to find them, as they were reminders to tell you about the next few tenants (reminder to fascists: "tenets") of my **Second Sluthood**, both of which concern hypocrisy (which is where my mind goes when contemplating politicians of ANY stripe). They are:

*Tenet Number Ten: Thou shalt not buy (literally) into the couture con of fake clothing sizes, which is that industry's way of sucking up to female shoppers by telling them they are two sizes (at least) smaller than they actually are.

This deception dawned upon me a few years back, when I noticed that, even though I had actually been gaining enough weight to go up to a size ten, the tag on the garment that looked to be my size read "size 6." I checked some other outfits. Same thing. It was infuriating to realize just what a vanity-infused, self-absorbed little (uh, big) pea brain these "bottom line" people believed me to be. And it continues without comeuppance or consequence for them.

For example, just last week, as I was perusing the endless channels on my endlessly-channeled TV, I came across one of those idiotic "magic diet" commercials. The satisfied customer—a young woman in the requisite "after" bathing suit—proclaimed, "I'm a size two! I haven't been a size two since high school!" Of course, *any* woman could look at her and see she's at least what used to be an eight. Maybe even a ten (who knows to what extent even I have been brainwashed?) Best case scenario (*vis a vis* a lot of Scarlett O'Hara-esque sucking in, along with a "Mammy" to zip her up), a six. And, a la the Lloyd Bentson-Dan Quayle debate of 1988, I desperately wanted to pronounce to this vapid, simpering shill of the Size Nazis, right through the television screen and into to her pudgy little ears, "I've worked with size twos. I interact with size twos every day. Honey, you're no size two."

Wake up and smell the Chanel, ladies. If you have had to question the tags on any garment—or even if you have not, do this one thing: just get naked, stand in front of a mirror (preferably a three-sided one) in a very brightly-lit room radiating an eco-friendly fluorescent glow, and conduct a private and thorough reality check.

Those lying size tags would not be necessary if not for the fact we Americans are so damn big and fat. Nor would the preponderance of infomercials about miracle diets. Which brings me to **Tenet Number Eleven: Thou shalt never go on a fad diet, buy a book about dieting, give up any food you love, or mute in any way the hedonistic pleasure of epicurean sensuality.**

Yes, Americans are lard-asses, and no, I am not advocating obesity. But for god's sake wake up to the fact that if you really do want to lose weight all you have to do (assuming that you have no congenital, glandular, or other medically challenging condition, is two things: eat less and move more). You heard it here first, America. All those fad diets, with their attendant books, juices, recipes, pills, powders, energy bars, tables, schedules, graphs, cards, colors, and other accoutrements do NOT work any better, and, in most cases not nearly as effectively as taking in less (as in eating) and moving around more (as in exercising). And it's—gasp!—free! Women who obsess about diets and fat grams and carbs and calories, who are always and forever pinching the fatty areas of their arms and thighs to check their density, who chit chat about the latest book written by the latest con artist who is going to magically make them look like the latest hottest supermodel (who probably looks to be five paces out of Dachau)—these women are toxic, or, at the very least, shallow. They are lemming, sheep, schools of salmon swimming against the genetically encoded current of their most basic human desire: food.

And while I am on the subject of vanity, allow me to offer up

**Tenet Number Twelve: Thou shalt never, not for even a slice of a millisecond, consider plastic surgery (well, excepting the instance of a horribly disfiguring accident).

I am pugnaciously passionate about this one, and deeply disturbed by my generation's denial of the inevitable, their refusal to stay in their own character. All the nipping and tucking and stapling and peeling and lifting and augmenting and botoxing and dermabrasing in the universe will not eliminate the fact that, hey, you are going to get *old* and *die*, so you might as well die well. Which is to say, gracefully. Each grooved crinkle, every weathered wrinkle should bear witness to the fact that you have lived a genuine life and are proud enough of it to put it out there. It galls me to gag that my generation, these baby boomers who were so pivotal in turning society on its head, who took to the streets for civil rights, who were instrumental in ending a war are now going Anti-Natural. Why not decide that aging is beautiful and change that attitude as well? My god, if you can go without shaving your legs and armpits for a few years, surely you can stand some wrinkles.

And another thing—the dirty little secret (for those not of a bent to shove their "work" right in front of your crow's-footed eyes) of having had "work" done is never a secret. We can always tell who has had "work" done, and if you continue re-forming your face past a certain age (sixty-something seems to be the tipping point) it is not only unattractive, it is downright bizarre looking. Witness those aging actresses (and the growing legion of male actors) whose faces are now a startled stretch of skin pinned into their scalps, stretched so tight the seams might give at any second, sending muscle, nasal cavities, eyeballs, everything cascading forth as from a skeleto-muscular horn of plenty. In the 1800s these women would have traveled with the Barnum and Bailey sideshow alongside the Amazing Alligator Man, the Bearded Lady, and the Thing in the Jar. Please, Hollywood, New York, suburbia, I beg of you, stop the insanity!

I declare to heaven, my bosom is literally *heaving* with spent passion. Ah, well, we all have our pet passions to go with the Slut's passion for petting, and I do have a tendency to digress.

So . . . as I was saying, hypocrisy is a mo-fo and I do hate it so (could this be the beginning of a future set of rhymed couplets? Ah, a poetic stirring is slipping through my soul. A gentle rap, perhaps?) Hypocrisy is the lackadaisical underminer of logic, the floundering fly in the anointment of the truth, and the fetid fiend from whom we all must flee. Yes, we all have an element of it in our worldviews, but hypocrisy is kind of like candied cherries in Christmas fruitcakes: there are either way too many, rendering the cake inedible; or there might be so few one can at least choke down a slice that tastes fairly good. But no one ever leaves out the candied fruit altogether, lest it lose the "fruitcake" designation. It all depends upon the recipe one follows (or better yet, avoid making fruitcake completely; everybody hates it).

Alas, even as I have taken myself to task (as earlier admitted, so **cut slack**), so have others accused me of the strange fruit of hypocrisy, for any of a number of transgressions. A religious fundamentalist might say I am a hypocrite because I reconcile being a Slut with spiritual cleanliness, while a rigid feminist could say I am the "H" word because I claim to be one of *them* whilst singing the praises of the power of the poontang. Hell, Opal even called me one when I introduced her to my concept of dubbing her and the gang my "token" friends, but of course this is a perfect example of her lack of a sense of humor and her tendency to take things, including the Bible, a bit literally.

"Tokenism goes against everything fair," she asserted. "*Merit* is what counts. You are being hypocritical."

"You are confusing my choice of a word for my slutty band of merry women friends with what you make of Affirmative Action."

"That's right. It makes us seem like we were chosen only because of one thing."

"Everyone but you were chosen for having the unique ability to run with the slutty thing. It goes to imagination."

"Oh, so I have no imagination. Well I guess I have enough to imagine what kind of Hades you would catch if you referred to someone as your 'token black' friend."

Which brings me to <u>Emerald Gray</u>. Emerald is one of the top saleswomen at the real estate agency that was my part-time employer for so many dead years. She is one of those Type A personalities who goes through life with the energy level of an Indy 500 pit crew, whether attending to job (*sell*, *sell*, *sell*, the vile idea of retirement being a decade or more into the future, although since the burst of the real estate bubble, along with her squirrelish habit of saving money, she has been seriously considering it) or family (husband—retired foreman at a paper mill, three kids—all decent human beings except for the bitchy youngest daughter; all in college, two cats—both Siamese, one dog—Chihuahua). She talks fast, eats fast, drives fast and *is* fast (but only with her husband; she has been faithful to him for forty-three years, or so she says). She offers a certain perspective—that of the happily faithful wife—that I have never known and never hope to know, I of the bouncing boudoir, I of the bumping of grinds, I of the revolving door of amorous assignations. And she has a rare man who apparently has been faithful as well—or is at least clever enough to have never been caught at anything assignatious, and

133

Emerald is not the kind of female who would ignore any of the tell-tale signs—and there are always plenty of signs, usually juxtaposed with a woman who lacks the inclination, imagination, or mental wherewithal to actually see them (yes, I speak here of myself, within a myriad of others).

Like Opal, Emerald and Jesus of Nazareth are very close; like me, Emerald is more of a liberal political bent than Opal, who, as evidenced, is quite conservative; and, like me, Emerald is fundamentally furious about the state of Christianity. At the same time, she walks with a bounce in her step, the swing of the pendulum having gathered its momentum, the tick of time having brought it long and loud into the realm of reason once more—enough that the 20th century folk persist in pulling ever harder against the evolution of the empathy gene.

Emerald is second in line of succession, in terms of longevity as a friend, only to Opal. And no, she is not my "token black" friend. Even I would not be so crass as to express our relationship in such a demeaning manner that flies in the face of current social niceties, however flimsy and furtively dishonest such racial niceties are. No. Emerald is my token mostly-African-American-with-one-quarter-Creek-Indian-and-a-dash-of-somewhat-white Louisiana-Cajun-raped-in friend, who does not want to be called "African American" and insists upon "black." I think it goes back to her "black is beautiful" big afro a la Angela Davis youth, and she is quite adamant about that ethnic indicator.

"What about being politically correct?" Opal chided her, getting the rise she sought.

"PC is BS," she said. "I've never been to Africa, don't want to go to Africa. I mean, I'm sure it's a beautiful country, but, shit. I'm a Louisiana girl."

I've tried to tell her that maybe she just hasn't had her Alex Haley moment.

"Just because some big ass writer went gallivanting all over the place digging up ancestors doesn't mean we *all* want to. Fuck Kunta Kinte. The only 'roots' I'm about are turnip roots."

She's had the "label" argument many times with the bitchy daughter, Nicole, who is a freshman at Florida State and, unlike her mother, *is* "African-American" and intends to at some point follow a DNA trail to her relatives across the Atlantic.

"She told me I wasn't respecting my ancestors, and that is eroding our culture," Emerald fumed. "Can you believe that bullshit? So I told her I reckon I wasn't eroding our culture when me and my friends were walking across the Edmund Pettis Bridge, you're welcome very much. Not to mention all the work I did and continue to do for Barack. And do you know what she did? Do you know?"

I allowed that I did not. Know.

"She rolled her eyes! Ooh, I wanted to pop that cocky little cheek! But I said we're going to live and by god let live. I said I ain't only over that bridge, I have over*come* that bridge. I said you be as African-American as you want to and I'll be all old fashioned like a mama's supposed to be. She can wear the braids and the beads and make a fuss over Kwanzaa and the whole nine yards. But we're going to let Emerald be Black with a capital 'B'—hell, I'll be Blajun if I want to be. Or Native Creek Blajun. Or Black Creek Cajun, you know, to honor my Native American blood and the old white-ass coon-ass who raped my great, great grandmother."

"And her response?"

"Oh, she knows when to stop with me, so she went on her know-it-all way. I ain't nobody but me and it is capital R-E-A-L."

"But not PC," Opal goaded.

"Anybody that gives up a personal principal just to be PC can put their head up their ass and kiss their guts goodbye, because they're gutless."

Yes, as diverse as our politics or our religious beliefs are, there are some critical—yea, essential—values upon which we insist, which I maintain goes directly to Sluthood. Ergo, in the time-honored tradition of, say, Moses descending Mt. Sinai with his cement tablets of God's commandments, come I with the **tenets** of Slutty Independence and to another friend of mine, one who sacrificed her independence and therefore her ability to see reality, sadly to her detriment (just as yours truly did for so long).

Diamond Jones, my most recently acquired friend (we shared a therapist), is also my token genius (IQ: 157) friend, living proof to me that one can be scintillatingly brilliant and still, um, fuck up one's own life.

Dr. Diamond is also a mamma—thrice a mamma in fact, but one who did not think through the having of the children until they were seven, eight, and thirteen. And of course, the return date on kids expires long before age thirteen. It isn't that Diamond is not a good mother or that she does not love her children. Quite the contrary. She is devoted and responsible and nurturing. But she did not give childbearing much thought at all, did not factor in how much of herself she would have to surrender, did not count upon the breakup of her marriage, and does not have the kind of Type A personality that enabled Emerald to "have it all." Certainly, she had the kind of drive that served her well just out of college, when she was starting her practice as a psychologist, but it would also work her into the ground as she strove to be—lights! camera! (drum roll, please) aaand—super-mommy!

I should point out here that while both Marble and Emerald have children as well, they have always been very relaxed about it all, not in overdrive to be some kind of mega-mom (Emerald has the overdrive, but not the inclination toward that unrealistic ideal of mommyhood), and the ever-looming mega-grandmom. Diamond, however, never had a relaxed day in her life until her kids were grown and gone. Determined to be the best mamma, she did what they call "it all" (unfortunately for her she almost never "did" her husband; certainly she never did any "jobs" on him); the successful career (though admittedly not near the success it could have been, and, as she is coming to realize, as she enters her **Second Sluthood**, can still be); the professional organizations; the networking; the pooling of the car from sports event to sports event and lesson to lesson; the shooter of trouble; and, ultimately, sadly, and predictably, the neglecter of her husband. Now mind you, I do not advocate infidelity, but one has to wonder, when these manic moms are racing to out-do one another, what, in the name of all that is truly tingly, has become of their husbands?

Sadly, today's parents are not living in an adult, grownup universe the way they used to, and if mamma or daddy is fully engaged in all aspects of the offspring universe, then how can they be engaged at all with one another? And we are surprised when either the mamma or the papa who ends up being excluded in that love triangle finds a more fulfilling relationship elsewhere? Ah, yes, this is another unpopular opinion of mine, the notion that all is not black or white, that yes, infidelities are often not just predictable, but sometimes, *sometimes* even understandable. Now, before you rant and rail about what the lying bastard or the whoring around bitch did, be mindful of the fact that (1) yours truly has flippin' *been* there and (2) a "reaction" is just what it says it is, "re" "acting," acting repeatedly, regardless of what would be productive: thinking in the now. The knee jerk reaction to blame the straying partner and absolve the overly-devoted-to-the-kids-to-the-point-of-dysfunctional parent defies reality, spins the wheels of logic in the slick mud of convention and entrenched attitudes and mores. Well, I say convention be damned. And you know what? Diamond agrees.

"I don't regret having children," she says, "but if I had it to do over, I would have had an expanded time and depth with my husband."

If only she'd had access to **Tenet Number One** in her youthful years!

"When Gary left me I spent two years being angry the major part of every day," she says. "I mean, the nest had emptied, the kids were gone, and that's when he tells me he's going to be with the woman he has loved for twelve years—and that woman is not me."

And so she commenced bad-mouthing her ex to her grown children, effectively poisoning her own relationship with the kids for whom she had sacrificed, quite wrong-headedly, her self; for it is etched in stone, occurring in all circumstances, regardless of the magnitude of any real or imagined transgressions, that any divorced spouse who speaks ill of his/her ex-spouse in the presence of shared child/children will fall dramatically in said child's/children's estimation(s). But, one might say, what about the time she—no, it matters not to the offspring. But, another might argue, he was a sorry piece of—again, it matters not a dollop. But do you know what he did to me? Nothing your ex ever did is bad enough that your child will appreciate your going over it, let alone repeatedly, *ad infinitum*, *ad nauseum*.

Diamond's moment of insight came when her twenty-four year-old-daughter, upon hearing the latest diatribe of misery and regret and blame from her mother, said simply, "I have no memory of you and daddy ever laughing together, and you're still not even trying to laugh. Please, mom, you've got to get over yourself."

"That," Diamond says, "got my attention. I saw myself fixed under a microscope, swabbed on a slide with the aperture set at 200x. I realized Gary and I had ceased to be engaged with one another. What little sex we had was perfunctory. The conversations were routine. We never, ever laughed. My god, without laughter it's obvious a relationship is dead."

And all as a result of her over-involvement with her children. It is a condition that affects parents of both sexes and homosexes, though when manifested in a father it typically reveals an overbearing jerk, the kind of guy who will whack a referee over a bad call against a son, or curse a teacher who does not give his daughter preferential treatment when it comes to discipline. And since it is more often than not a mothering issue as opposed to a fathering one, I usually call the condition "mad maw disease," although there is a subgroup of "mad paws." And this country, I fear, is in full-blown epidemic mode.

I can hear you berating me for assigning myself the role of High Priestess of Parenting when no living being was ever contracted from my tenetless womb, no amniotic-encased little bundle of perineum-ripping joy. "How is it that this childless, self-professed self-helper has the credentials to tell me how to be a decent parent?" Answer: credentials? I don't need no stinkin' credentials. Not with Diamond as a friend and psychologist who "validates" my observations. Not with two decades plus of witnessing parent-child dysfunction in my capacity as a knowledge-giver. But there are many reasons why you parents should zero in on this mini-diatribe, chief amongst them the fact that no one, and I mean *no one*, is as narrow-minded and unable to be objective about children as their own parents. Many will claim they maintain objectivity and fairness, will ramble on and on, citing examples of how they have stood firm and seen the big picture. Well, guess what? Your point of view is tainted by the sticky-webbed double helix of genetics, or mayhaps its fraternal twin, adoption bliss overkill. You are not objective. Besides, there are tons of experts out there who do not fit your description of what makes an expert: dog experts who don't own dogs; fashion experts who are sloppy dressers themselves; wedding experts who have never been married; education experts who have never been educators; terrorism experts who have never been terrorists.

When Diamond realized her own role in her husband's infidelity, her life took a turn, and she began to re-emerge as her genuine self, stopped dwelling on lost years, and is now more confident and capable than ever to administrate her thriving clinic. And she inspired **Tenet Number Thirteen** in the Manifesto: **Thou shalt not go on and on and on and on and on about your offspring.**

Those of us who read and think and have lives do not want to hear every detail of little Bunny's sweet sixteen party or grandson Jason's winning touchdown or how toddler Tootsie got into your make-up and was so-so-so cute and cuddly with it smeared all over her cherubic little cheeks that you melted into motherly or grandmatronly mush. Sad to say, Diamond was eat up with a bad case of the third person—answering questions about herself with tales of the children. There was no first person in her life until her therapist and I pointed it out to her.

To all you breeders out there, please: when you have the urge to tell a tale of one of your heirs, think "bullet point" as opposed to "epistle." It truly is not as precious to us as it is to you. And for God's sake keep the photographs and e-images to a minimum. Nothing is more intrusive than being expected to gush and coo and effuse over pictures of bald-headed babies and snaggle-toothed kids and tuxed teens all pimply at the prom. If at all possible, simply e-mail them so we can skip that step where we get put on the spot, all eyes on us, a bated-breathed audience waiting for some over the top reaction to these visages of supposedly human creatures at various stages of growth. Or, better yet, we can hit "delete" and be done with it proactively.

As noted, I am not a mother. This was a deliberate choice, one for which I have not a single iota of regret. And I have nothing against mothers, in spite of the mother whose craziness I am still forced to tolerate from time to time. Hell, as you can see, some of my closest friends are mothers, but they are multifaceted and interesting women and not of that ilk (yes, I know I've vented already, but sometimes a person just ain't finished where vents are concerned) which marches into schoolhouses to make excuses when seventh grader Georgie punches a kindergartener on the bus, or to bicker with the judges when little Margie does not make the cheerleading squad, or demand to know what's wrong with the teacher when "straight-A" Sammy makes a "B," which is, in truth, yesteryear's "C" pumped up like a blood pressure cuff in order to keep mommy dearest or daddy bestest from stroking out over a less than perfect child.

One can long for the good old days when parents lived in blissful ignorance while their children navigated the seas of social and educational interaction on their own, without mommy or daddy trying to constantly smooth the way, interrupt reality to create illusions, in the name of "parenting." Is it any wonder so many of our youth are apathetic, roly-poly gadget-hounds, unable to think for themselves, veritable cow turds on the promising green fields of life? We have over-doted on them, overindulged them, over-defended them, overfed them, and overdosed them on so much "stuff" that we have endangered our own American "species" to the point that, once the great merger of the races and nationalities occurs, I fear we will be culled right off the bat. Yes, Darwin was right, and our own peril is nigh.

To Diamond's credit, she took stock and is the one friend with whom the bond is on a truly guttural level, our having both been at that point of decimation, of having the universe swallowed into the black hole, of reconfiguring, finding some kind of aforementioned reality, and rising from the ashes. Yes, most of my friends have had bad experiences with men—but for the most part they were either younger at the time and/or their men were more short-term. Not Diamond. She knows that when one has had her unshakable faith in a decades-long relationship taken down to ruin, then one is not experiencing the typical "broken heart." No. In such extreme instances the bruising goes to the atria, the ventricles, and that once mighty chest-wall beater repairs itself much more slowly. Diamond and I know this well, and we are sisters in that regard, grateful that we are not stark, raving mad. Just a neurotic twitch or two.

Speaking of which, we all need someone in our lives to keep our relative (in)sanity in perspective, and that would be <u>Micah</u>'s role. And yes, at one time Micah had a last name, <u>Lang</u>; but, as with Cher, Madonna, Prince, *et. al.*, once one establishes oneself as enough of a standout that anything more than one nomme is redundant, that will be done. Micah is my aforementioned token crazily creative male homosexual friend. He's a little bit OCD, a little bit phobic, a little bit manic, a little bit country, a little bit rock and roll. Like moi, he is a connoisseur of the theatrical. For example, he has a pet rooster, Cogburn, whom he routinely puts on a bejeweled leash and takes for long walks. I maintain that he only does this because he likes to say, "I am going to now *retire* to the out of *doors* as I must go walk my *cock*," with a grand flourish.

Micah is only the most in-demand interior designer on the Redneck Riviera, pursued by everyone from the blue-haired bluestocking crowd to the up-and-coming first house on the beach crowd—at least back when there was such a crowd. The fact that he is well above water during these hard economic times and devastating oil spill times is not in the least surprising, since he was for years established in none other than—yes, NYC—complete with Manhattan showroom, huge rent-controlled apartment a block from Central Park, home in the Hamptons, famous clients (can you say, "Jackie O"?), write-ups in *Architectural Digest* and its knock-offs, flights to clients in Las Vegas, New Orleans, London, etc., etc. But alas, after too many years of partying, preening, and prostration over the break-up of an eight-year relationship, he sold his business and came back to his Gulf Coastal roots—uh, tidal pools. "I thought if I had to stress over fabric swatches or gold plated bathroom fixtures with just one more rich bitch I would commit suicide—or 'off' a rich bitch," he says. "And now I'm Jimmy fucking Buffett."

And he sort of is, with a twist. The Hawaiian shirts are typically worn with white linen shorts instead of jeans, and there are no flip-flops in his footwear realm—strictly topsiders, softened, worn into comfort. And he is relishing his own **Second Sluthood**, doing what he does best—raconteuring, creating scenes, pressing against provinciality, going over the top, where yours truly dwells so often. Like moi, like us all, he has a vice or two. He partakes in occasional tobacco usage as do I, but he extends his partakage to the leaf of the cannabis plant, which sends Opal into seizures. She seizes less lately, however, because I added this tenet to the Cunts' Commandments:

Tenet Number Fourteen: Thou shalt embrace thy vices and the vices of others.

Opal tried to claim she had no vices until I dragged her to the walk-in closet where she keeps her six hundred dollar vibrator and reminded her of her on-line lust-fests (which a true slut would not for one second consider a vice; a straight-lacer like Opal, however . . .)

"Okay, but I already **cut slack**," she said, referring to her giving up on "curing" Micah's homosexuality by bringing him to Jesus.

To which Micah replied, "Honey, you can cure meat and you can cure a case of the clap, but you *know* you ain't going to cure a queer. And you sure as hell won't get *this* queer to forego the ganja. *Embrace* the ganja."

"But it's not *legal*," she protested.

"Neither is oral sex, not in this state," I said.

Micah rolled his eyes, "Tell me about it."

"And don't forget about that Christian Taliban maniac who wanted to ban all sex toys." I nodded toward her closet.

Opal's eyes narrowed. She glared at me, then Micah, and took a deep breath. "Nobody messes with the Black Baron," she growled.

"So you'll refrain from pounding on your pulpit about the Happy Pipe?" Micah asked.

More of the Opal glare.

"Come on, sweetie. Look at it this way," he said. "Think of it as my inner heterosexual having a torrid love affair with Mary Jane."

She perked up immediately. "There's really a heterosexual in there?"

Dear, dear Opal. She does struggle with Slut world.

Yes, **Tenet Fourteen** goes a bit further than the mere **cut**ting of the **slack**, but one has to consistently come down on the side of freedom. Let me say I want to distinguish here between "vices" and "debilitating addictions," bringing the simplicity of moderation back to social intercourse. The Slut does not bat an eye at anything done in moderation between consenting adults, and she often overindulges in what used to be "guilty" pleasures (remember, guilt has gone out the window, along with fear, in these our golden years).

As one who attends to the muse, I must emphasize that vices make for interesting fictional characters. In the real world they do the same, just as quirks make for delightful afternoons. I cannot imagine begrudging anyone his drug of choice as long as he is not robbing, maiming, or killing someone else to get it; or operating heavy machinery once he has ingested it. Indeed, I look forward to the day when heroin addicts are given sterile pik lines. However, simply for the sake of argument, I shall stick to those vices that are legal—alcohol and tobacco and assorted other "sins" such as gambling, the frequenting of strip clubs, and the practice of any of a number of sexual fetishes, etc; and those that *ought* to be legal (the aforementioned ganja, say, or prostitution, though some of my posse would disagree).

First of all, real Sluts do not believe in Sin beyond the obvious—physical attacks, murder, theft, lying, outward meanness and the like. Beyond that, "sin" is a term wrapped up in religion, and it is patently un-American to foist one's religion upon anyone. The Day of Reckoning is long past due, when certain laws still on the books in some states (such as laws against all oral sexual acts, "abominations" like homosexuality, certain sexual appliances—which gives me another mini-pause: What if we simply handed out vibrators to the Holy Rollers? Would that not keep their gutter-dwelling minds busy for a while? Well, the women, anyway? Just a thought) should be purged. Case closed.

Alcohol, too, falls into the "sin" category that gets fundamentalists frothing at the prayer-hole to press for more restrictive laws such as those banning sales on Sunday, which is thoroughly unconstitutional. But it is with that nasty habit of smoking that the area gets gray in a haze of second-hand fumes, which are used, it seems to me, to fan the flames of intolerance to the extreme.

Here I must step up and give my own self a pat on the back for, even during that decade (yes, ten years) when I completely gave up cigarettes, I was always kind to smokers, having come to the belief that the only thing more demonic and evil than smoking was the self-righteousness of the reformed. If all the tight-assed little twits who run around shooing away the big bad smokers directed even a fraction of that energy toward the *real* polluters—say, chemical plants, oil refineries, paper mills and the like—we would find ourselves living in a much cleaner environment that would render the curling wisps and billowing clouds from a few fags inconsequential.

I am not encouraging smoking; I am merely encouraging kindness. Bring a bit of wisdom into the mix. If, for example, there are two individuals smoking cigarettes in an open but nonsmoking area where there are fifty nonsmokers who are frying fish, grilling burgers on gas cookers, burning toxic candles, and spraying bug repellent, just let it ride. If there is a smoker in a well-ventilated restaurant—or an open courtyard, say—in a city full of carbon monoxide fumes, exhaust, and natural gas, along with god knows how many hundreds of other poisons floating in the ether, one has to ask, what's the point? And why not go after those other, billions of times more prevalent, poisons? Before moving on I should probably address something many of you nonsmokers might well be wondering: after ten years of not smoking, why did I take it back up? The answer is simple. I wanted to. Which goes to the crux of the thing: let people do whatever they want in the area of vice—with the leanest and most reasonable of regulations—and keep these off-colorful layers in the wonderfully weird weave of our world.

Besides, when I took up writing at the century's turn, I could not imagine how to do it without smoking. Writers are notoriously addictive personalities.

One final word of caution to the aforementioned tight-assed twits: If you insist upon demonizing smokers to your offspring, making said smokers out to be "bad" people, these progeny of yours will one day discover your lie, for when they encounter some kindly soul such as myself, one who takes the occasional puff—always courteously, of course (as in having six very buff, half naked men fanning the fumes away with palmetto fronds)—and lo and behold, they *like* me-they *really like* me, there is a good chance they will rise up in revolt and become chain-smoking, pole-dancing homosexuals (or whoever else it was you taught them to hate).

Oh—and everything I just said? That goes for Micah's marijuana, too. Legalize it, create pot farms, sell it, and tax the shit out of it. Think of the boost to the economy! Besides, Micah deserves it—and he has the money to pay some serious taxes, which he would gladly do, as he is pointedly honest. Every woman needs his kind of honesty.

"You are a *born* bohemian, sugar darling," he might say in a dramatic drawl that spills across any conversation like some thick and exotic liqueur, "but I am not *feeling* the chapelle du *jour*," which is a reference to my hat-wearing habit. Indeed, I have a separate closet full of hats and caps, which, along with plenty of jewelry, as already admitted, are my silly indulgences, and Micah never fails to offer a critique.

"The chapelle du jour *screams* 'Slut' and it is *divine*, my sistah," he will say; or, "Take it off this instant and call an exorcist! What demon inhabited your body in the night and whispered *that* chapelle du jour into the sleeping ears of your usual sense of style?"

"Surely it is not that bad," I might counter, knowing, of course, not to quibble with his expertise.

"Honey, you clash so much you clang when you walk!" And here he might put his palms over his ears. "*Do* make it stop!"

And, of course, I do as he says.

Because he comes to the Gulf Coast with a New York City stamp of approval, Micah has tres entrée with the upscale set. He often attends polo matches at Point Clear with Marble and Brannon, the aging moneybags she married. But while Mr. and Mrs. Gotrocks take the events a bit seriously, Micah makes no bones about his reason for joining them. "I simply *adore* watching pretty *men* on their magnificent, studly *steeds*," he drawls, rolling his eyes and making kissy lips. He is an incorrigible flirt. He also enjoys borrowing my hats and stamping divets with the ladies.

But Micah has more heart than to allow himself to be all superficial, all the time. He has a caring streak that extends to anyone he meets who happens to be having a bad day. Couple that with his adeptness at program management/stage direction and you get an intrepid problem solver. For example, I accompanied him to his twenty-fifth year high school reunion in a very small town in southwest Alabama.

"Please, sugar darling, *do* come along to hold my *hand* so the big bad rednecks don't assault me!"

"That is such a crock. Weren't you class president?"

"Yes, I was *popular*, but there was all that bad business last year when I got *drunk* and asked *Spike Gonads*, who was once upon a time this tackle or *guard* or something, and *such* the homophobe, to slow dance. It did *not* go over well."

I agreed to go and restrain him from flirting with danger.

Unfortunately, a rainstorm caused the traditional parade to be cancelled; and, because the school's principal decided against having said parade the following day, Micah organized one of his own. He got a permit, invited the high school band and floats and cheerleaders to try it again, "borrowed" an antique Rolls Royce from a friend's car barn and rode in it with the queen herself, the girl who spurred him to action. "My God," he enthused, "when I saw that poor, *poor*, girl, with the formal gown, and the little *tiara*, and the title, just sobbing and sobbing because she would not get her moment in the spotlight, it just *killed* me. I had to do something."

So he threw a homecoming parade and got to be kind of a co-queen to boot. But his motives, rest assured, were pure. And he did return the car.

Together, this inner circle of my good, good friends makes up a family whose members are all at different stages of healing and, therefore, different levels of Sluthood; and that is what determines the pecking order. Yours truly rests firmly at the top, not because I am the most "together" but because, hey, as most emphatically pointed out earlier in this rendering, I am the one who came up with all this, "this" having sprung from my brow just as Athena sprang from that of Zeus. I suppose Emerald would have to be dubbed most "together" and therefore pretty Slutty; but Diamond and Micah are both coming along, licking the wounds of lost love, as we all must. It is possible that dear Marble will always lag behind the curve, at least until she can let go of the need to have money transfused into her blood, a need that has given her a kind of emotional anemia. And Opal? My dear non-biological sister of youth and adolescence, who has stuck by my side throughout lo these many dank decades of death? I am afraid her position on the low end of the pecking order is permanent.

Nevertheless, to quote Sister Sledge, "we are family."

Chapter 5: Virus in the Hard Drive: Fear Be Gone, or Be Loved

I CONFESS: I am a bit of an agoraphobe, a condition that strengthens as I dance toward death. It creates an inverse to my dogged philosophy of spurning fear while embosoming hope. Consequently, I further fear you might hurl a most despised epithet at moi: "hypocrite."

Please do not hearken to that old bugaboo, judgment; for I truly do say unto you that in light of having a gene pool that reads like the DSM (for those among my legion of readers who have no experience with mental illness, this would be the *Diagnostic and Statistical Manual*, the Holy Bible of the shrink community), a bit of phobia is, for yours truly, phenomenally understated as a mental glitch.

I know, I know. I have offered up a credo for Sluts, and the purging of guilt and fear is requisite. But everything is relative, and I have come a long way, baby. So as long as there is forward movement, I believe it is acceptable. Do not brand me with the hot iron of hypocrisy simply because I am flawed; we all are. We all are complicated. Honesty, dear reader, honesty.

And yes, I am a little bit phobic, but it isn't as if I go into convulsions upon stepping across my threshold or claw out my eyeballs at the thought of the town square. "A bit" phobic, selectively, and, even though, as stated, I feel myself sliding further down that path (okay, I said "forward" movement, but do let us forgive the backslider for she is

155

lovable), I have decided to simply embrace that part of myself in the knowledge that none of my fearful quirks interfere with any of the activities I value.

Mayhaps you are wondering, "Why, R.P. Saffire, what has an uberheroine, such as yourself, to fear?"

I am afraid to say it is fear itself, so I will say that I have a few minor, rather irrational ones, to *wit*:

I have no desire to travel, but, if I must, I prefer to drive or take a train. I absolutely, steadfastly refuse to fly. I realize that book tours involve actual touring, so I am simply willing to forego whatever monetary benefits might accrue should I fly to, say, Des Moines, to hawk my wares. I care not. Once one is over fifty, it behooves one to do only what one goddamn well pleases. And I have decided, after watching the demeaning behaviors exhibited by whoring-around authors at book fests and such, Ruby Pearl Saffire is, as the youth say, "over it." I will not attend a one. Nor will I give speeches. I will not do anything that might involve having to be medicated or subjugated in order to do said thing.

A side note here: I recognize the fact that there are individuals out there who benefit mightily from medication (as I most assuredly have); however, it is my contention that too many Americans are not only a bunch of big, fat gluttons, snorting and snuffling at the aluminum feeding trough of the world; they are also self-absorbed, over-medicated pagans worshiping at the altar of such glutted, money-grabbing gods as Merck, Eli-Lilly, and Astra-

Zeneca, having been thoroughly brainwashed by the advertising shills of said money-grabbing gods. Anxious? "Ask your doctor." Bladder issues? "Ask your doctor." Restless leg? "Ask your doctor." "Want to grow **thicker eyelashes**?" "Ask your fricking doctor." Meanwhile, wars go on, women are mutilated, children starve to death.

End of digression.

Back to more pressing, life-altering questions, such as: Does R.P. Saffire have any other major or minor phobias? But of course, blessed voyeur. There are most assuredly one or two things with which I regret I must contend. For example, I am not fond of bridges, tunnels, heights, closed-in spaces; not fond of massive collectives of humans intent upon one focus, as in, stadium crowds, shopping malls, pilgrimages to Mecca or any other holy place, including Wal-Mart, where one stands a chance of being trampled to death; not fond of open spaces, as in, the ocean, the desert, the sky (I love to *look* at them all, but simply do not want to be *in* them, and, in the case of the ocean, do not even want to be *on* it, and so, until we are able to rearrange molecules and self-transport, *a la* Captain Kirk, I am at peace with the fact that I shall never see the sights in Rio, London, Hong Kong, or Tokyo); not fond of large things, as in, machinery, factories, skyscrapers, elephants, New York City; not fond of loud things, as in, the roars of the jets (sky sharks, living to kill) that are certain to come plummeting down upon me from their unnatural perch in the cumulus corridors they prowl, the cement-shattering tat-tats of jackhammers that are sure to sling some freakish, fatal projectile into my Slutted brain, the overbearingly obnoxious blares of fuzzed bass thumping from the cars of teenagers whose parents never taught them one whit about manners and who feel compelled to drown out all that is sweet in the world with their tricked-out car stereo systems. The point is that I recommend that both major and minor mental illnesses be brought out of the dank attics, out of the lair of the pharmaceutical industry that is hell bent upon medicating us all into a Brave New World of socially retarded stupor, and into the fresh sunshine of acceptance, wherein our antics and oddities are celebrated as something like "personality quirks."

And, with my "personality quirks," I manage quite nicely and remain content the vast majority of the day. I encounter bridges and tunnels and overpasses and the like without dissolving into watery-kneed panic, usually keeping my emotions within a range that spans from mild discomfort to shortness of breath born of a pre-anxiety attack. It is with the aforementioned notions of navigating clamoring crowds or of climbing aboard auto-piloted aerobuses that the trap is sprung that sends me into unbearable misery. Ergo, why put my heaving bosom and my battle-weary brain through such palpitationous poisonings?

Unfortunately, I am a metaphor for our society, given our culture of the past decade or so, with our color-coded terror having paralyzed us into dumbed-down, nose-picking, non-decision-making.

Until the magic of the e-world with which I flirt began to create "springs" during which the masses moved against dictators and such, and "trending" became the new Life Force.

"It was *Dub*ya," Micah oft opines. "Or, rather, that vile little bitch Karl Rove and his Dark Master, Cheney. They had us scared to take a *crap* because some wayward *terrorist* might reach up through the plumbing and *gnarl* our testicles."

I do not take issue with his assertion, as it is clear that so many "good, red-blooded Americans," as Bizarro Ozzie would say, simply shut down after 9/11 and handed over their rationality to a band of bitches in britches. Even I succumbed to that phobia for a bit, looking askance at swarthy citizens who might be concealing a vested explosive or intent upon sprinkling a microscopic dusting of anthrax about my neighborhood. But after about a year of this, and especially after my dear, dahlin' American troops were sent into—what country? Oh yes, the one that had absolutely nothing to do with 9/11—my senses began to become un-numbed.

"But what about 9/11?" Opal has demanded on more than one occasion (sometimes much repetition of fact is necessary before learning takes hold). "They invaded us!"

"No, that's the wrong 'they'—we were attacked by the 'they' from Saudi Arabia—and besides, it's *terrorism*—a secret, underground, worldwide network, not a specific country," I reply.

"So?"

"So we'd better infiltrate the hell out of it. That is the only way to counter—inside the belly of the proverbial beast, don't you know. And from this moment on, I simply refuse to be afraid. And least of all, afraid of Al-Qaeda."

In the midst of all my other fears, irrational and not, I decided not to give any bomb-wearing, jihad-yelling, Western-hating miscreant any power over me, as in creating any sense of terror in me. After all, that is the goal of the terrorist. I decided to let my terror of looming incontinence override my terror of crazy folks from another continent, for verily I say unto you, terror is an emotion that almost always trumps clear thought and good judgment. Therefore, any so-called "leader" who pulls that card (terror) from the deck is seeking not to lead, but to manipulate. By the same token, every time that certain questionable "news" channel crawled the color-coded terror level across the television screen, which was not infrequent during the first several years, they were aiding and abetting the enemy by doing—what, class? Correct: Creating terror.

What happened to: "We have nothing to fear but fear itself"? That is the mark of a true leader, one who keeps a level gaze on the struggle and refuses to capitalize on the darker instincts of the human race. We can do this, by gum. We are in it together, by golly. These are the mottos of *my* "America First."

"But if we don't fight them over there we'll have to fight them over here," Opal parrots.

"Do not utter that sentiment," I command. "I have been there and I have done that. I well remember the Vietnam years. The 'love it or leave it' fascist years."

"You always overstate," Opal snaps. "The term 'fascist' is inflammatory. It's un-American."

"If the term fits," I counter. "And anyone who would stifle my constitutional right to free speech by branding me un-American would most definitely be a fascist."

"Well. Suppose I call Mr. Obama a fascist? Some folks have."

"Oh please, they call him a fascist *and* a communist, which proves their ignorance, since those ideologies are at totally opposite ends of the political spectrum. Hitler threw the commies in the concentration camps, for god's sake."

"Oh, the *drama*," Micah laughs.

Thankfully the country seems to be coming out of that adolescent drama, that contest of seeing and noting in the National Slam Book, who belongs to the patriot club and who does not. It all seemed to be calculated by whether you (1) wore an American flag lapel pin, or (2) placed a yellow ribbon magnet on your automobile, or (3) boasted a "Support Our Troops" sticker on your shining chrome bumper. As for number 1, I tend to hearken back to how effectively those zany Nazis used symbols as a way of silently strong-arming their ever-retiring population. And, while numbers 2 and 3 are kindly sentiments, the implication seems to be that if one does not feel the need to

161

advertise said sentiments, one might be thought unpatriotic.

"Nobody had better call *me* unpatriotic," Micah drawls. "You show me one of those *buff* soldiers and I will salute the hell out of him in my most special way. But even though I do so *love* to see men of *might* all dressed up in their desert *gear*, I simply cannot allow my lust to cancel out the human *carnage* of this wild goose chase that should have ended in Afghanistan with that *pituitary* case Bin Laden at the end of a sturdy American rope, swinging ever so gently in the desert *breeze*. So it turns out it took a big-balled *prez* named Barak to show that bomb-loving sand flea to his watery grave, with the fish and other ocean-going parasites picking over his bones."

Micah takes 9/11 even more personally than the rest of the posse. He was living in New York City at the time. And he was quite tickled when a bullet blast to the eyeball put Osama, not in a paradise with ever-how-many virgins, but, literally, sleeping with the fishes.

"I think Bush did the best he could—well, I have to fault him for New Orleans, but aside from that I really think it's easy to criticize from where we sit," Opal maintains.

Micah leans forward. "Honey, that's our job, to scrutinize the Bush. And I'm here to tell you, that Bush was absolutely *swarming* with crabs. And I fear our dear current prez—the brilliant, *hot* one— will *never* deign to de-louse this country of its crabs. He won't put them in prison, where they belong, getting routinely butt fucked."

"That's gross," Opal says.

"Not if done properly, sweet pea. I just fear that the *real* criminals will never pay."

There's that "f" word again: Fear.

Fear is counterproductive. Fear is the opposite of hope. It is the stuff of darkness and nightmares and human frailty. It is something the true Slut must hurl into the abyss, along with dieting, plastic surgery, and playing by society's stale rules. Whatever your political stripe, from fascist to republican to green to democrat to independent to socialist to communist to anarchist, if you are an aging (gracefully) Slut, it is critical that you toss away fear (or, like moi, as much as you can manage), along with its first cousin, guilt, in order to march proudly, confidently, head held high, shoulders square, determined to have yourself the time of your life, toward the ending of your life, your deliciously, richly revived and energized life.

Your re-born life.

It's like re-booting a computer.

And speaking of re-birthing/booting, here is a little sidebar about my longest-held friendship :

Like yours truly, Opal is also "born again," but in the conventional sense, as in Born Again in Christ, as she was during the 1970's "Jesus Freak" era, her philosophy finally veering solidly away from mine, which was all partying, all the time. Throughout our twinkling twenties and thwarted thirties we engaged in passionate discussions about sex,

163

politics, and religion, while at the same time—imagine this!—maintaining our sisterhood in spite of that deep divide (something our God-bless-America society as a whole fails to do anymore). By the time we sidled up to our floundering forties we were much easier in our differences, having allowed them to marinate like a fine filet mignon in the red wine of our affection for one another, and now, in our flamboyantly fantastical fifties, we see it as a humorous shade in the clashing colors of our odd-coupledom. Or should I say, ménage a trios: me, Opal, and Jesus.

He talks to her, Jesus does. She insists that he has no problem with any of her carryings on, does not give one good, godly hoot about her online sexcapades, her six hundred dollar vibrator, or her swilling of wine of an evening. I believe she only hears what she wants to hear, but more power to her. As for me, as my track record with marriage and men proves with certitude, I could never be true to one religious icon. As sure as I committed my life to Christ, I'd be cutting my eyes at the Buddha, seductively winking at Lao-Tzu, crooking my "come here, cutie" finger at some white-collared clerical cutie, or flirting with a silly rabbi (I would insert a clever and sacrilegious Mohammed moment into this context but that has not served certain other writers well, and, while I do not give a good goddamn on one level, well, let's just say that we all have trouble living up to our ideals).

I consider myself eclectically baptized, having undergone a catechism of catch-all communions and cancelled confirmations, a spiritual glutton at the buffet of belief, with Lucky Safire as my rudder. I've always had a tendency to take everything in, throw my arms wide and give life a big, heavenly hug—before I joined the un-dead/un-alive zombie world, that is. Opal is much more centered and resistant to change and so traditional I believe she will have the resolve, even as she is lying on her deathbed, to write thank you notes in advance for all the lovely flowers sent to the mortuary chapel for her own memorial service. Opal and I are complete opposites in almost every way, yet our puzzling pairing has lasted a lifetime thus far, maybe for reasons as deep as the bond between us or as shallow as the fact that I like her name (she was named for her mother's birthstone). Names are important, as I might have mentioned earlier.

Opal's status as a cyber-Slut might seem like a rather gargantuan inconsistency unless one understands that Opal is only as biblically challenged, only as loopy as the next good Christian, or as anyone else (yes, including moi) is. She attends church every Wednesday evening, Sunday morning, and Sunday evening, and she logs on at all hours in between. Her husband Bradley, who was an excruciatingly boring Baptist deacon and owned a financially fruit-bearing Ford dealership, passed away four years ago but she was at it—this internet addiction—long before then. My thinking is that her refusal to call herself a sinner and get re-born again, over and over, as so many do, goes to an admirable consistency in her character. What I refer to as faux (Jesus) Freaks, such as serial philanderers who get saved after every affair in order to get back into the Little Woman's good graces are a dime a dozen. And don't get me started on the Tex Watsons of the world. If one can be a bona fide Manson gang murderer and later find salvation, thereby gaining interviews on Christian television, then surely Opal is going to make it to the Pearly Gates.

But, once again, I digress.

I used to theorize that Opal's commission of virtual sin is what kept her from committing it in reality. The truth of the matter is that she is perversely frigid; i.e., she loves sex, the idea of sex, and the flush of the orgasm, but possesses a deep aversion to one of the key instruments of heterosexual sex; i.e., the penis. And I feel somewhat responsible for that.

From the time we were sneaking up on adolescence, furtively, armed with Disneyesque booklets all about how our tender young bodies were a-changing, Kotex pads and elastic belts all laid out on our beds without a word by our Eisenhowerian mothers, we were doing counter-surveillance at the public library. We plundered the medical books, finding photographs of puss-spackled genitalia, engorged testicular tribulations, and enough jargon associated with itches and discharges and burning and lesions to make us completely suspicious of the entire messy, inflamed business. I cringe when I think of the rotting and disfigured phalluses I thrust in front of

Opal's horrified face, the descriptions of fevered, oozing, reddened and agonized vaginas I read aloud, searing images of syphilitic sex and gonorrheal gyrations between her increasingly neutered neurons, which, at some point, must have begun firing the fight or flight response, thunderclapping in lightning strikes throughout her cerebral cortex.

And then I read *Valley of the Dolls* and realized we had been mining the wrong section of the bibliophilic catacombs. Fiction—*adult* fiction—had the real answers, and so I read on, sharing passages with Opal. Here were words which added an allure, a promise of some kind of breathless release to the attendant unpleasantries or miniscule risks involved.

Opal, however, was not so easily moved. "I wouldn't let someone pick my nose, now, would I? So why would I let someone—I just—No! Nobody is going to put anything inside of any opening on this body."

Finally I plundered the mysterious box up high in my father's closet—the box my nut-ball mother referred to as "Sodom and Gomorrah," the box that held an assortment of *Playboy* magazines and paperback books that had to be hidden away lest someone get the wrongheaded idea my parents might ever be intimate with one another. "What if the house catches on fire?" my mother would say. "What if the firemen find Sodom and Gomorrah? What will they think of us?"

"That we're good, red-blooded Americans," my father would reply and go back to reading his newspaper.

I watched for the opportunity. It came, as it were, and I managed to pilfer Sodom and Gomorrah, taking only one thin paperback so as not to arouse suspicion. It was a little piece of porn called *Innocent in Chicago* and was engorged with all manner of trembling, throbbing, tingling, hardening, panting, undulating and quivering, beginning with a young girl and the family canine in Chapter One. Pay dirt.

"Guh-ross!" Opal would let fly after every scene she listened to me read, her body language finally betraying her prurient engagement as she leaned forward, eyes glassy. But, "No one is ever putting one of those nasty things inside of me." And by all accounts from her she was, in fact, loathe to allow Bradley "inside of her" except on the rare occasions when she felt sufficiently guilty about not doing her "wifely duty" that she would come to my house for a pep talk and several hits—okay, a whole bottle—of Annie Green Springs. Once primed and numbed, she would return to the martyrdom of her marriage bed and take her medicine—or rather, have it administered unto her.

Hypocrisy is a perpetual peeve of mine, but I suppose we all drink from that water fountain to a degree; it is not marked "Christians only," after all. And even though we disagree on the expression of religion and I think her fundamentalism reeks of hypocrisy, Opal is a living example of my philosophy: do whatever the hell works for you and yours, as long as there is no harm to others. And by harm I mean general bloodshed, not the occasional out-of-joint proboscis.

Which brings me to Jesus.

The years I spent in darkness were mostly spent in front of a television, where I found a very deep and perverse fascination within myself, a driven urge to study and dissect and peel back the hideous layers of the realm of those most unhinged, rabidly power-mad, and divinely devious of our society: the televangelists. It started as a lark, back in my college days, when my friends and I watched Jim and Tammy Bakker's *Praise The Lord Club*, for laughs and to wage bets on when Tammy Faye's mascara would commence to running; but over the years, once the sham marriage (my own, not Jim and Tammy's) was well underway, I began to see true evil lurking there, in the shimmer of the fevered sweat born of a rant of salvation, in the haloed sheen of a sculpted coif, in the Bible-tinged words telling the poor and the sick the only way to peace was through the Lord Jesus Christ and, by the way, send cash. "Jesus loves you," they would drone before launching into a riff about how God would splay you open in the pit of hell for a peacock's tail's worth of sins. I kept hearing two at-odds messages: (1) God the Father loves you; (2) be very afraid. And, as I am wont to do, I reached into my poetic soul to try to capture the anger, to put my spirit into the spirit of those who were/are so

169

very certain that they alone have the list of Sinners, who, In the Hands of an Angry God, are on the fast track to the lake of fire in the bowels of the Underworld. It goes like this:

The Rapture [According to ultra-fundamentalist WASPS (White Anglo-Saxon Protestant Shitheads) across the Bible Belt and the Heartland] (A song to be sung to the tune of "Farmer's In the Dell")

Allegro vivace
The queers are all in hell
We said, "Don't ask, don't tell
An A-bomination-O!
The queers are all in hell

The whores are all in hell
Their bodies for to sell
Hey, ho! We told you so!
The whores are all in hell

The porno fiends are there
To grow their palms with hair
Lust, musk, from dawn to dusk
Eroto-cross to bear

The smokers would not quit
And so their souls aren't fit
Now va-cate the Pearly Gates
To roast on Satan's spit

Allegretto
The devil takes a drunk
In lakes of fire he's sunk
No bloody booze down here
For alcoholic punks

The doper won't be freed
He smoked that wacky weed
No food for eternity
That's Dante's hellish creed

The black folks are in hell
Makes heaven oh-so-swell
A whole race we did displace
Without a fare-thee-well

Allegro furioso
Now Satan takes a chink
A Buddhist commie pink-o
Here's how, hey Chairman Mao
The masses on the brink

Hindus, Jews and monks
And pagans, popes are sunk
Shinto, away you go
Ye godless gooks and punks

Oh, Cheetah's kin will bleed
Their evolution creed
Bonzo's descendants-o!
The humanists' Bad Seeds

The "secular" "mainstream"
Quote: "Christians" on "our team"
Will gnash teeth in disbelief
A liberal's bad dream

Adagio
But heaven is so bare
St. Peter's in despair
Hey, you! Please listen to
The power of our prayer

Now something is amiss
There's fire and steam's hot hiss
Not Us! No! We don't cuss!
We don't belong in this!

Adagio patetico
We drank, we smoked, we screwed
We secretly liked nudes
But thought if we borned-again
Hellfire we could elude

A-las!

Thus, as I contemplated the sizzling fires of this place called "hell," I was highly and mightily confused, especially when I began to wonder just who might *not* be cast into Hades. Around the same time, I crossed a shadowy boundary into the world of mental illness. I began to believe those maniacal ministers on the tele-tube were talking directly to me. I didn't know I was in a deep depression; I only knew paralysis, going through the motions, sharing my fascinating knowledge about parsing sentences and picking apart paragraphs with eighth graders by day, showing the dumpy houses I was pushing before graduating to more and more upscale markets by night, yet morphing into a vaporish, ghostly presence that was partner to the barely present ghost of my husband. And verily I say unto you, the bleak landscape of depression comes in many unrecognizable forms, even in the form of a beloved schoolmarm/successful salesperson skating the surface of life like a water bug on a fishpond, staying but a ripple ahead of being food for a baby bream. Two years with a therapist, a hysterectomy, the recognition of the lie of my life, the ejection of the liar in my life, and plenty of P&P (Prozac and Premarin) cocktails from Dr. Jimmy finally snapped me out of that.

And so, after spending the latter 1990's residing in the pit of PTL hell, with the hellish spawn of PTL, the Christian Broadcasting Network, I joined humanity once again. When I "came to" I immediately "came to Jesus" and declared my freedom from guilt and fear, those two emotions one must refuse to feel in order to be a successful and fulfilled Slut. The feather boa of spiritual eloquence can only come from the slinging off of the cloak of dark emotions. And it is this pure freedom that enables one to become empowered to drink from the fountain of youthful indulgence.

173

In shedding this mythically Eden-esque snakeskin, I saw Jesus in a new, clean light, his intentions unsullied by pulpits, pews, piety, and price-gouging. Those *WWJD?* bracelets were all the rage at the time, and I recoiled whenever I heard smarmy fundamentalists using the expression, which they threw around as cheaply as Lent gets thrown around, as in: "I'm giving up my cell phone for Lent!" or "I've decided to give up polyester for Lent!" Really. Did Jesus really die on the cross so that you could honor him by depriving yourself of your technological toys or stay-pressed pants? Further, would he ever even contemplate what he "would do" if faced, for example, with what for you (judging by what you gave up for Lent) might be a life-changing decision? Something like, say, a choice between *Leave it to Beaver* on Nickelodeon or *Sex & the City* re-runs on another channel? Just how petty was he? Or was he actually discriminating in the area of pronouncements about how others lived and what they did? Wait a minute. He kind of didn't throw around a lot of harsh judgments, right? Hmm. By golly-gosh to Glory, what *would* Jesus do, and, more to the point, when and under what circumstances? Also, what would he *not* do?

As I have ventured into my **Second Sluthood**, well aware of the fact that Jesus took care of/up with the Miss Kitties of the Fertile Crescent, I have come up with a few suppositions. These are only suppositions, mind you, not suppositories to be crammed into your rectum, migrating up and up, until stuck in your craw as absolutes; Opal agrees with some of them but disagrees with many of them and she, after all, hears from Jesus on a regular basis. Still, I assert that these are sound examinations of the braceleted question: *WWJD?*

First of all, Jesus would not mind that I do not capitalize his pronouns, as in "Let us give Him all the Glory." I would simply write, "Let us give him all the glory," because he wasn't some egomaniac who would expect that. He was adamant about the simple life, choosing pastoral settings in which to share loaves and fishes, an overall laid-back, low-key kind of king of kings.

Jesus might have serious problems with the capitalist industry—be it music, television, film, book sales, whatever (if the bottom line is profit, which is kinda how we roll)—that has grown up around the religion named for him; oh, sure, he might like some of the Christian rock songs but would have difficulty with promoters, agents, producers, people selling *WWJD?* bracelets, etc. Of course, if the profits went toward feeding the poor or healing the sick, well, I'm thinking he would most likely be down with that.

As for the publishing world in particular, Jesus would surely find the notion of being "Left Behind" nothing short of befuddling and probably downright disgusting, since he repeatedly described his daddy as being all about love and mercy. Where the "Christian romance" genre is concerned, well, I like to think the Christ had/has a fine-tuned sense of humor and so would get quite

175

a chuckle out of it, especially when he reflects upon the titillating anointment times he had with Mary Magdalene.

Jesus might think that someone who owned more than two or three mansions, all tricked out with car elevators and such, mansions big enough to house the populations of a third world country or two each, was taking the whole wealth thing a little too far and might want to entertain the "brother's keeper" concept. Just for a jolly good lark.

I take back what I said about music; Jesus could appreciate that the term "Christian rock" is an oxymoron (I hearken back to his sense of fun); after all, he was quite a rebel in his day, and rock has historically been and continues to be nothing if not rebellious. Besides, I like to think he would have impeccable taste in music.

Jesus would not ride in (unless it was getting him to a remote leper colony over rough terrain), let alone own, an SUV, not to mention a fricken' Hummer.

Jesus would not scream that homosexuals are an abomination; he would certainly not disrupt any funerals to do so.

Jesus would not mind that a Slut like me uses foul language; he would be more concerned with healing the lame, raising the dead, feeding the multitudes, etc.

Even though he would probably reiterate the "Love thy neighbor as thyself" standard, Jesus probably would not think it necessary for one to show that love if one loves oneself in an over-killish kind of way (example: a tight-templed refugee of a severe facelift wants to provide such a self-indulgent surgery for the lady next door).

Jesus might feel compelled to throw a Moneychangers-in-the-Temple style hissy-fit if he encountered any of the following:

- Mega-churches of the "Six Flags Over God" variety (The Vatican would qualify)
- "Prosperity" preachers
- FEMA
- A liposuction clinic
- The culture of celebrity, Hollywood, and the wholesale selling of souls, selling of blowjobs, and selling out friendships for movie deals
- Anything on a television (unless it showcases really important information, strong writing, and/or sharp wit; I'm certain that *The West Wing* would make the cut, for example)
- A Las Vegas High Rollers' room
- Any fundamentalist member of the Christian Taliban bent on waging a holy war or a "culture" war or, hell, probably any kind of war against, oh, anybody
- Any vehicle costing over, say, thirty grand, the aforementioned

"fricken' Hummers" in particular (because of the war connotation)

- Anne Coulter

Those are just a few of the things that come to mind as I contemplate the *WWJD?* question, and said contemplation inspired within my bosom yet another tenet for sluts. Hence, **Tenet Number Fifteen: Thou shalt heed the WORDS of the Christ (and any other like-minded spiritual leader, which pretty much includes all of the major religions).**

I wonder if our very vocally extreme Christian brethren have really read those few quotes (you know, the words in the red typeface; the quotation marks indicate what actually emerged from the actual mouth of the Lord, however many translations ago) in the Bible that contain the passionate words of the Christ, words about refraining from judgment, loving one another, tending the poor and the sick, the "huddled masses" (Lady Liberty's quote; not J. C.'s) as it were. But I suppose I would not be very effective as a Slut if I were to follow my other true calling of stepping into Mother Theresa's shoes, placing my palm against the fevered brow of the downtrodden. Perhaps in my next life, if I am born with as much ambition as she. Besides, Sluts are just as necessary as saints, Sluts can even *be* saints, can even be the home of the Saints, as is the case of the great, nasty, lively, pitiable, unique, surreal city of New Orleans, Louisiana, which, as it turns out, I must include after all, because it showed me something exquisite about life in America and about my best friend Opal, long before that city was knocked down by a self-righteous bitch named Katrina . . .

Chapter 6: Networking: Globalization and Oil Spills and Floods—Oh, My!

. . . A SELF-RIGHTEOUS bitch named Katrina followed up by a corporate cock named BP. A one-two punch: water and oil. While the crude continues to grease up the wetlands, NOLA proper grinds its way back toward some morphed iteration of what it once was. And if New Orleans is going to come the rest of the way back, she's going to have to be a monumental Slut.

Of course, NOLA has historically been an outrageous Slut. Let bug-eyed, combed-over television preachers rant on and on about how God used a bunch of water to punish the fornicators, drug dealers, and whores; let them liken the entire city to a whore with their Satan-inspired venom. The truth is, New Orleans was and still is a Slut and will never disappear as such. Okay, she might be in such straits that she will have to do a little whoring around to claw her way back, but she will return to a full flowering of Sluthood. Unless the four horsemen of the apocalypse keep on a-ridin' into town—developers, bankers, carpetbaggers, and eminent domain.

About a year before Hurricane Katrina Opal accompanied me to the Tennessee Williams Literary Festival. We were sitting at Café DuMonde, having the requisite beignets and Chicory coffee, soaking our senses of adventure in the steamy atmosphere that only New Orleans, the aforementioned Slut of the entire country (Las Vegas being its disease-ridden whore, of late attempting to be more "family friendly" but coming off rather pedophilic in my humble opinion), can offer. Jazz notes riffed and drifted out of the humid haze of the morning and wrapped around the little tables, encircling all the patrons with strains of sensuality.

"I need a man," I said.

But Opal did not respond in her usual way, which is: "I need a face lift." Instead, she was engrossed in some sort of sneaky surveillance project only she understood, quick-glancing around the open-air restaurant like a skulking counter-spy with an expression something like confusion morphing into muted panic.

"What on earth is the matter?"

She leaned in, still watching all about the place, furtively but obviously so, and lowered her voice. "I was just noticing . . .

"Yes?"

The low voice became a whisper. "Where are all the—"

"For heaven's sake, spit it out. I swear, sometimes your 'dramatical' reticence makes me want to piss in your greens."

"Okay, okay," she snapped, then went back to the undercover agent whisper. "Where are all the *white* people?"

I am accustomed to Opal's odd, ethnocentric outbursts, but this one caught me off guard, probably because Opal would never have consciously put herself in a situation in which she would have to wonder where the white people were. So I did a visual sweep of the area in question. And indeed, the café was a veritable collage of cultures and colors and costumes, the vast majority not of primarily Western European influence. Some partakers of the chicory looked to be of Asian extraction, others perhaps had been genetically spawned near the stomping grounds of the Jesus, and still more probably had their roots in the African grasslands. There were burkas and yarmulkes within spitting distance of my big floppy straw hat. And there was a whole palette of epidermal hues: deep cocoa, buttery bronze, lemon tea, iced ebony. Very few palefaces—a thimbleful, maybe. It was nice, in an exotic, out-in-the-world sort of way. But I had to address Opal's question: where *were* all the white people?

I decided to play a match for the high ground. Since neither Opal nor I ever had children, I raised my coffee cup in a rather vocal, exaggerated toast. "Here's to two childless white girls who contributed to the extinction of the entire white race."

A few of our neighbors laughed and raised glasses, appreciating the irony.

Opal sucked in a gasp that nearly stripped the tablecloth neatly from beneath the plates and utensils. "We really *did*, didn't we? My *God*!"

She promptly ordered a Bloody Mary.

Those readers from certain other regions of the country (or from Atlanta, Georgia), need to know that Opal and I live in a small community that is not unlike so many others across the Southeast's coastline, a community with a preponderance of white folks who really have no clue that, while, once upon a time, immigrants "assimilated" into the melting pot of American life, America is now being "assimilated" into the cauldron, in some places simmering, of the world. Furthermore, the majority of those with no clue are going to be experiencing the kind of panic my friend manifested in the days following our foray into the French Quarter.

And then there will be those others who will certainly take it further, who will turn to suspicion, violence, and what I believe will unfortunately be a mini-Armageddon, a little dress rehearsal, as it were. You see, there are thousands upon thousands upon potentially millions of a certain substantial segment of white males, all over the country, who are this very second (certainly if they reside in the Southeast) driving around in mud-splattered pickup cabs on top of tires as big as my house, males who had deer blood smeared across their faces when they came of age by slaughtering a buck, alpha males who can thin their own herd as easily as they can slice the throat of an animal. These men, whom I know well, are, at their core, obviously, mere blustering, swaggering bullies who really do believe that high school football matters in the world and who will be absolutely chilled to the marrow with raw terror when it dawns upon them that they are being—oh, the humanity!— *outnumbered* by people of assorted other tints and hues. Actually, since the 2012 election, the awakening is somewhat underway; it seems to me they are in a bit of a state of shock, but that shall certainly wear off and things will undoubtedly get very, very ugly. Nothing preys upon the testicular bravado of the southern racist (probably any racist, eh?) than other-hued people (it used to be black people only, but with so many cultures and interracial marriages and the like, the paradigm has obviously done a little shudder), homosexual people, and the idea of loss of power. Just Google "Aryan nation" and see what you find.

And yes, I have just delivered a harsh stereotype, and, in the interest of fairness, I will say that there are many decent, upstanding salt-of-the-earth types who thoroughly enjoy huntin' and fishin' and racin' and muddin' who are truly good and kind and gentle folk, folk who wish for peace and equality now and forevermore, on into perpetuity, in the name of all that is holy, God bless us every one, amen and amen. I ain't talking about *them*. I'm talking about the sons of the White Citizens' Council and their demented spawn, those with a rich family tradition of lynching and strong-arming and hate-mongering and who really are still out there. And let us not forget their mega-evil sponsors, those of wealth on the top tier, those who, back in the day, orchestrated the bombings and burnings. Those vestiges still remain; they are not a mere figment of my imagination, as Opal often suggests (Opal also consistently seeks to deny the decidedly brutal history of the South).

In any case, someone needs to tell them (the spawn of Klan) it's all over but the shouting.

Or not.

And while we are in the neighborhood, this is a good time to make mention of the little sluthood commandment that is **Tenet Number Sixteen: Thou shalt indeed have 'that conversation' that has not been had, the one our forty-fourth president says we still need to have—you know, 'that one' about race?**

And if black folk in general say 'that conversation' needs to occur, then we white folk need to suck it up, face the music, grow some gnads, and by god *have* it—because *we* don't get to say when it's 'over.' It is not as if we earned that right by suffering some kind of genocide, and I am mightily confounded by those crackers who, in their refusal to really read and understand history and the collective consciousness, insist that the need for the chat is 'over.' Particularly now that we have an Af-Am prez, which is akin to outright stating: "Look at me. I am a dumbass racist." But I am certain that Jesus loves them anyway, even if he has to really, *really* try.

Anyway, I was not surprised that Opal noticed the racial makeup of this little island in one city, NOLA. I, like you, was somewhat struck by the fact that she had not really noticed, before that moment, that the world really was in hueful flux, had been for quite a while, and, as is the case with any other trend, had finally made it to the Gulf of Mexico, each state bordering the water vying for the honor of being dead last among the lower forty-eight.

Ever since that revelatory moment of clarity, Opal has been terrified.

So Opal began stocking up on things, storing them in her basement—canned food, bottled water, toilet paper, radios, flashlights, batteries, toilet paper, liquor, handguns, toilet paper, medicines, Clorox, and toilet paper. She is certain there will come a moment of critical mass, when the masses critical of the entirety of her race will pour onto her property, confiscate her home, and sexually assault her before she is mutilated—the whole "rape and pillage" scenario. Now, mind you, we aren't talking about the typical variety of "stocking up," either, as in, for a hurricane. Everyone along the Gulf Coast has the requisite stash of supplies in advance of those named buzz-saws that are usually a mere pain in the rectum and occasionally knock out the power and water for weeks at a time, becoming a huger pain in said rectum.

And then . . . there was . . . Katrina.

And Opal went into overdrive, investing in more of the above, along with a lot more liquor, first aid supplies, and, in particular, much, much more toilet paper.

"Honey," I said, "I truly admire your devotion to the thong caddy. And that Sam's Club card is really coming in handy!"

"I know you think I'm crazy, but I'll bet you'll be over here pounding on the door when the End Times come."

"Only if you take down that 'no smoking' plaque."

"I can't do that. I love you too much to do that."

"I'd rather have a raw ass then," I said, thinking I might at least start stocking up on Virginia Slims.

It was turning into the Cuban Missile Crisis of the twenty-first century. She bought three generators and began hoarding gasoline in rows of red plastic, yellow-spouted containers in her garage. She began networking online with rabid survivalists, but danced back from that foray when she found herself in Neo-Nazi chat rooms and began receiving unsolicited invitations to Klan rallies.

I even took to singing a little ditty I composed to the tune of "America the Beautiful," just to get under her "appropriately-pigmented" skin, of course. It went like this:

Aryan the Dutiful

How beautiful my white sheets are; I love that Fox News spin

A starched white hood upon my head conceals a toothless grin

America! America! We claim you for our own

We won't abide no fierce gay pride; the spics can all go home

The constitution got it wrong and Jesus Christ did, too

Have malice for your fellow men if they're not just like you

America! We won't let go! We are the Chosen Few

We'll act a fool, no Golden Rule will make us love a Jew

Our testicles depend upon the racist tripe we spawn

The rebel flag's our sole defense to fight the blood Red Dawn

America! You've gone to hell! Please reconsider it

Equality and liberty and freedom don't mean shit

Yes, the rhyme is simple and the content repugnant, but it did the trick in getting under Opal White's lily-white epidermal shrink-wrap. But it was the news images on television, of people on rooftops and interstate overpasses, begging to be rescued, of the desperation at the convention center, the whole messed up mess of it that upset her most. She did not, however, rush out and slap a "Save New Orleans: Impeach Bush" bumper sticker on the shiny chrome bumper of her silver Cadillac El Dorado as so many others did around that time. She did not even peel off that obnoxious "W The President" sticker (and has not, to this very day, well into Obama's second term, peeled it off) that doubly sticks in my craw. She merely turned to me, eyes puddling a helpless ducting of tears, and sobbed, "Where did all those black people come from?"

"Well, I'm guessing most of them are descendents of the slaves our forefathers brought here in chains."`

"Don't get me started, Ruby Pearl Saffire. My people were town folk. Merchant class. They owned no humans whatsoever."

I did not launch into an explanation of the socio-economics of sharecropping or the agrarian model of capitalism or institutionalized racism. I did, however, point out that these newly discovered, dark-skinned denizens had been living in New Orleans for, oh, generations.

"But I never saw them—in such numbers, that is—when I went there. And I've been visiting the French Quarter all my life."

"The French Quarter? Now, really, Opal, don't you think folks living somewhere around the poverty level might have concerns beyond a wild weekend of partying and puking with Phi Mu and Chi Omega tittie-flashers in a sea of underage drunks?"

She squinted for a moment, shook her head, and wrote a two thousand dollar check to the American Red Cross. Conscience salved. No need to become a cross Red American and engage in class warfare.

Of course, as previously indicated, Opal is not alone in her fear that white folks are most certainly going the way of the dinosaur; it is probably one of the most un-discussed fears the blue-eyed set carries around in its collective bosom (and when it is discussed, it is done so in code, as in "culture war"). It is a truth that has caught them, those who do not remain in full denial (like the aforementioned mouth-breathing masses who are just now beginning to be nudged awake—by the blathering Bill O'Reillies and Sean Hannities and—excuse me while I puke—Rush Limbaughs of the air waves—to envision the shift toward their own minority-hood), quite by surprise, even though sociologists have written for years, yea decades, about population shifts and the blurring of the edges of separation between all the races. And, while I am not naïve enough, as also previously stated, to think that it will be a simple, nonviolent process, I do want to believe that, if and when humanity emerges on the other side of Chaos, we will all, ultimately, become a lovely shade of walnut with honey-colored eyes and all join hands and sing the Coca Cola song, in perfect harmony.

One can dream.

With the displacement of the whole of New Orleans, and in particular the Lower Ninth Ward, a new tsunami of terror washed over my xenophobic friend, especially after the local news reports about the influx of those inner city (read "Negro") citizens into our rather rural south Alabama county. "My god, will they ever go back?" she wondered, eyes once again rounded into an expression of the head-lighted deer variety.

I resisted the urge to point out that, when she and I had butted points of view in a discussion of whether the Ninth should be re-built, she had commented, tone iced with disgust, "You just watch. The government will build back the whole thing and hand it to them on a silver platter."

"Silver? Really? You think it will be silver?"

"You know exactly what I mean. It being government housing and all. It's because they're black."

Whereupon I had launched into a tirade about how it was *not* government housing, how at least half of the Lower Ninth residents actually owned their own homes, how the government and the insurance companies and the eminent domain and the love of profit would surely get in cahoots long enough to compel some real estate criminal to bulldoze the whole place and throw up a bunch of pink and turquoise and aqua stucco condominiums. As for the *real* government housing, I continued, no doubt it would become prime real estate and make some profiteer a Mississippi River steamboat load of cash. (I have noticed in subsequent visits that much of it has, indeed, been bulldozed.)

Now, however, after her 'will they ever go back?' question, I was much more restrained, doing my Zen breathing, and holding my smile along with happy thoughts. I lit a cigarette, leaned forward, and whispered, "Wouldn't it be wonderful if the government built it all back on top of a huge silver platter on pilings?"

"Well I think that's exactly what should happen."

"Silver platter and all?"

"Absolutely."

Amazing what self-interest can do to one's political point of view. Still, Opal did not begin a petition-signing campaign to aid the storm's homeless and displaced. She did, however, buy two or three more guns and even considered hiring a bodyguard, "a cute one, of course."

Needless to say, Opal was predictably quite livid about the influx of Mexicans around the same time. She became so intense about it for a while that she said she was having sexual fantasies about Lou Dobbs (minus the penis). Never mind that she has a Mexican yardman, a Mexican housekeeper, and a Mexican who works on her cars. She even calls them "my Mexicans" and allows that if her basement were not so full of the accoutrements of survival she would take in a family, allow room and board for work done.

"A legal family?"

She blushed. "Well, it would certainly be cheaper if they weren't, you know?"

"Wow. Then you'd have your really and truly and very own 'my Mexicans'." Once again, self-interest wins out.

"That's the best way to do it," she enthused. "Just two parents with several children—old enough, you know, to pitch in."

"You won't abide by the child labor laws?"

"Don't be silly. They wouldn't be here *legally*. So they'd be that much more grateful and work that much harder."

"Oh, I see. Circumvent the law altogether. Works for me." I had long ago recognized when it might be fruitful or entertaining to debate Opal and when not.

She did not take the cease and desist cue. "I wouldn't be breaking the law in a criminal way, of course."

And *I'm* supposedly confusing. "How so?"

"I mean, it's not like a *real* crime. Like robbing or killing. Or even reckless driving. All it is—is just getting housework done."

"And sundry other jobs," I offered.

"Yes."

"My goodness, Miss Scarlett, you've certainly thought this through."

"Yes," she sighed, getting all dreamy in the eyes, staring off into la fantasia deliciosa. "If only I had room in the basement."

"Why don't you just throw up a little old row of shotgun slave shacks out back?" I asked. "You could sit on the deck, sip on mint juleps, breed them, and teach them Negro spirituals."

I do hope you voracious readers are not getting a completely bad impression of Opal. You see, Opal White embodies the typical Caucasian-female-of-a-certain-age attitude prevalent in the belt of the Bible and scattered across America in places like rural Indiana. She means no harm, would never

193

really use any of her arsenal of guns on a fellow human, would be outwardly polite to anyone whom she met. She was just brought up that way. She is not an active, vocal racist; she is a passive, well-meaning, *unaware* racist, the type of which there continue to be so many, particularly in our redneck of the woods. In short, she just doesn't "get" her own racism. Ergo, the need to have "that conversation."

Unfortunately, there are many active, vocal and aware (as in, this is a conscious choice) racists among us (in the South and beyond) here in the twenty-first century. These are the ones—white, black, terrorist, Aryan nation folk, whatever—who ought to be spayed and neutered (aw, shucks, go on and kill all the terrorists and ethnic cleansers and be done with them) and I would be happy to sign a petition to that effect. If, however, I chose to distance myself from the unaware racists, well, my potential readership here in white-bread land would dwindle considerably. I would be quite alone, since most white Southerners' (particularly those of an age) reflexes jump straight to defensiveness when the subject of history arises. They fairly (or, rather, unfairly) leap to avoid making that leap into serious, studious soul-searching. "Well, I'm not prejudiced," they will say, followed by, "but," followed by proof that they are, indeed, prejudiced. One often hears another cliché: "Oh, I am color blind," they will say. Which is a big fat bold-faced lie, of course. We all see color— unless, of course, we really are literally color-blind, and even then one could discern with what *shade* of person one was interacting. And these people truly do walk among us, as leaders, breeders, and, yes, teachers, who bring such baggage into classrooms.

This leaves the segment I inhabit, of like-minded souls, who try to remain aware of and modify and distill down our, yes, "prejudices," to also distill down our perceptions of those we truly do love, like Opal, and decide whether we will take them with their warts. Even Ruby Pearl Saffire has a few warts, even the occasional big, crusty, hairy wart of judgmentalism that can become a neon green tumor in no time if it's not burned off post haste, along with the wart of (see Chapter 5) hypocrisy. As much as I am loathe to acknowledge these presences upon the grid of my spirit, I do take moments—long ones—in which to examine the stain of bigotry in the loose threads of my socially-woven self. I find it to be both productive and humbling. Therefore, while it is true that I take Opal with her warts, she could argue that she puts up with my warts as well, so it all sort of balances out when the day is done. At least she and I are hanging out and having a lark and a glass of wine and conversating instead of shouting over one another like they do on the cable "news" programs and talk radio.

Opal and I have common ground. We shared a childhood, we shared adolescent secrets, we shared subterfuges as teenagers, covered for one another when caught in a lie, supported one another through heartbreak and loss, and, when the first one of us catches the bus to the Other Side, I am certain the other will feel Left Behind.

If I may wax philosophical for a few lines, I suppose it is the common ground that really matters. I am guessing there is some kind of instinctual herd mentality defense mechanism (I have no clue what I am talking about here, but it seems to make a kind of collectively unconscious psychological sense in my own addled mind) that stirs a resistance to adding other strains into the bloodline. And, while I am in no way, shape, or form any sort of a blueblood, I do lay claim to a few patches of powder blue in the gene pool, the blue of it having something to do with what passes for "class" in this country but which I choose to view as an explanation for the occasional inherited quirk, such as insanity, that pops up in the branches of the family elm (my mother's side, of course; Bizarro Ozzie comes from more noble, honest, working class roots). But I suppose that family pride is one of those common ground things that tend to run through the family of us homos sapiens. I find it a travesty that we humans zero in on the petty little differences—religion, or who wants the most cookies—to snipe and ultimately war over. In the larger, future survival sort of scenario, there is only one word for most of our conflicts: "silly." Yes, "silly" is a perfect word for avoiding the common ground.

After Opal had her revelation at Café DuMond we slutted around that Slut of a city, from the ticky tacky voodoo stalls full of incensed spells and Marie Leveaux legends to the art galleries where we waded into images that pressed at the pulse of our friendship, laughing and remembering. We had the obligatory red beans and rice. We treated ourselves to a Creole meal at The Gumbo Shop until we could eat no more, cramming the scraps into a Styrofoam box. Then we set out for the Hotel Monteleone, past street musicians, drunks, and tattooed gutter punks pierced to the gills, the marginal folks who bracket our lives as reminders of that other reality, the folks on the fringes, the marginal, the cast off, the out cast. One beat up old-timer, clutching the neck of a wine bottle, clearly a citizen of the streets, approached us, gesturing at the take-out box Opal carried. "Y'all gonna eat that?"

My dear, dear, lily-white, toilet-paper-hoarding friend did not miss a beat. "No, sweetie, you take it. And be sure to enjoy. I assure you, it wasn't cheap."

I felt an undulating swell of warm feeling growing ripe within my—yes, my bosom. The fact that Opal puts on much of her self-centered stinginess made me go all mushy and near teary. But just when I was on the verge of giving her a hug or an "awww" or even an elbow jab kind of "shucks" thing, she turned to me, furrowed brow, a genuine look of concern on her usually cattle-placid face.

"I hope he's drinking white wine. I don't think red would work at all with that meal, do you?"

Chapter 7: Undo Edit/Clear/Replace: Coming Back from the Dead

YES, dear, dear reader/voyeur, the example of Katrina with sauce du crude oil serves as a metaphor for yours truly, from Slut to destruction to re-Sluttification. This tome is a clarion call for defiance, rejuvenation, the red meat of living, light on the grease, handed unto you from the once dead, moi.

Post-Hand Job, yours truly was not unlike the life-departed shell of a blown-away city or a flown-away cicada, not Katy-did but Katy-**done**, clinging to the shingled and sapped bark of a pine stalk, a shell drained of purpose, destined to fall to the ground to be battered by the elements until it dissolves into the mush of the forest floor. So I grieved like a howling widow, went to work and performed my tasks without any spirit, came home and simply sat, swilling wine like a pickled simpleton. On the weekends I sat some more, occasionally summoning the will to arise and force-feed myself or go to the bathroom. Summer came and I was still sitting, day upon day, until I had my come-to-Jesus moment with dear Opal and my come-to all the gods of all the religions of the universe with Lucky Safire.

Did I arise from the ashes at that moment, chipper and endeavourous? Of course not. But I did take unto myself a plan. I visited Dr. Jimmy, who was appalled by my bony frame, commanded that I re-take up the habit of ingesting foodstuffs, and referred me to a divine shrinkologist to help me tackle the depression that was fast becoming the Depression Era.

Did I dive into the writing of precious poems and sterling stories? Of course not. I did however undertake an allegiance to **Tenet Number Eight: Thou shalt cut bait and fish** in order to re-connect with my very soul. I began by composing, each day, a single, self-affirmative sentence and writing it three, four hundred times, thereby establishing the habit of writing while simultaneously re-framing my sense of self. What, you might ask, were some of these sweet sentences? Here is a Whitman's sampler of them:

"First and foremost, I am going to be just fine."

"I have life and friends and creativity."

"I have a flat stomach!"

"I am going to revive as would a Phoenix."

"I will not think of the last twenty years as a waste."

Due to the tone of negativity in this last declaration, which did not dawn upon me until I had scrawled it, oh, two hundred and thirty-three times, it morphed into:

"I have learned much over the last two decades and am wise beyond my years."

You self-help junkies know precisely from where I come. The brain is a soup of chemicals sloshing from neuron to neuron, fixing within the matter of the gray a certain set circuitry that, over time, locks into either a melodic rhythm of seratonal sibilance or a dissonant dialogue within itself, dipping and spiking in counterproductive cadences. The former offers the service of keeping one outside the range of supposed disorders in the *Diagnostic and Statistical Manual*. I did not belong in that number, if ever I did in the first place, my cerebral chorus having clattered into a cacophonous concert of chemically serrated synapses, so that my cranial eco-system had succumbed to a severe climate change. I had to (relatively) "re-sane" the membrane, as it were.

This is where the Ruby Pearl Saffire philosophy intersects with the trite and true truisms of the most blatantly shallow self-help treatises: *people can change*. Most people *should* change, as good change is indicative of mental and spiritual growth. Many people want to change while others fight change (these are the hopelessly helpless). But the sad truth is that too many of the well-meaning change-wanters are too damn lazy to work at being happier. Writing a few hundred sentences takes a nice little bite out of the day, when one could be whipping up a batch of cookies, tending to the zinnia beds, spending quality time with the tyrannical little off-sprung tykes, or picking one's nose. Of any excuse I would say, simply: no sale. For what an ultimately better, more perfected, self-aware baker, digger, parenter or picker one would be armed with insight, effervescence, inner strength, and new life!

In other words, don't bitch about the sentence-writing. Sentence yourself to it. And you don't have to steal *my* sentences, which include:

"I am destined for laughter."

"I have no need for bitterness."

"I am one kick-ass female."

And

"I have pretty, pouty lips—all of them."

Come up with sentences that apply to you. Draw them from the depths of your emotionally battered and burdened bosom, spilling them into the cleavage of your own re-claimed person-to-be. And—this is very important—do not simply *write* the sentences. Think, yea, *meditate* upon each poise of your pen or pencil, branding the flow of words upon your brain until they become one with the primal tides that ebb and flow within that wayward organ. And verily I say unto you, in a matter of days you shall notice subtle shifts; within weeks you shall sense a turn; and after only months you shall find yourself in the midst of a self-appreciation you have not known in years, if ever.

If you don't, it could be that you are simply too stupid to grasp any insight that is dashed into your face. Such people do exist, although they rarely do a lot of reading; ergo, it is likelier that you shall, indeed, "get" yourself.

As a result of, of all things, writing sentences.

I found it ironic that I was using the classic teacher punishment tool, the writing of the sentence, as in, "I will not chew gum in class" or "I will not be hurtful to others" or "I will be thankful, every single second, that I have as my teacher and guide one Ruby Pearl Saffire, she of the scintillating intellectual might that will nimbly shepherd me into the rosy dawn of a new day, a full life, and my own nirvana." But far from using the sentence as punishment, I was using it as a reward, a revival, a reinvigorating resurrection. The venom, however, had to be slowly purged, and lo, it so did suck. Anger is a nasty, gnarly goblin, and, while the content of the sentences-upon-which-to-speculate must always, always, be uplifting, I am not naïve or demented enough to have you believe the nasty brew of betrayal fizzles into the fifth dimension. Poof!

Alas, as a festering boil upon the bowels of your being, anger/guilt/bitterness/pain/etc. must be lanced into a slow-as-molasses outpouring of said vitriol. It might be something of a joust, but well worth the win, having the possibility of morphing, as did mine, into a re-connection with some past hobby, knack, talent, or gift.

Slowly and surely, I began to weave other kinds of writing into the grid of my sentence-writing time, purging as much negative energy as poetically possible through verses with such titles as:

"I Hate Your Guts!"

"You Trashed My Truth and Lied Your Way into the Maw of Hell"

"Can You Please Run Your Car into a Wall Now So I Can Collect the Insurance?"

"Have I Told You Lately That I Hate Your Guts?"

"I Hope Your Limp Dick Rots and Shrivels Like a Dried Jalapeno Pepper"

"And Falls Off"

"By the Way, I Hate Your Guts"

You get the drift. These were impotent little tirades, aimed at an impotent little man, and I am loathe to share them with you, as they are tres embarrassing, both in the level of intensity and in the lack of literary polish. Suffice it to say, their expression did the trick in peeling back layer upon layer of bad, bad "stuff" and opening my soul like the trembling budding of a rare tropical bloom, poised upon the periphery of a grand flowering. By the time I got through my country song phase, the Hand Job poems had all but disappeared, the petals began their unfurling, and, as noted, I retired from the teaching profession, having scored enough divorce settlement money and real estate dollars to sustain myself.

The blooming continued, as I struck out— slowly—into the world of writing, to the occasional conference or book fest, only to strike out in the finding of any inroad into the publishing world. Alas, the vast majority of agents and owners and editors were not looking for raw talent with which to build a body of work, to guide and nurture and groom into a towering figure of great literature, to be studied for succeeding generations as a purveyor of universal truths. I admit to doing a little nosedive at the realization that here was yet another non-verdant façade, that money and celebrity had infiltrated the pristine beauty of the well-written word. Everywhere were hawkers and hacks and egos and prima donnas. No talent abounded, and the almighty dollar ruled the day.

The dream had become a lie.

I should not have been surprised, given that we are living in, not only a culture of fear, but also a lying culture, one which is a stunning metaphor for my Life with Hand Job years. Just ponder it! We have information hurled at us constantly from television sets, radios, computers, and smart phones, slices of the culture of celebrity clattering about in our brains until we can barely gather the good sense to try to sort through the information we really need in order to make good decisions. The "news" channels recite soundbites without delving very far into anything like real facts. I remember, once upon a time, when news people had ethics, served the public, as opposed to preening and regurgitating. There once was a thing called a "follow-up" question, which oftentimes clarified for the public that it was hearing a politician's lie. There used to even be a specific kind of reporting called "investigative" (you could look it up), which might inform the public about the poisoning of migrant workers with toxic pesticides, the deadliness of American automobiles, or the criminality of a particular politician. Now we get mostly fluff, such as movie stars and murders, two things which absolutely do not affect my life in any way, shape, or form (okay, crime *rates* might, but not the specifics). And, along with those two very un-weighty topics, we get talking heads that drool out the drivel of politics—which *do*, by the way, affect my life—without much investigation or scrutiny.

I held out hope that the fact that Washington had been finally injected with a big dose of intellect and rationality would give me reason to expect reporters to do the same, although I am still suffering the narcissistic commentators, mass-produced morning show hosts (where do they manufacture these people?) who routinely botch up the syntax and chat about all the un-news going on in the country or repeat the same "talking point" handed down from on high, over and over, in endless subversion of what little *real* journalism there is anymore.

Then there are "the internets," which host an electronic buzzing of bloviating bloggers, useless urban legenders, and all manner of rapacious rumor mongering. Certainly, yes, there is truth there to be found on the net—much more truth than one finds, say, on the Bosom Tube—but unless one is savvy enough to know the most reputable, reliable sources, one has to sift through mountains of fictions in order to find it. The result is that someone goes a-Googling, has an answer in seconds, and accepts it at face value, thinks (s)he has the truth, when in fact (s)he is smack dab in the middle of a world of smoke and mirrors.

And so, just as Hand Job presented me with a false version of reality, you, dear peruser of all things literary, have been given the same treatment by the mangled media, political pricksters, and the whorish hacks who attend to both. And is that not a delicious irony, my sweet peeping toms? He who became a blood-sucking hack in Alabama state politics, charged with the spinning and spamming of our localized culture, gummed up our own marriage with that ilk of deception, and, by all accounts, continues to gum up Miss Denial's sexless relationship with him. I know this because Hand Job continues to attempt to broker a rapprochement, a reconciliation, a "deal;" and I ask the questions I have asked in the past and continue to ask. And, surprise-surprise, I get the answers I got in the past and continue to get.

"Don't you love me?" he asks.

"Have you come clean in the other compartments of your life?" I query each time.

"Not exactly. Not yet," comes the sheepish reply.

"Why sugar-pecker, then how could I even *consider* answering such a question?"

Sometimes he is downright pitiful, but I refuse to budge. After all, if he has not even fully come to honesty, much as one would come to Jesus, then what in the hell would be in it for me, other than a repeat performance of my dead years? Honesty equals liberation and is codified by **Tenet Number Seventeen: Thou shalt allow honesty to set thyself free!**

Honesty would certainly get Hand Job an answer and is my feeble attempt to offer him the salvation his soul craves. But how would I answer him? Tisk-tisk, blessed reader. That is an answer I dare not give away, as he is certain to pick up this parchment just to see what has been written of his wretched existence and the future of said existence. For now he is a hulled cicada, in a hollow, Katy-did die kind of universe. In the meantime, I continue to scoop up blossoms of the sensual escapades that fall into my eyeleted apron from time to time, making up for good times long time lost.

Katy Can!

Yes we can!

Chapter 8: Scrolling for Input

AS my post-millennial writing portfolio grew, along with it my desire to get it "out there," I found within my bosom the need for critique, input, feedback. Naturally I took my blossoming tome (a novel—but at that point a mere short story of fiction about a gigolo who further disrupts a rather dysfunctional family) unto the Dirty Half Dozen, and read it aloud. I learned very quickly thereafter this was the exact *wrong* crowd to judge my work in an objective fashion.

"You are *merely* the Scheherazade of the written word," Micah gushed. "You must tell me one thousand more or I shall go on a murderous rampage."

"It's incredibly good," Diamond affirmed, adding, in her shrink tone, "and it's certain to be therapeutic."

"You'll be *famous*," Marble enthused, "and the money will pour in."

"Especially after you go on Oprah," Emerald added.

And Opal? She crinkled her nose, furrowed her brow, and posited, "I'm not so sure about the sex part."

Yeah. A gigolo. No sex. Right.

It was not my friends but other *writers* and denizens of the publishing world I needed, so I hit the literary circuit in earnest. At one conference I found myself, light of $350, in a private session with a "professional" editor, Bohemia Burgmeier, with whom I shared this, my **Second Sluthood**, in its nascent form. She was from some hot-shot la-de-dah New York City big-house publisher, thus the reading fee for the thirty-minute sit-down. A sub-fifty-ish looking, full-thighed in fashionable denim "expert," she wore fake fingernails, long, (below the shoulders—for a woman past the age of forty this is verboten) frosty-highlighted hair, and a NYC attitude. She was indeed quite the know-it-all, a sarcasmagoric shrew as well, and she would not be tamed.

"It's about rising from the ashes," I offered, in our pre-consultation.

"Nobody can tell *me* about rising from ashes; I've done it all my life!"

Whereupon she launched into a very sad tale about being abandoned by her self-indulgent parents and raised by an aunt, whom she called "Auntie Em," a hard woman who ran a hog farm upstate and used Bohemia for labor, doing hog-sloppin' and such. She was particularly hard on her mother, who was "a horrible person" who "never knew the first thing about loving a child." She went on to tell two more tales about being a party to two separate marriages, the first to a ne'er do well and the second to a very wealthy but abusive architect. By then our introductory time had expired; however, she did agree to read the manuscript, even though, she declared, "We've pretty much seen it all in this genre."

At our next confab, she had changed her tune a bit. "You could be on to something," she said, "but it definitely needs tweaking."

I hung on to her every word. This was an expert, instructing little ol' me.

"First of all, you cannot make reference to the South until halfway in. At the very least a third. Otherwise you've turned off most of the country, especially New York! Hel-*lo*? Where the publishers are?"

She also said, more than once, "Your preposterous prose is ponderously purple."

"I shall wear purple," goes the line from Jenny Joseph's poem on the existence of an elderly renegade. It is only just and fitting that my words be colored as such. Being (shudder) "subtle" is obviously not my modus operandi. Therefore, I spoke directly and to the point: "I find your rabid prejudice against my roots supremely offensive. You are a big city supremacist, that's what you are."

"Oh, puh-lease."

"These bigoted ideas have been programmed into your—"

"I'm following a model that has been proven time and time again."

"Into your vocabulary, into your mind, into your very spirit. If you are a religious woman I would advise you to get down on your knees and beseech the Lord or some-such for forgiveness."

"Have I mentioned that your speech is as purple as the prose?"

"And if *you* were the object of that kind of stereotypical scorn I suppose it would be just fine."

"Once again: Puh-lease. Look. With extensive editing this might have some potential. I mean people might get a—what do you call it?—a 'hoot' out of—"

"God, you sound like Miss Jane Hathaway talking 'hillbilly' to Elly May Clampett."

"—out of this book if you let them get hooked before you say you're from—" she took a deep breath and, with the weight of the Northeast on her shoulders, slowly exhaled, "the *South*."

"But haven't you heard? There *is* no South anymore. We're all the residents of the big blue marble. Universal feelings. Universal attitudes. A glut of belly-flapping, baby-booming, golden-parachute-dragging Americans going global."

"Doesn't matter. They will automatically think this is one of those hokey grits-and-corn pone, you-might-be-a-redneck-if, blue-collar-on-one-end-antebellum-blue-blood-on-the-other stereotypical kinds of things when they get a whiff of your, um, region." She actually wrinkled her nose as if catching the scent of eau d' sour buttermilk.

"Well, I certainly am not 'hokey.' Hokier than *thou*, yes. Hokey, no. And if they automatically assume anything, well that speaks volumes about them as fellow members of the human species. So my attitude is simple: fuck 'em."

"Brilliant strategy. *That* always works."

"Has it ever been tried? Could there be a huge billboard: 'Fuck you. Yours Truly, Ruby Pearl

Saffire'? A very simple, direct message, in black and white. Some kind of very sleek and sexy font. You know, very New York, which only adds to the delicious irony."

"Are you insane?"

"Perhaps it is time to think insanely—not merely outside the box, but as if there were *no* box in the first place."

"How do I get you to understand that if it's perceived as regional—"

"But it truly is not regional! Since when did sex and desire and resurrection become regional? Answer: not regional. Damn it to hell."

"Have you approached any publishers or prominent writers at these—conferences?"

"Of course. But it's a very exclusionary business, you know. A lot of men with very big egos and very small penises who are still, in the twenty-first century, threatened by the poontang."

"I know. I know."

"The preponderance of males is appalling! And I have seen it at work at these conferences and festivals and such—the cronyism, the exclusivity. It's rigged against women." I could feel the two of us bonding, a warmth building within my bosom, an opportunity arising. "I mean, imagine the aspersiveness of the term of non-endearment: 'chick lit'."

"Absolutely. All the more reason to—"

"And each of these men, these 'old sports' in that network, each one really is operating that way as a direct result of having either a very small penis or a very large closet."

"I know that and you know that, but you have to trust me and play the game."

"Shit, I quit playing games when I told my gynecologist to suck out my uterus along with the whole nine yards of Fallopial-tubed ovaries with his itty bitty vagina cleaner.

"Another thing about the manuscript . . . as entertaining as this all is, I just don't see how it's all going to hang together."

"So my thoughts jump a bit."

"A bit? A *bit*? Your thoughts *within* thoughts jump—a bit."

"Ain't it fun?"

"Fun, yes. I just don't know how many readers you will be able to draw in to them—the thoughts. The preponderance of parentheses!"

I gave her my Hannibal Lecter smirk and wink. "*Love* ya alliteration."

"And the italics and the goddamn semi-colons!"

"I'm willing to do a semi-colonostomy. You see? I can compromise."

Sadly, she did not react but continued, "And you want to add self-help to it all? Who are you to offer advice? You're not even a therapist."

"Neither is Dr. Laura, and I make a hell of a lot more sense than she does."

"Not the point.

"And have I mentioned that you use the comment, 'I digress' far and away too frequently?"

"This conversation continues to be so alliterative. I do love that."

"And the word 'bosom'!"

"Because it's such a warm, squishy, comforting little word. Look. What wouldst thou have me do?"

"Make a choice. As it is you go from talking about sex to talking about religion and politics. And some of the writing is something like humor. Some is social commentary."

"So? This is one funny, sex-ridden society we live in, don't you think?"

"And then you throw in those crazy poems!" She threw out her arms in a sweeping show of exasperative redundancy.

"I feel certain that professorial types will love my *Roadkill Trilogy*."

A heavy sigh from Ms. Burgmeier

"And women of an age will love my little 'thong' ditty. And if you can't laugh at a few lines about an extricated uterus, well, you don't deserve a sense of humor."

Of course, Ms. B. took grave offense when I confided in her my refusal to fly the friendly skies. "That's it. You'll never get a contract."

"Oh, surely there will be someone out there who can accommodate my trivial little eccentricities."

"*Ever*," she reiterated. "My god, it makes you look like the yokel they will take you to be."

"There are plenty of tres sophisticated, Mensa society folks who fear to fly. I shall research this and report the good company to you."

"That's not the point. These days it goes with the territory."

"What territory?"

"The contract. The *con*tract."

"Oh. That 'con' word. Again, I am not one who is full of respect for the corporate world—even publishing."

"You will be seen as 'difficult'."

"I care not."

"Why stack the deck so completely against yourself?"

"Have you not read my book? I do not live my life for any corporate entity or lying man."

"You also need to know that you'll never make it without an agent."

"So I hear."

"Without an agent you are doomed."

"Your fear mongering puts me back in a Bushian state of mind. I will not live my life like that. Hell, I'm already a bit agoraphobic."

"I just don't know why you insist on thumbing your nose at the whole business."

"Because it's a whore, a rank capitalist, intent upon sucking everything into a big, greedy pile of nothing."

"You're making a huge mistake. But if you manage to finish this—thing, send it to me. I'll give a look. If I think it can make us some money, I'll be all over it."

"I cease to give a good goddamn. I will not be a whore."

All true-blue sluts have integrity.

In the end, I felt I had been duped, clipped, taken, flimflammed—"shrewd" by the shrew. Yet the encounter was a valuable object lesson in what has been an ongoing theme of this manifesto and now becomes **Tenet Number Eighteen: Thou shalt cease to give a good goddam.**

I can feel the incredulity of those readers who might have made the attempt to write for publication, the ones who prowl the book conferences watching for crumbs to fall into their ink-stained palms, the Stigmata of the un-chosen ones. It is a little-known subculture, this legion of would-be literati who ebb and flow behind the literary scene, who do not yet realize that personal power can be easily seized once any particular person ceases to give a good goddamn. Which goes to the essentiality of being a pure, unadulterated (but un-adulterous) Slut (as opposed to a whore, which is what the publishing industry actually is). Ergo the initial blog, which was at least a way to get the work "out there":

October 28

Yes, it has been a while, and I suppose it's only normal that I continue to resist this cyber-world of ethereal, electronic flotsam. Opal keeps telling me to just get a fresh pedicure and move my feet, get a fresh manicure and let my groomed cuticles curtsey, then sashay and promenade (or a seductive tango, perhaps? A steamy striptease?) across the keyboard, and she's right, of course.

216

One must exercise one's reaches for talent, to be better and better equipped when the fruit is within one's grasp. One must lean at the ready into opening possibilities. Build it and they will come, so—lo, I come unto you with my poetic waxings.

But I do use the term "poetic" very loosely—as loosely as my flaccid breasts rest, beneath my dotted Swiss bed jacket, upon my aging chest, in fact. Rather than sending out deep musings of contemplation or despair, I have chosen to send *up* several classic poems by using their rhyme and meter to paint verbal images of something with which I am most familiar, road-kill. I have grown up on Southern soil and seen, on a daily, yea, oftentimes hourly, basis, the asphalt dotted with carcal renderings in various stages of decay. Some days it seems as if one cannot drive the length of a doublewide without seeing some mushed up mammal gummed into the highway, eyes popped, tongue hatching maggots. This imagery is fire-branded into my brain, quite possibly into my DNA, and such random, unacknowledged death screams for nothing less than a poetic obit, particularly when one has been so knocked-down as to become one with the road-kill in empathetic ennui. That is what I was thinking when I conceived my *Roadkill Trilogy*, three common targets of mortal trafficking: a deer, an armadillo, and a 'possum, each a symbol of all the fender-whacked creatures (both animal animal and human animal, like moi) that have gone before and will so subsequently go into that good night. So please, gentle reader, place thy tongue firmly against the inside of thy cheek and be kind to the author.

ROADKILL TRILOGY

<u>One: The Road Forsaken</u> (inspired by "The Road Not Taken" by Robert Frost)

Two lanes diverged on my path to food
And since I could not follow both
To seek a salt lick, there I stood
And gazed down one as long as I could
To where it curled through the piney growth

Then took the other, antlers high,
For it was the one with fewer cars
To bend their bright bumpers around my thighs
Or sling me aside with their massive size
Or strap me on hoods to show at bars . . .

The pulp hauler's rig was stealthy, geared low
As my hoof tapped the asphalt's gravel-lined curve
Its horn cut the night with one blaring blow
Fixing my fate in these woods of woe
For a buck dodges shots, but not a truck's swerve

I shall be telling this tale with a sigh
To fallen fawn in heavens hence
The blacktop forked in the woods, and I—

218

I took the lane few cars did try
And the timber trade made all the difference.

<u>Two: I-465</u> (inspired by "465" by Emily Dickenson)

I heard a Fly buzz when I died
The tires upon the road
Had tracked across my back until
It flattened from the load

The cars swashed by—and oft upon
The shards of my half-shell
And nothing but a puny nub
Was left of my fine tail

An armadillo always dares
To tread where asphalt lies
Yet knows he beats the raccoon's chance
Of being food for flies

And so a fly began to buzz
The carcass that was me
The moon at once went out—and then
I could not be to see

<u>Three: O! Possum!</u> (inspired by "The Highwayman" by Alfred Noyes)

The night was a cauldron of blackness

Stirred by oaks and pines;
The moon was a faded glimmer
Of a glare that lost its shine;
The road was a ribbon of moonlight
Over the wiregrass plain;
And the possum came a lumb'ring, lumb'ring, lumb'ring,
The possum came a lumb'ring up to South Broad and Main.

His bulging black eyes were surrounded
By brittle and mottled fur;
His claws clicked the asphalt gently
As he sidled up to the curb;
His coat caught the starlight's sprinkle
Across its gray-matted sheen;
And he watched with a doomed man's wide eyes, his heart pumping
Death's dread reprise, his thoughts on the vehicle lurking,
Ahead, but just unseen

Just up the road she was primping
Her curls with her deep red nails,
Still bathed in the glow of the neon
From Bobby Joe's Honky-Tonk Hell;
She drove the Camaro her boyfriend
Had bought for her skanky white ass—
It was Bess, the bar-keep's daughter, the bar-keep's big-haired daughter,
Checking the crimp of her mousse in the mirrored rear-view glass

The radio screamed Lynyrd Skynyrd
As she wiggled her spandexed hips,
A Capri Menthol Light bobbed and dangled
From her glossy-wet Maybelline lips;
Her vodka and tonic rode shotgun
With the weed for her buzzed-up brain,
And the bass thumped the car's vinyl
dashboard, electric guitars screamed
   a wild chord, the Camaro downshifted and rip-
roared
   Straight through South Broad and Main

The chrome slammed his rodent-like body
Straight into the asphalt earth;
He bounced and he scraped and meandered
A pinball's most dizzying mirth;
Like tumbleweed pitched through a windstorm,
He rolled from hither to yon,
Landing with all four feet skyward,
Claws beckoning Heaven's pink dawn

And the legend lives on in the flatlands
Of the doomed marsupial's pain—
How the possum went a-tumbling, tumbling,
tumbling—
The possum went a-tumbling—
All over South Broad and Main.

And that is my *Roadkill Trilogy*. In a moment I
shall hit the button on my keyboard that will make

221

it impossible to take back any of my words, which will be snatched into the invisible network that will transport them, as if by some kind of voodoo sprite, unto you.

And so I push on, to literary fests and author events and seminars on how to get published. And still the strange, lonely-eyed, slouching man hangs at the fringes, never speaking up, just watching, sometimes catching my glance. I do not believe he is dangerous; he is merely odd and solitary and apparently of a literary bent as I see him everywhere, have run across him at dozens of panels and lectures and author events.

For now I am most deliciously spent, making ready to send my wan words to you, dear, dahlin' reader/voyeur. Hold them gently, cup them in your thoughts, take them to your bosom, and know there are many facets to Ruby Pearl Saffire, perhaps many more even than the poetry, social commentary, and self help I have thus-far promised. We shall see . . . we shall see.

I hearken back to that blip of a blog to remind you of the degree of my insecurity at the time. I marshaled the level of security it took to even *make* that early effort, but compare that woman with the one who continues to emerge, the one splayed open and willing before you upon these pages, having **ceased to give a good goddamn**. *Yee-hah!*

There was something else about blog world: the symbolism was simply too rich. Blog? Bog? My life in the swampy quicksand of mediocrity followed by the effort to re-join the masses, only to find them in a larger mire of their own making? My musings could serve as a reflection of what so many out there merely "attempted" to do with their ramblings (all the while believing they have something to say; I, on the other hand, really *did* have something to say). It can illuminate the life's theme, life's truth, which I have finally discovered: one can rise from the aforementioned ashes, reformed and wise to all the bullshit. The re-taking of the wilted will. The re-making of the splattered soul. The recouping of the cut losses. The swelling of the sense of urgency I have to spread the Good News of how and why we must cavort, *undignified*, through these dimming latter years of ours.

And then, fortuitously for the brief blog (I thought, clearly incorrectly, at the time), the universe took yet another turn:

December 3

I do admit to being rather sluggish in posting these entries, yet I have been looking forward to recording this one, as there has been a development that seems to move the narrative of this blog into an interesting direction. Thus, the life story I am creating takes shape, hopefully shape-shifting into an even more pleasant direction.

223

Patching together a new reality is oft times distracting, although occasionally all it takes to feel renewed is stepping into one of my post-divorce collection of thongs. Let me reiterate that it only happens occasionally, but the occasions, like labor pains, seem to come more and more frequently—occasions when the slipping into the thong is like slipping into a more authentic self. Is my crowning and subsequent re-birth around the corner and just between the thighs? I have taken to wearing appropriate underwear, as my mother always says, *just in case.*

And I was wearing one of my favorite thongs—purple paisley edged in black lace with "cuddly kitty" stitched on the front in black script—when that strange, lurking man—the one from the conferences—accosted me in a food court at the mall in Albany, Georgia, as I snouted forth from every mucous membrane in my Miss-Clairol highlighted head. I shall now relate said encounter:

I had arrived at the food court with a hard-core jalapeno/habanera monkey on my back, hankering for the spicy buzz I seek from time to time. This desire for a mouthful of fire cannot be overstated enough; I daresay that crystal meth has no stronger a hold on its addict of choice than my very own pugnacious little primate. Ergo, when the urge strikes, seconds are like unto minutes, which are like unto hours, all the more frustrating as immediate satiation is critical. Since there were no authentic restaurantes mejicanas in the immediate vicinity, I settled on a Taco Bell, ordering a cardboard square container of nachos denuded of cheese along with several packets of the extra spicy salsa and a couple of additional cardboard squares, resisting the temptation to plead with the pimply teenager behind the counter: "Come on, man, hurry—I'm fuckin' hurtin, dude!"

I took a seat at a table near the fountain and proceeded to whip up my own lethal blend of dipping sauce, squeezing the contents of the fast food packets into one of the cardboard squares, adding a generous amount from the bottle of Triple XXX sauce I always keep on hand in my purse (as a flask is to an alcoholic, thus is my stash to moi). I set upon the feast and in short order my brain was humming, my ears were popping, and the world was fading into a gray background as I rode the endorphins into Epicural ecstasy while the eyeballs and membranes poured forth. Time fell away. Nirvana ensued.

The endorphin frenzy was beginning to abate when a calloused, ragged-nailed hand bearing a rather threadbare but apparently clean handkerchief appeared before my crossed eyes. "You look like you can use this," a gravelly voice bore into the receding buzz.

I looked up and saw the familiar image—a forty-something male, not unattractive though not remarkable looking either, dressed in rumpled clothing that was not yet disheveled, not unlike the garb of a Columbo, a la Peter Falk—the man I had seen at more than a few book fests, trade shows, and such. I struggled to collect myself and managed to respond, in a stuffed-up timbre, "Excuse me, but are you perchance stalking me?"

His face did not change its rather flat expression. "I don't stalk. I investigate."

This jarred in me a bit of irritation, sending me into a higher-functioning mode. "Well are you investigating me? Because I assure you I am a law abiding citizen, a good, red-blooded American one."

"Take it," referring to the handkerchief.

"Thank you. Won't you pull up a chair?" I undertook the wiping of the eyes, the blowing of the nose, then, "Fortunately for all concerned, I do not drool in public; however, in the privacy of my own home, and with enough habanera—"

"Can't stay."

"Well you most certainly cannot exit until you tell me for what I am being investigated. Is there a law against my salsa fix?"

"No investigation of you, not in the larger narrative."

"But you are a law man? I myself am a writer who is determined to be published." I was also determined to get some kind of reaction from him. I gave him a slow once-over. "Have you a big gun?" I raised an eyebrow, then winked.

He did not actually roll his eyes, but I saw a flicker of that gesture. "I'm a P.I."

"Oh, like Magnum! You must lead an exciting life, what with car chases, leaps from rooftop to rooftop, stealing down dark alleyways through a hail of ammunition. I used to enjoy the occasional detective show on the tube of the boob."

"Television? Nah, wrong genre."

"What do you mean?"

"Nothing. I've got to move on." He turned to leave.

"Wait—do you have a name?" I put out my hand. "I am Ruby Pearl Saffire."

He took my hand, and my intuitive self felt a bit of potential in that touch. "Scarpete. Just Scarpete."

"That is an intriguing name." I let my fingers brush his palm as he released the handshake. I rarely let opportunities to flirt pass me by these days, particularly if I sense potential intrigue of any kind.

He did not respond, just nodded a couple of times, then, "Well."

"For what purpose do you attend these literary events I have been also visiting?"

"I told you. I'm an investigator."

"Investigating what?"

"You ask a lot of questions."

"Isn't that deliciously ironic, since it is *your* job to ask them? And so I shall reiterate: investigating what?"

"Can't talk about it."

"Aw, come on. I love a good mystery."

"Told you. Got to go." He began to walk away.

"Yoo hoo, Mr. Scarpete."

He turned, with something akin to exasperation upon his inscrutable countenance.

I waved the handkerchief as a damsel would in farewell. "Perhaps we shall meet again."

"Maybe," he shrugged, but one corner of his mouth ticked upward as he turned, an upward tick that most assuredly was the potential of a making smile. Then he continued to walk away, as the fountain's cascading waters tickled my senses into a burgeoning curiosity about this being who was crissing and crossing my little world.

But then and there, in the Albany Mall, I only sighed, considered options real and imaginable, contemplating the intricate nature of interpersonal dynamics, and finally opted for what came most naturally: I unscrewed the cap on my bottle of Triple XXX and mixed up another batch of bliss.

After that, nothing. Zero. End of internetical spelunking and back to what I considered the more virtuous non-virtual world—for about six years.

And even now I prefer to find immortality in a more tangible way, to produce an artifact that might well be excavated out of a library by some twenty-third century archaeologist space traveler studying the Lost Civilization of Planet Earth. If all goes according to plan, then I shall go down in herstory as one of the final voices of the long-forgotten Age of Books, as an advocate for the slow-connect intimacy of pages turned, syllables on paper, an activist fighting for the continued existence of words crafted for one work to be taken as a whole; not a little series of yaps and yammers, tweets-twitters-and-twats, brilliant as some of them may be, crucial to civilization as a few of them likely are, that flash onto a screen and hang there before the click of an icon exes them away. Fortunately for me, I still live and breathe in the Age of Books, albeit as it wanes. Communication, like a tiger, still comes in many stripes. And, just as a leopard is not likely to change its spots, neither is a shriveling up, soon-to-be little old lady such as myself likely to become more than what she was originally intended to be: a social commentator/self-help guru/would-be poet/author with a nature hell-bent on Sluthood and book writing as opposed to blogging and such.

Yes, there is a story—a rather compelling one—about the strange, scruffy man who would oddly re-surface in my life. I did not suspect at the time that we really would meet again, would, in fact, engage in a rather riveting duet of discourse carrying within it the potential of intercourse, which I shall surely share as my story is shaded throughout the upcoming pages. But first:

Continuing on my odyssey in Literary Land, I decided the place to be was in a real creative writing program with a real instructor (as opposed to some big city full-of- herself editor or some impersonal internet site), and plunked down some more serious mullah in order to attend a class at the university. What I expected was guidance, constructive criticism, mentoring, all the warm fuzzies upon which we humans thrive. After all, when one is putting one's deepest musings, often even one's inner tyke, upon the table for all to scrutinize, then one is tres vulnerable.

What I got in this three hour weekly seminar was a vicious, evil little man determined to chip away at the spirits of the ten students under his tutelage until they were completely broken down (it's a good thing I had **ceased to give a good goddamn** by then).

Dr. Jaime Prique Blanco (I added the middle name; I have no idea what "prique" means in Spanish; to me it simply means "prick") was of the school of thought that proffered writing programs should be hazings of cruel twists of verbal daggers plunged deep into one's pathetically willing students' hearts. The role of the professor was to be one of ultimate authority, a supreme, all knowing voice of he who is to be sucked up to, groveled at the feet of, emulated, and feared. Often he would stop a reader after the first paragraph, or even the first sentence, proclaiming the writing "trite," or "hackneyed," or "just plain horrid." On other occasions he might let a student go on and on, all the way to the bitter end, before proclaiming the story to be "language usage of the all-time low variety."

Of course he had a couple of "pets"—both male (he was particularly brutal with the females)—whom he praised from time to time but not enough to make fear a stranger to them. I watched in horror as he reduced his brood, one by one, to mush. Yes, at every turn emotional anguish was prepared to be heaped upon any victim, including yours truly.

"Obviously you aren't serious about writing," was his only lisping comment after my first offering, a bawdy chapter from my novel.

I had been observing Satan for three weeks by now and had decided that I was not about to do the dance to which he was accustomed. I was his elder, which is quite a good card to have in one's hand; the others were practically children. I said nothing, but locked my formidable, little-old-lady gaze onto his.

After a few beats he leaned forward, attempting intimidating body language. "Well? What do you have to say?"

I replied in a most pleasant tone, "I was not aware that a question was posed. And I do not care to respond to the rude comments you feel compelled to make."

His face went red. "Then get out. This is a *seminar*. A discussion."

"I am quite aware of what it is. After all, I paid hundreds of dollars in order to have a seat here and I shall not be leaving until I decide to leave. Or perhaps not at all to leave." I gave him my sweetest smile.

"Who do you think—" he sputtered, then, surely perceiving his disadvantage, "Suit yourself."

"Thank you, Mr. Blanco," I replied, as perkily as possible. "I'll do just that."

"*Dr.* Blanco."

"Yes, of course. Do forgive me. I had forgotten."

Yes, I had bested him, and the others knew it, expressing their admiration of my spine outside of class. "You simply have to **cease to give a good goddamn**," I advised them when queried about my ability to face him down in such a calm and gentle manner. I was unable to contain myself, however, when a darling little girl named Michelle was disemboweled before the group.

She had shared a synopsis of her short story with me, expressing all the insecurity he had fostered within her thus far. It was a compelling tale. She confided that it was inspired by her father's death—very full of those all-powerful inner tyke issues which equates with the opening of one's heart. I truly feared for her.

Lucifer stopped her half way in. "Is this drivel *going* somewhere? Or is it just you, publicly masturbating?"

She was speechless. Deer. Headlights. The making of tears.

"You are a merciless prick!" It came out before I could check myself.

"I beg your pardon!"

It was too late, of course. The words cascaded from my forked tongue. "You are just the kind of prick who screams to the world, 'Look at *me*. I have this teeny-tiny *prick* so I must compensate with a pathologically *huge* ego that requires the fear and adoration of a bunch of willing young people, who will one day realize what a sham is being perpetrated upon them'."

"You—you—" he stammered, red-faced, purpling darker.

"Or perhaps you should be saying, 'Look at *me*. I am a self-loathing homosexual has-been who lives in a *humongous* closet and can only sadistically humiliate the young men who look to me for guidance because it gives *me* something to think about whilst masturbating in the shower whilst my beard cooks breakfast. As for the young women, why don't I simply accuse one of *them* of *emotional* masturbation when I am threatened that she might be supremely more talented than I, who have a mere *two* published novels, however many forevers ago, under my belt, the first of which was desperately *self* published'. Yes, Mr. Tightie Whitie, I have done my research."

I looked at Michelle, who was gazing at me, wide-eyed and drop-jawed, as were all of the others save Lucifer, who stood and bellowed, "You! Get! Out!"

I scooped up my notebook. "You're goddamn right I'll get out, but not on *your* orders. I'm leaving because this has been an utter waste of cabbage and I intend to march over to the registrar this very second and demand my money back and I urge everyone else to do the same. I do, however, want to thank you for the opportunity to make a rather dramatic exit, which I do *so* love, you pathetic little, impotent, *impotent* prick!" I then shifted tonal gears. "By the way, Michelle, your story is masterful. Ta-ta, all. *Buenas tardes*, Prique." And I gave the door a mighty slam.

233

I could go into much detail about Dr. Blanco's preening and feyness and boastfulness and plucked eyebrows and inflation of past personal successes, but the little prick deserves no further ink. I had originally planned to include him only as a footnote in this manifesto, but my indignation seized hold of my fingertips.

The silver lining: I am pleased to report that I was successful in getting a goodly portion of my money refunded. As for the other students, I fear they all remained to complete a semester's worth of verbal gutting and dismemberment, for alas, they were young co-eds, with a god-complexed professor to please. I, however, was done with academia in particular and input in general.

Let us now move forward to

Chapter 9 Enter-shift-insert . . . NOT!

WHEREIN it is revealed that one should always follow **Tenet Number Nineteen: Thou shalt engage in banter (particularly if thou art possessed of a sharp intellect) for verily I say unto you, "It is sexy."** And it can lay some interesting ground work.

It turns out that the scruffy man, one Mr. Scarpete, he of the food court salsa assault, a conversation which was a serendipitous foreshadowing of didactic dialogues to come. Our brief but spicy encounter had left me unsettled and pleasantly intrigued, there in the Albany Mall back when the century had turned only two years old.

You can imagine my surprise when, a full five years later, I began to catch glimpses of him around my hometown. At first I questioned myself. Surely this was someone who merely *resembled* him. No, the appearance and garb were nothing if not distinctive. I next wondered whether I might be having some sort of hallucinatory episode—a flashback from the long-ago dawning of the Age of Aquarius, perhaps? Once I was satisfied that he was not a remnant of a foray into the counter-real world of lysergic acid, I was prompted to revisit my initial concern re: stalking. This concern was assuaged, however, when I noted that he was obviously not looking for me, as he did not even seem to notice me, seemed fixated upon something altogether different, something upon the periphery of his world and mine. He would have to actually notice me in order to follow me in a stalkeresque manner. I had taken him at his word, and rightly so, there in the food court of the Albany, Georgia, Mall, that he was not any sort of delusional obsessive, for I would happen upon *him*, not the other way around, catching a glimpse of him in Julwin's, the local diner, or perusing the area papers at the News Stand, or entering Page and Palette, the independent bookstore here in town that manages to compete with the Barnes and Noble up the road a piece. And it was most jarring that he failed to notice me, paid precious little mind, a twist that sorely vexed me as I am nothing if not noticeable, bangling and bubbling through any venue that presents itself.

Finally I could take it no longer. When I saw him in Bruno's, expressionless as before, picking through cold remedies on the medicine/toiletry aisle, I was emboldened and indignant enough to charge right up to him.

"Excuse me, Mr. Scarpete, but do you not remember me whatsoever? Am I not a memorable character?"

He looked up, seeming startled, yet back to deadpan in a beat of a heart. I mentally noted, in pure private dick style, that his cart held six Swanson frozen meals, an eighteen pack of frozen fish sticks, several frozen chicken pot pies, a loaf of Bunny bread, a large package of bologna, a tin of Folger's coffee, a large bottle of Hellman's mayonnaise, and a case of Miller High Life beer. "Sure," he said in a nasally, stuffed tone. "I don't forget faces. You're the writer chick."

"I am *not* a fluff of poultry, sir! A writer, yes. And I have a name. Quite an elegant one, actually."

"Have you ever done any of these?" He coughed and indicated the shelves upon shelves of Tylenol, NyQuil, Robitussin, lozenges, chest rubs, syrups, capsules, tablets, *ad infinitum*.

"Enough to know that one has to wonder why we Americans need so many goddamn choices," I retorted.

He appeared to be wearing the exact same garments in which he was garbed in Georgia, but I resisted the temptation to comment. "Uh huh." He turned back to the shelves. "Cold's interfering with the job."

"What job is that?"

He continued to scrutinize the shelves of elixirs, potions, and witches' brews, mumbling to himself in grunted syllables I could not begin to understand.

"Perhaps you did not hear my query. I inquired as to what your job might be. I mean I know your *job* job, but not what brings you here."

Still he puzzled over the medicinal products. Naturally my frustration was fervent by now, yet I began to notice that it was laced with something else, something beyond my initial curiosity and ponderance in Georgia, for it is a rare, rare occasion when I, R.P. Saffire, having undertaken the endeavour of engaging a member of the opposite sex, am ignored by said member. It brought me up rather short but ever more determined.

237

I touched his shoulder, "Mr. Scarpete—oh!" He had startled quite strongly at my touch, which gave me a jolt. "My goodness, I was only attempting to get a response from you. I am certainly not launching a physical assault."

He had turned toward me and in his eyes I caught that strange, almost surreal expression of something akin to sadness that I had first noted during our former encounter.

"Yeah," he said, turning back to study the products.

How does one explain something as subtle as attraction? Was it his aloofness that was beginning the familiar stirring that would ultimately play havoc with my pheromones? Was it his resemblance to Peter Falk-as-Columbo, albeit graying and without the glass eye? Was it a spiritual connection sprung from past lives? I do not pretend to know, and yet we have all (hopefully) felt it. Since I could not, of course, reveal this attraction, I said only, "These products do nothing but treat your symptoms. I would recommend aspirin, vitamin C, bed rest, and hot toddies of bourbon, honey, and lemon."

He took a box of Tylenol Cold from the shelf and pointedly dropped it in the cart.

"Well, they're *your* sinuses. Don't blame *me* when they go to cement."

"You're a regular Flo Nightingale, aren't you?"

"Actually, no. I am not a nurse by any means. I gave all my husbands strict instructions not to get sick and die before *me*, as I would not be up to the task of caretaker."

"*All* of them?"

I took this to be an interrogative as to the number and so I obliged. "Four. But I don't really count the first three as I was a child, and the last one was a sham, so it turns out I am quite the marital virgin, n'est-ce pas?"

"Uh huh."

"I truly do urge you to consider my carefully considered prescription. It worked in the olden days, the toddy, and that awful stuff you have literally chunked into your cart is more like unto poison."

"You like to tell people what to do, don't you?" But he said it with a smirk, a rather endearing one.

"As a matter of fact I am writing a book of that very genre—with social commentary and poetry thrown in, of course."

"A book, huh?" He was immediately infused, in spite of his swollen nasal passages, with a shadow of a demeanor of genuine curiosity.

"Oh, yes, quite an intricate and quirky little tome, much like moi."

He pulled out a handkerchief and trumpeted a blast of mucoul renderings into it. "Maybe we could talk about it sometime."

Aha! I had him. "Well, sugar dove, if you can tell me my name I might just consider it."

He smirked again, endearingly, again. "Like I said, I don't forget faces or things or people. It's my nut."

"Pray, continue."

"You are one R. P. Saffire, who enjoys her salsas to the point of pain."

I had to laugh. "Is it not ironical in an exquisite manner that the tone of our two only conversations has been set by certain snottings?"

His smirk quirked upward, but that seemed to be the extent of his ability to laugh. Intriguing *and* challenging.

I pressed on. "What sort of work are you doing in my part of the world?"

"Just doing what I do. Asking questions."

"Prithee, about what?"

"Just looking for somebody, that's all."

"Well, fish eggs! Is it top secret, classified, for somebody's eyes only, a threat to national security, etc?"

"Can't say that it is."

"So tell me, Mr. Scarpete Columbo person, for whom are you looking?"

"Hard to explain."

"Attempt."

"Not many people would get it."

"Surely by now you realize I am not 'many people'."

Another tic upward, the very slightest, of the mouth. "You don't seem to be."

"Before this conversation goes a syllable further, you must riddle me this: are you a complicated man?"

"Complicated?"

"Yes, complicated."

Something akin to a whispery snicker escaped his guard. "Lady," he said, "I'm about the simplest mug you'd ever want to meet."

"Well that is quite the relief. And my guardian angel will be delighted to hear it." And as an aside to Marble, I did not mind at all that he had addressed me as "Lady;" it was kind of cute, actually.

He did not react.

"So? Whom are you pursuing? A drug runner? An escaped murderer? One of those mythical Islamofacsists? Jimmy Hoffa? A body dumped? An identity thieved?"

"Something like the latter."

"Do go on."

"Yeah," he said, wiping his nose with his handkerchief, "I'm looking for an identity."

I waited, refusing to prod further, and he did not disappoint.

"I'm looking," he said, "for myself."

Chapter 10: My Domain: A Single Tax Colony—In Ala*bam*a?!?

YES, a man from the periphery of my life wandered into my little corner of the world on a quest for self, or so he said. This twist would be enough to render a work of fiction not "believable," a too-convenient plot turn. Fortunately, this is nonfiction and is therefore true. If some of you Thomases out there are having doubts, well, Chapter 10 is too far in to decide that you do not believe that I am putting my honest adventures out there, into the bibliophilic bog, for you to slog around in. And my words should guide you, motivationally equip you to traverse said quagmire without feeling the quicksand pulling you into a self-defeating morass of mediocrity.

I have told you a bit about my little corner of the world, a place that I have to say is decidedly Southern in flavor while being an aberration for the region as well. I reside in Fairhope, Alabama, the oldest and possibly the only single tax colony in the country, at least it is as this book goes to press (there are forces afoot to dismantle it). It is a town filled with flowers, art galleries, and quaint shops on the eastern shore of Mobile Bay. I was drawn to this place because it was settled by a band of Utopian free thinkers, intellectuals, socialists, who believed the waterfront was for everyone to enjoy, and all the property in the town would be leased as no one should *own* the land. In the early twentieth century some denizens of the town made their way down the bluffs at certain appointed times, shed their clothing, and took their communal swim *au natural*. Aha, I thought, upon hearing of such customs, these are *my* people.

Of course, when I describe the history of the place to people I meet in other parts of the U S of A, they are shocked. "You're telling me this is in Ala*bam*a?"

I rather suspect that many of you, my beloved readers, also harbor the belief that I am lying. So feel free to do a Googling of your own, research my claims here, and I shall be vindicated.

So much for the unlikely bit of my domain. I wish that I could say that the nude bathing continues, that the high ideals live on, but alas. Fairhope has warped into a much more conservative place than its founders ever imagined, overrun with development that has somewhat diminished in activity since the nation's financial woes began, Hummers that still unabashedly put excess before the eyes of all, and SUV's still bearing "W" stickers, even though the rest of the nation, lo, the world (many white crackers are not only "anti-intellectual-elitist," but they also take great pride in stupidity; witness their love affair with yet another "C" student, Sarah Palin), has long since recognized the utter mess that man made—which is, after all, what alcoholic personalities do—make messes for those around them to clean up.

There is a strong, independent element in this experiment-in-socialism former village, and artists and writers and eccentrics abound. This I love,

243

along with the fact that, as I write this, as the post coital flush of the president's second inauguration fades, I sense a change in the air—even here in white bread land—a shift in the currents buffeting the bohemian season, and I am heartened by the lift of the collective spirit. (Although now, with the election 2016 on the horizon (Rah, Hilary!), I look back on several years of insanely executed intransigence in the political sphere. The Teabagger Effect. Alas.)

Back in ought seven, though, my heart was not prepared to be spirited away by Mr. Scruffy Scarpete—not yet.

A few weeks after our encounter in Bruno's, in my domain, this man Scarpete phoned me, having been given my cell number (by moi), having openly admitted that he did not believe in carrying around such technological wonders; for all we knew, he insisted, these marvels might well cause genital warts, burst appendices, and popped eyeballs, let alone the brain tumors we *did* know about. He used an antique—a pay phone (the sad little shotgun shack he rented in a ramshackle neighborhood did not offer telephone service) to invite me to meet him for a late lunch, which I did. And, dear reader, what began as a couple of rather odd conversations got, as Alice herself observed down one such rabbit hole, "curiouser and curiouser."

This rather endearing, rather enigmatic character did little talk of the chitting or chatting variety, which suited me just fine, as I find such meaningless drivel an utter and horrific waste of time; but our talk turned down a rather strange, philosophical literary lane, and I beseech you, beloved reader, stay with me.

He quizzed me relentlessly about the mind of this writer, starting out with fairly ordinary questions.

"You have done a work of fiction?"

"Oh, but of course, sugar sleuth! Sadly, it has not seen the light of day in publication world, but I am determined that it will. It is a comic tale about a dysfunctional family not unlike that of yours truly."

"So your characters are real?"

"But of course not! Realistic, yes. It's *fiction*."

"How do you come up with your characters?"

"Goodness, this feels like an interview, as if I am on stage."

"Whatever floats your boat." He took a gulp of coffee. "Where do the characters come from?"

"They spring from my brow, much as Athena sprang from Zeuss's."

"Come on, come on. Give me the real skinny. You're not talking to an audience at some book festival."

"Well, no, I am sitting in Julwin's. I have just ordered a catfish plate. You have not ordered anything but a coffee. Did we not come here to do some lunching?"

"Caffeine. It's all the fuel I need right now."

"At any rate, I do not need you to point out that we are not at a book festival."

He cupped his palms around the white mug. "Lady, can you just be real?"

I found his addressing me as "Lady" *this* time somewhat distasteful, finally forging a bond with Marble and her law enforcement experience. Still, I managed a retort. "I am the most genuine article you will ever encounter!"

"So answer the question."

"All right. My characters are composites of people I know and people I make up. They are all in little pieces that come together, much as the pieces of moi finally came together after a hellacious bounty of heartache and labor."

"Hm. So they live in the imagination to be 'thought up'."

"Of course."

"Is that where *I* live? In your imagination?"

"Don't be silly. You are real."

"How do you know?"

"Because this book in which you find yourself is nonfiction and therefore true, and so you are real. My heavens, do you not even know that you are real? What kind of a sleuth doesn't notice a thing like that?"

"A literary one."

"A what?"

"A literary one. One who is looking for himself."

"You are confusing me."

"What's the title of your novel?"

"Heavens, you are rat-a-tatting me to death with all these questions. It makes me hearken to my childhood—not a place I am wont to frequent."

Indeed, the rapid-fire quality to his speech put me in mind of the Bizarro Ozzie and Harriet dialogue meshed in my brain, along with that clipped, 1940's movie dialogue that is so grating to one's nerves. Still, one had to be intrigued.

He did not remark on my remark but looked at me intently, tapping his fingers on the slick glass table top, waiting.

"Alright, alright. The title is *The Fall of the Nixon Administration* and it's—"

"It's a political book?"

"No, of course not."

"Then why do you give it such a misleading title?"

"It's not misleading, for goodness sake. It's symbolic. It is a literary novel."

"Did you have the title before you had the characters?"

"Actually, no. I had a gigolo with a bunch of chickens whom he named after all the president's men—you know, Haldeman, Mitchell, Dean, that bunch—plus a wealthy widow with a prissy, disapproving daughter not unlike my prissy, disapproving sister DeBOrah. Although there are certainly many authors with whom I have chatted who will testify to the need to have a title before they can even pen word the first. I, however, find that the muse will deliver an appropriate title unto me at the magical moment. And where is this conversation going?"

"It's what I do. Questions."

247

"Ah, Mr. Scarpete, but you have revealed to me your quest—to find yourself. If you were a more youthful individual I would recommend that you go to Europe to 'find' yourself, as so many of my acquaintances did in the 1970's."

"You give a lot of advice that isn't asked for. Could we get back to the questions?"

"We most certainly can, but only if *you* answer a few. After all, it is hardly fair to hog them all. And by the way, as I believe I have already pointed out to you, I offer advice in the capacity of one who is writing a book emphasizing self-help."

"Bullshit."

"I most certainly am writing such a book!"

"Self-help books are bullshit."

"I shall let that rather rude pronouncement roll off my back and say only that there will be no shit of the bull in *my* tome. But answer me this, Dirty Harry: Where do you come from? And what do you really mean by 'finding' yourself? We both know you do not mean it in the usual sense."

"No." He furrowed his brow, tucking wrinkles deeper into themselves. "It's not easy to explain. Most people—"

"I am not 'most' people, as I have also pointed out before. Such repetition!"

"Got to repeat. Go through the clues. Over and over."

"In order to?"

"Crack the case."

"The case of the missing you. Don't you think it's time you finally, really and truly and honestly, explain?"

He shifted nervously in the booth, squinted his eyes at me as if sizing me up—again.

"Come on, Mr. Scarpete. You are conversing with one Ruby Pearl Saffire, a born again Slut who is writing her own life as she lives it, so I am constantly finding myself. I sense that you have a story that is just as exquisitely interesting as mine."

The smirk I had found so endearing made its first appearance of the day. "You could say so."

"I shall. So?"

"Okay, okay. Here's a hypothetical: Let's say there's this private dick who's pretty fucking logical, thinks on his feet, can figure things out. This author created him, right? Then the author is murdered, and this P.I. has to investigate it—the death of his creator—to find out as much as he can about his own story as he can—because all he has is this one story to go by. And a life is a hell of a lot bigger than a story."

I was dumbfounded, first of all because he had just strung together more words than I had ever heard him utter; and secondly because of the envelope he was pushing. And yet I could follow this line of thought; it even made an odd sort of sense. "Are you saying that you are fictional?"

"I guess."

"Well, that certainly squares with the quantumish physics of my neighbor, the Mayor of Waterhole Branch."

249

"I'll have to check out this mayor."

"But did your author create the mayor? Did your author create me, too? I don't think so."

"Can't rule anything out."

"So I'm not real, just realistic."

"Or maybe you're just a fictional author of a crappy piece of nonfiction."

"I am beginning to feel a bit insulted by your rather negative analysis."

He grunted.

"Have you no apology to make?"

"You make a lot of demands, don't you?"

"I simply do not understand barbarians, that's all."

"You're kind of prone to exaggeration, aren't you?"

"Dear Lord Jesus Christ, wherever are you from?"

He gave me a blank look.

"I mean, you are obviously an interloper here, in these Southern climes."

"Look, Missy, I know better than anybody that I don't belong here."

"Clearly. Your lack of manners is atrocious."

"Now she's Emily Post," he muttered to his shoulder.

"How long have you been talking to your arm pit?"

He stood up. "Look, I thought you might be willing to give me some information. I didn't know it would be a goddamn contest. Well, maybe I did know."

"A contest? Not at all. For a sleuth who must observe and deduce you certainly are far off base with that conclusion."

"Then what would you call it?"

"My dear dick, that was what I would call banter. Banter is fun. It's sexy. It's witty social intercourse."

That drew one of his mini-smirks out of him. "Here's looking at you, kid," he said flatly, warming my bosom with his lead-ballooned effort at witty banter.

"Do give me a call, Mr. Scarpete. I'm not through asking you questions, so some witty intercourse would be much enjoyed."

I thought I heard a piece of a chuckle as he left.

Obviously we parted that day without ever settling on reality, let alone manners; and yes, dear reader, I admit to being rather taken with this man of mystery while at the same time sizing him up to be one of those of the "emotionally unavailable" types (in spite of his insistence upon his supposed simplicity) that some women—in past times even moi—are damned and determined to draw into a relationship. We are rarely successful at this endeavour. Still, as an exercise it could be entertaining for a while, so I told myself there were certainly dialogues in the future about the nature of matter and the cultivation of manners.

Do not fret, gentle reader. As earlier conceded, the Old-Southy, stale manners I so abhor should move ever so gracefully into the tainted past and reside there forevermore, amen. But do let's keep alive the basics, those of the "do unto others" variety. This need not be regional; I am certain that throughout this great land of ours there are millions upon gazillions of beings who yearn for kindness, pure and simple, having grown ever more weary of the crass corruption of social discourse.

Still, this is the South, this my domain, where stale and fresh manners still reign, and where the tendrils of all things good and bad continue to tickle the soft underbelly of the place. I am afraid that a chapter on My Domain cannot unfold without a few nods to its flavor. Ergo, my insistence upon laying it before you, to enjoy, chortle over, delight in, be repulsed by, and even despise, as you see fit. In my R.P. Saffire way, via verse, I offer the lay of the land unto you, beginning with a simple ditty (inspired by one Joyce Kilmer's "Trees") immortalizing the creeping green vine that tangles across the countryside, mangling the scenery along ancient, cracked and buckling highways, now as dead as the towns that once hububbed them. I give you:

Ode to Kudzu

I think that I have never knew
A vine as lovely as kudzu;
Upon the Southland's red clay breast
It winds and curls and roams and rests

Some sing of cornbread, greens and pies,
Or pine-woods nights 'neath August skies,

But none embodies trashy treasure
Like the creeping kudzu's pleasure

Yet Southern grandeur is not safe
From the vine's voracious strafe
For antebellum homes are tinged
With plaster walls all greenly singed

And even Scarlett's pantaloons
Were itchily with green festooned,
Her corset on her tiny waist
Had help from kudzu's rooted paste

'Twas brought to us from Asian lands
To fight erosion of our sands,
Yet roots set in and inundated
Fields and farms—growth unabated

No shears nor poisons can unglue
The mighty kudzu's hold so true
It grows on metal and cement,
And asphalt poles and firmament

Its miles of leaves cling near and far
Anchoring each rusting car
That decorates the dusty yards
Of rednecks, loggers, thieves and bards
(Like me)

No double wide would be complete
Without its tendrils curling sweet
Along the hedge and chain-link fence

Around the dawgs and Uncle Spence

For though many a dawg has disappeared
Beneath the vines, all emerald-tiered,
To meet St. Pete in a nobler way
Could not be done, no need to pray

And Uncle Spence, his chaw in cheek
Was sittin' do-less by the creek
When one marauding kudzu vine
Took Spence to Glory, to Heaven's 'shine

Don't get me started on all my kin
Who left this earth with a kudzu grin;
For the vine has super powers
To endure past seasons' flowers

It circles angels' halos gold
And bears the hot and scoffs the cold,
To transport spirits from the earth,
Those of lightness, those of girth

Magnolia leaf and scuppernong
Or bob-white's trill, cicada's song
Cannot embody Southern truth
Like Creeping kudzu on the roof

Some say I'm crazy, I'll admit
To boast of kudzu's grasp and grit;
But Willie Shakespeare would agree
There's no richer source of poetry

Yes! The mighty vine is here to stay!
I'll sing its praises night and day!
The only thing that nears its thrills
Are hordes of Southern fire ant hills

But I digress—please bear with me
If only God can make a tree
Then kudzu is not far behind
For only Job can make a vine

Of course, when I shared my verses with Bizarro Harriet, she sniffed and said, "A poem about kudzu? When there are azaleas everywhere? And magnolias? Look upon the beauty of the world and sing praises about *that*. Will you never write something that could be submitted to the *Ladies' Home Journal* or *Good Housekeeping*?"

"Are they still in circulation? In print?"

Bizarro Harriet rarely "gets" me, completely skips over my tendency to parody, to go a bit beyond the top, and thumb my nose at all that is supposedly decent but is in reality the source of much travail. Therefore, she shall never truly "know" me, her child, the fruit of her womb, the ripper of her perineum (I take great joy in the fact that she needed eight stitches after expelling my angelic little fetal self).

BH shall be reading the poem below for the first time, if she even bothers to read my tome. She will surely find it distasteful, but the people described are the very ones I find distasteful: ignorant racists, who continue to wave their Confederate flags and

255

spew unintelligible venom that continues to taint the culture with its arrogantly sub-human poison.

A side note: Did you know that there are two or three gigantic—no, GIGANTIC—Confederate flags flying along the interstates of Alabama, on private property, of course, whipping the stars and bars in the GIGANTIC statement they invariably make when displayed so prominently and so desperately, and verily I say unto you, it shames me and the vast majority of (intelligent, educated) others to no end. So, again, the spirit of evil persists, even into the twenty-first century, and, again, if my little cluster of words, modeled after Vachel Lindsay's "The Congo," offends anyone as "caricaturish," I care, as I am wont to say, NOT.

The Tensaw –or– "Who's Your Daddy?"

Fat freckled bad boys
Drinkin' in the yard;
Rib cagey coon dawgs
Lappin' liquid lard;
Dirt pore grampaws,
Shootin' at some squirrels,
Buttermilk babies
Born to little girls;
Borned-again me-maws
Hopin' for a sign,
Whore-hoppin' husbands
Cheatin' in a line—
Then I saw the Tensaw

Crawling through the black,
Cuttin' through the pine trees
With a murky track—

Tar paper shacks
All slantin' in a row;
Trash fire kinfolk
Baskin' in the glow;
Inbred cousins
Screwin' 'til they tard
Red dirt young'uns
Playin' in the yard—
Then I saw the Tensaw,
Curlin' through black
Carvin' through the clay banks
With a murky track—

Slope-head cretins
Headin' for the malls
Long-chinned half wits
Grabbin' at they balls
Big-hair bar girl
Hunchin' on a thigh
Bubba-boy racist
Tokin' on a high;
Nashville lyrics
Twangin' through the night
Bulgy-headed bad boys
Lookin' for a fight—
Then I saw the Tensaw
Churnin' through the black
Cuttin' through the swampland

With its brackish brack
Then I saw the Tensaw
Churnin' through the black
Cuttin' through the swampland
With its brackish brack!—

Hoecake an' Hot Wheels
Killin' they first deer
Corn-fed young'uns
Bloodied ear to ear
Slack-jawed Klansmen
Wishin' they was young
Lynch mob memoirs
Rollin' off they tongues
Gaunt-ribbed bird dawgs
Writhin' in the mud
Hard eye fist fight
Blood-burnin' stud

THEN I SAW THE TENSAW
CUTTIN' THROUGH THE BLACK!
CRAWLIN' THROUGH THE SWAMPLAND
WITH ITS BRACKISH BRACK!

Then I saw the Tensaw
Clawin' through the black
Clingin' on the swampland
With its brackish brack

There is a need for a couple of the tenets of
Sluthood to further address the venom of the Old

South. I give you, first, **Tenet Number Twenty: If thou art a racist, homophobic cracker, thou shalt reveal thyself by speaking out throughout the eight years of the Obama administration.** (By the way, so far so good). Come on, we decent folk really need to know who you are—especially those of you who keep it in the closet (and you know who you are). Take heart—you can do it. Just look around and you will see that a lot of notable professional albeit smarmy talkers are doing it— Limbaugh, Medved, Ingraham, all manner of talk radio flotsam whose yammering heads are exploding right about now. Cartoons depicting the president as a dead gorilla or picturing the White House lawn laden with watermelons, songs about "magic negroes," viral e-mails sent by Republican senate aides, and any other manner of—"I'm a racist!" would be greatly appreciated. It's just time for you to lay that heavy burden down by the river, praise Jesus. Oh, and while you're at it, let's give it up for the Queer Nation. Yes, all you closeted conservatives, come out, come out, wherever you are. It's not as if you are fooling anyone—at this point it's getting to be rather sad to see such self-loathing. And those poor wives! They deserve to be set free for their Sluthood years.

Second, in order to thoroughly ensure that the Old South might Rest in Peace, is **Tenet Number Twenty-one: Thou shalt use thy good china EVERY day—and even mix in the *good* good china.** Don't you get it? You are going to die, and you really *care*

259

about cracking your china? Talk about being a dumb cracker.

Priorities. *Please.*

There are just some things about the South that have simply got to go, but there are also flavors and customs and expressions and endearments that must, please God, stay. My job is to communicate them both. And so, dear reader, between my "Road Kill Trilogy," the two ditties above, and the trilogy of countrified verses below, I do believe I have succeeded in inserting a goodly slice of regionalism into this epic tale of moi. I put it before you here in order to illustrate the strengthening sinew of my spirit, how my soul went from shattered to shit-kickin'—and also on the off chance that some scion of the Nashville scene might pick up this tome and subsequently want to purchase one of my next three offerings as lyrics and salve my ancient pain with a bit of cash. It could happen (although I kinda know nada about the music biz).

The first, though written from a male perspective, is cynical and full of the anger that bubbled all about me like a cannibalistic stew of simmering, psychological blow-darts. Do consider my broken spirit and keep me in your kindness, comforted and accepted.

SINsincere

[Ahem. The verses are intended to be sung slowly and mournfully, while the chorus is of a decidedly lively rhythm.]

You go on and get outta here
Ask me do I give a care
Take your kitty cats and your candy jar
Give me back my dad's guitar

You go on and get outta here

Nothing to fear itself but fear
All you been is a symbiote
Tell your poor old mamma that's all she wrote

(Chorus)
Cause you're a lyin,' double dealin,'spirit stealin'
mis-stake
A playin,' cowboy layin' critter that I gotta hate
Just come a little closer and I'll hack you with a
butcher knife
You're so smarmy in that army of the girls that
had to break me
And your clever endeavour to deceive just let
me break free
I'd be a goddamned shit-fuckin' fool to want you
for my wife

You go on and get outta here
Move on out of this hemisphere
Take your estrogen pills and your lingerie
And your sick obsession with Jon Benet

You go on and get outta here
Send me an Air Express souvenir

Take your vitamin drinks and your plastic shoes
Tell the bar stool boys your happy news

(Repeat Chorus)
You go on and get outta here
Cause it's a sin to be so insincere
A sin
Insincere
Sin

The point of view in the next ditty is masculine also, and the fact that the first two songs are such reveals volumes about my loss of a deep, female identity. It is intended to be lively, ironic, and speak to the betrayal of long-term commitment. As I reflect upon it now, it seems that I had to become a child (ergo the childhood imagery) once again before I could re-emerge as an adult of the female persuasion.

Sounds good, anyway, in an on-the-couch kind of way.

She's In the Money Now

School house love notes, kissin' by the raincoats
The lunches and the cloakroom caps
Red hair and freckles, mamma gave us a nickel
For every porch fly we slapped
Cheese wagon chuggin', Lucy and me huggin'
Near the 'mergency exit doors

Childhood sweethearts, soul mates and counterparts
But she's in the money, now

(Chorus)
She's in the money, now
And I can't figure how
He's got her love to see him through
Along with his Jones and Dow
She's in the money, now
Guess I was too low brow
Used to call her Baby-Baby broke like me
But she's in the money, now

Steady sweeties through high school, I was lookin' real cool
With Lucille on my arm
The backseat was rockin' an' her fishnet stockin's
Set my blood to a wild fire storm
We pledged our devotion throughout the locomotion
Of makin' love and how
We forever would be one on one
But she's in the money now

(Repeat Chorus)

Well, a Cadillac rolled in, driven by my old friend
Never thought that they would cut my throat
Diamond things and new money, ain't it kinda funny

How easily love is bought
When he gave her a Jaguar she went for the jugular
She whispered me a hot stock tip
And my one on one come all undone
When it passed across Lucy's lips

That she's in the money now (Chorus)

Yeah, my love market crashed when he offered up the cash
And she's in his money now

And the final piece of the Country Song Phase of R.P. Saffire's Self-Reclamation Trilogy is a lyric in which the lies are confronted and the moving on is undertaken. Praise the Lord!

Pit Crew Rendezvous

Well he's revvin' up his engine and mine won't spark
He's off to the races and I'm stuck in park
He got a souped-up Chevy and a tattoo of ol' number three
He's just too fast for me, guess I always knew it
I thought a ring and our promises would get us through it
But he's made another lap to the ladies on his lovin' spree

Well they're fast and they follow the NASCAR circuit

If his frame needs a-jackin' they know just how to work it

They can lube all his joints, pull his plugs and make his pistons fire

They can pressurize his tires, change his oil and his filter

They can make him blow a gasket and then put it on kilter

My heart-achin' toleration's comin' right down to the wire

CHORUS
He's a wanna-be racer in the Alabama Gang
And his pit crew harem has him doin' his thang
Yeah, he's pullin' off the track for some service that I can't do
His gasoline is pumped by a flashy little redhead
And a bleached blonde bimbo rotates his retreads
Yeah, his crank shaft's turnin' my departure into overdue
One cools him down when his radiator's boilin'
Another straightens him out when his spoiler ain't spoilin'
Gotta S T P
Puttin' up
With his pit crew rendezvous

Alright, the green flag's flappin' and I'm wavin' bye-bye

I put my sugar in his tank and my kneecap in his—thigh

When he comes crawlin' back he can pucker up and kiss my caboose

You know the mix he's concocted has wrecked our carburetor

And the vows he's broke make him a cheatin' altar-nator

Yeah, the belts and the hoses and the women are just way too loose

REPEAT CHORUS

But he ain't takin' no victory lap in this competition

Can't make the Winner's Circle if you ain't got no ignition

So I'll throw it down in gear and let him feel the meaning of "out-do"

And I'm comin' round the backstretch, kiss my dust

Got a hot rod Ford, California or bust

Gentlemen, start your engines, gonna show you a thing or two

REPEAT CHORUS

And speaking of showing you a thing or two, I would be remiss in the description of my domain if

I did not include my own private little corner of the world, where strangeness is celebrated, where the river comes in to be a branch, which passes my house to further upstream become a mere trickle.

I like this quiet place, laced in the Spanish moss that drips from giant oaks. It is the antithesis of excess and the cacophonous clamor of fast living. It is so magical there is even a song about it (just Google "Grayson Capps-Waterhole Branch"), and it is the setting for **Tenet Number Twenty-two: Thou shalt follow the teachings of the Mayor of Waterhole Branch, Alabama, who has this sign posted on his property:**

Be It Said Here Now:

The inhabitants of this piece of earth's land have seceded from all forms and levels of government. All are welcome regardless of social class, race, religion, political ideology, ideas of morality, level of education, economic status, state of mind, mood, mental condition, sexual preference, attire, marital status, age, habits, feelings of superiority or inferiority, degree of gullibility, weight, height, physical deformities, interests, type of personality, prejudices, intellect, spiritual bent, vocabulary, criticisms felt, legal status, ethnicity, reputation, and so forth.

Here there are no laws. However, anyone and all who mistreat any being, either real or imagined above, below, or upon the land, will be gently but forcefully required to leave.

The mayor is my neighbor, a delightful, curmudgeonly, womanizing, insane, aging boomer who writes books, turns junk piles into art, makes mobiles and wind chimes out of all kinds of things—old jewelry, women's shoes, deconstructed typewriters, clarinets, pianos, beer cans, whatever—does paintings on plywood and canvas and hangs them everywhere (even on the outside of his house, an old, old asbestos tile-sided, tin-roofed domicile); who at one point dug a moat around his porch; who has a mannequin sitting in one of his trees; and I have not even scratched the surface in describing his place. He has built a stage, dubbed "The Play-like Playhouse," behind his garage; hosts an event called "The Annual Shoe-burning" each year. The mayor has an intimate connection with New Orleans through his son, Grayson Capps, a wonderful, raspy-voiced, bluesy musician who had to re-locate to Tennessee after Katrina. The mayor, Everett Capps, is delightfully crazy, and his life and philosophy inspired the next three tenets of Successful Sluthood (as well as the previous Tenet Fourteen). These are

Tenet Twenty-three: Thou shalt celebrate thy insanity;

Tenet Twenty-four: Thou shalt not become attached to Stuff; and

Tenet Twenty-five: Thou shalt not be impressed by celebrity, fame, or fortune.

Sluts are not afraid to go fruitcake-y (regardless of the previous analogy in regards to hypocrisy) with abandon, recognizing that living in the moment is the only kind of life that makes sense in a nonsensical world filled with seconds strung end upon end until the end comes, and it will. Care not what those wound-up walking wounded amongst us might think; simply be in the millisecond, and if that should mean flinging off one's clothing to take a skinny dip in Waterhole Branch or screwing up one's courage and climbing a tree as a nod to childhood (do mind you don't fall and break a hip) standing upon one's head just for the hell of it, or you name it. Dare to be crazy. Immerse yourself in sensuality. Dive from an imaginary Hawaiian cliff into "divine decadence" (thank you, Sally Bowles). When you go before the Lord or the head guy/girl/being presiding over whichever version of Heaven you choose, be prepared to say: "You know, head guy/girl/being, I appreciate the life you gave me because I enjoyed the hell out of as much of it as possible."

And if you do not believe in heaven, just create a bit of it right here, right now. Who in his right mind would call that insane?

Real insanity, the mayor might say, is being a slave to Stuff, that American tradition of buying more and more and more and bigger and bigger and bigger and supposedly, but usually not, better. The mayor maintains that stuff is not even real, but is a figment of the imagination, since nothing at all exists but thought.

Well, maybe.

I say that, just in case it is real, to be so enamored of it seems a sad waste of energy, given that it is only a superficial manifestation of that which can only come from within our selves, the kind of fulfillment and peace and contentment that one can come to at any phase in life (witness yours truly). The Stuff will certainly not follow us into the afterlife, unless you subscribe to the "if you're a Pharaoh the stuff can go" or to the old "seventy-two virgins" (or is it "olives"?) kind of heaven.

Therefore, the mayor has always maintained that if Americans wanted to experience real freedom here in the Land of the Free, they would cast off the shackles of the banks and credit card companies by declaring freedom from so much Stuff—declaring their independence, that they require precious little in order to be happy in this life. Upon looking at the state of things now, it gives one pause to think: Too bad it's too late for so many.

Of course, Opal claims this brought down the economy, but she misunderstands. She tends to blame the victim, when the true culprit is a much bigger animal: corporate greed. According to the mayor, folks could still earn capital and spend it on things they truly enjoyed, but without all the superfluous clutter foisted upon them by slick advertisers and, in barrages of tree-killing form letters: "You qualify!" or "You're pre-approved!" along with the meat-dangled-above-the-hound's-nose fake checks for thousands of U.S. dollars (which, by the way, could soon become about as useless as Confederate money unless a shift in values rights its certain devaluation). These are the real criminals, these bribers and con artists who threw the promise of slop out at us big fat American pigs while we grunted and snorted and pushed against one another in the race to Wal-Mart.

And why were/are we so set on gorging on the myriad of Stuff in our culture while so many in the world are hard pressed to get water? Is it the perceived bigness of America, the sense of unending Stuff? Or is it that the aforementioned criminals are in cahoots with advertisers and a media obsessed with fanning the flames of fame? Hmm. This brings us to the **Twenty-fifth Tenet**, a warning to resist the American obsession with the creepy culture of celebrity. Because, hey, do we really gotta know what's going on with Brittney or Angelina or Paris or Lindsay or the missing white girl du jour?

Now I will admit that my friends and I, like typical girlfriends everywhere, will fall into the celebrity dish of the moment and have some fun with it; I am not stupid enough to believe one can avoid it completely without going into a Tibetan monastery, and even then . . . well, those madcap monks might be incense-sniffing, lotus-sitting *People* and *Okay!* magazine addicts for all I know. I like to take a dip in the pop waters from time to time, just to check what the currents are doing, which way the lemmings are being pulled. And let's face it, fame impresses, seems a little bigger than life, draws us in to something we perceive as special. As a result, I, like anyone else can list all the famous and semi-famous people I have ever met (not merely seen, as in, in concert, but met, as in, a proper introduction and the shaking of the hands; shaking the hand of a famous politician, even with an introduction, however, also does not qualify; it is too mundane). My very short list (only of the famous, not the semi-famous, and not counting politicians or writers met at, lo, the gazillions of conferences attended, or regional "celebrities"; and the chronological gap in said list speaks to my decades of hiding) goes like this: Jerry Lee Lewis, Joe Namath, one of Jackie Onassis' interior designers (okay, it was a degree of separation, but it's Jackie), someone who was on the Oprah Winfrey show many years ago, and another someone who was on more recently (again, it's Oprah), and John Travolta (Hey, he's been on Oprah, too—wow—that's three Oprah connections! What are the odds?!?). I suppose that whether this is perceived as a long or a short list is relative, and my only point in making it is to marvel at the fact that I remembered it at all (being of an age) as well as to make a confession: the most recent meeting of a famous person, Travolta, was the most disturbing to me, as it came on the heels of my rebirth, and, I thought, my ability to resist such foolishness. It also came via my association with the Mayor of Waterhole Branch.

The Mayor wrote several novels, never published, decades ago, manuscripts which lived and yellowed in a trunk until his son, the musician, put up some documentary filmmakers "passing through town" at his New Orleans hovel. Upon finding out one of them wanted to make a movie set in New Orleans, the son drove them to Alabama and dug out one of the manuscripts, a novel called *A Cream-White Occurrence Off Magazine Street*, which became *Off Magazine Street* when it was published right around the release of the movie, *A Love Song For Bobby Long*, named after a song written by the son, who provided more music for the soundtrack, and ultimately invited his parents and me to watch some of the filming. Thus the meeting with John Travolta, and I do recall reaching up (I was sitting in one of those requisite chairs with the movie title printed on its canvas back) and shaking his hand, and standing, but being sort of pulled up (by him, mid-handshake) at the same time, rising into these unbelievably blue eyes, and I swear, the effect was of a camera zooming in on a close-up of something (the eyes) that had been culturally conditioned into me and, of course, I responded like any typical heterosexual woman or gay man would, by maintaining a semblance of control while thinking: Honey, you (meaning J.T.) sure as hell are pretty. Whereupon I began to be disturbed. I did not want to be "typical," fawning (albeit internally) over a goddamn movie star. I had long since come to Jesus and the **Second** coming of the **Sluthood**, seen the light, and cast off such shallow notions.

"For god's sake. It was John Travolta," Opal said, the bent of her own personality taking her immediately to the response I had attempted to

273

resist. "How long did he talk to you and Grayson's mom?"

"I don't know. Maybe four or five minutes?"

"Five whole minutes?" (She sounded like a high school sophomore: "I saw Johnny outside the gym and he *smiled* at me!") "What was he like?"

"He seemed very nice." And that was true, though I hated to encourage her. I did not elaborate on the fact that he seemed very genuine.

"What did he say? What did he say?"

I could take no more. "He said to dress up like Olivia Newton-John in *Grease*, and he'll take you to a beach movie at the drive-in and neck with you and be your ready steady."

I did not remain disgusted with myself for long, though, because the next tenet of Successful Sluthood (and please do not criticize the fact that it sounds trite and pop-psychology-ish because it is something that is out there in the world of talk shows and call-in radio, but just because it is "pop" does not mean it is, by definition, pabulum) is the "seal the deal" tenet. If you ever need to go to the three most important tenets of Successful Sluthood, think Heart #8, Soul #5 and Seal the Deal #26. Hmm. Sounds like a line of perfumes. Perhaps I shall get some offers. Anyway, back to

Tenet Number Twenty-six: Thou shalt forgive thyself thy transgressions.

Forgiveness is a big fat hairy deal. Truly it is. It is even bigger for a woman whose husband was living at least a quadruple life, complete with other women (at least three of them at last count), but verily I say unto you, until you can do that whole forgiveness thing, to the best of your ability, you can not fully bask in the soul-saving silvered sunshine of a **Second Sluthood**. And while I admit to having a sliver or two of anger that I am loathe to purge pricking deep in my heart, I would argue that I am doing pretty damn awesomely, given the circumstances.

As for Mr. Scarpete, our consummation was not to be just yet. Out of sight, out of mind. So, having apparently accomplished his mission in fair Fairhope, he simply vanished, leaving me feeling a bit like Dorothy, who, about Oz, observed, "My! People come and go so quickly here!"

Chapter 11: Delete

YOU know, given the current economic climate (note: this chapter was written in and around 2009), I feel that it would be in very poor taste to dignify a Chapter 11 with any content; therefore, I shall instead sally forth into

Chapter 12: Surfing the "Nets": Putting Out and Putting It Out There

A MAN cannot break a heart that has not been offered unto him, and I had been barely getting to know the mysterious Mr. Scarpete when he mysteriously disappeared. Fortunately for me, however, men are everywhere, abundant, like unto ripened fruit that drops off the tree and into one's palm. Ponder it a moment. One does not even have to go a-hunting one. A desirable woman such as myself is bopping along, minding her own business, and *bam*! There is yet another man, with all the potential of providing a silly little thrill or a thrilling little silly.

Oddly, though, and jarringly, I had picked up on a Scarpete vibe that whispered to me that there was some kind of spiritual overlap there—and yes, I have witnessed the odd soul-mated couple here and there—rare, to be sure, but possible. And as a distinct possibility, dare *I* miss such a thing? I immediately called archangel Lucky.

"Come on, R. P., you know the answer to that."

"I do?"

"Well, *duh*. If that guy is your soul mate, it won't *not* happen."

"But you don't believe in soul matage."

"Come on. I don't *not* believe in it, either."

"So much negative play with the adverbs!"

"Anyway, what matters is that you *do* believe that sort of thing happens. And how often do you get what you believe in?"

"I didn't get Hand Job."

"Right. Did you really *believe* in him?"

"Oh, I get it—this is me, making my own story."

"Right. That's all anybody can do. What is it about the detective guy?"

"It's really strange. It's like you said. He's simple but he's smart. And I have the sense that I can learn about me through him, in a delicious kind of way, like you said."

"Cool."

"You're clairvoyant."

"No, just aware."

"So what are you up to these days?"

"You know me. Building huts outside Rangoon. Smoking a lot of really nice weed. Life's an adventure for sure."

"You know what? *We* are the soul mates. Us. You and me."

He laughed, "Did I mention I'm getting laid a lot?"

"Never mind."

And of course he is right. Life is an adventure, and I could never deal with Lucky's "habits."

I decided not to even puzzle over Scarpete's disappearance, knowing he would eventually be back if he was supposed to be, if the Fates willed it to be. I just did what any effective Slut would do: I **cut bait and** started **fish**ing. Even though I had been to quite a few conferences and book fests already, the posse had convinced me to do even more, to really plug in to the wonders of "the internets." This time I gave myself over to the web.

I absolutely adore the word, "surfing," as it transports me back to my Beach Boys days, surfer shirts, flying crosses, Swinger cameras, Midnight Sun hair products and blonde streaks, Coppertone and madras. Opal was right, she of the cybergasm and the nocturnal chat rooms. I could do this internet thing, yes indeedy. I could catch its wave and shoot the curl!

And verily I say the internet world is an endless and a truly wondrous one, for that is where I found and plugged into a vast network of writers and conferences and festivals and such. And I struck out upon, give or take, two years' worth of travels and travails, and, sad to say, I fear it came clearer and clearer unto me that I might easily strike out of having anything published, ever—and I refused to even consider self-publishing, for that way held wickedness, lack of editing, and fees. I was plying my wares in order to be paid, not the other way around. Still, I forged on, often with one of the Dirty Half Dozen along for the ride and for much needed encouragement, all the while filing away rejection after rejection.

Alas, the publishing world was like all other businesses, had even devolved further in the years since my "editing conference" with the Shrew. Long gone were the days of Maxwell Perkins and real relationships between writers and editors, when the agent was not anywhere in the photograph, in the golden era of the first half of the twentieth century, before the arts and athletics were altogether soiled by the love of the almighty dollar. Alas, I had been birthed much, much too late. But I pressed on.

Opal paid homage to our friendship by accompanying me to New Orleans, to the Saints and Sinners Fest, a heroic act on her part as she is something of a homophobe and that particular fest is LGBT. Of course Micah shepherded her through much of her irrational fear and helped me convince her that she should make the trip.

"Heavens," he said. "It's *Nouveau Orleans*. Did we not all make a vow to go to that *poor*, devastated place as often as possible and spend as much *money* as possible so that the economy might get a tiny boost?"

"Yes, we did," Opal said in an appropriately guilt-ridden tone, "and I do want to help New Orleans. It's just that—"

"What, sugar plum? Afraid the big bad bull dykes will pursue your femmy little fuzz ball?"

"Well . . ."

"You must be joking," I said. "Or maybe . . . you know, Micah, perhaps Opal's penis issues are not what they have seemed to be all these years. Perhaps they signify something else entirely."

He joined in, "Oh but that is so deliciously *ob*vious. How I can I help you, sugar plum? Just *fling* that closet door wide and embrace the you that is *you*!"

"Would you two hush!? I'm not a lesbian! This is how rumors get started!"

"Then do not protesteth so mucheth," I said.

"I'm used to Micah, is all. In New Orleans there will be no telling how many of them."

"*Them*?" Micah's tone dripped disdain.

"Micah, don't let this get you pissy," I said. "Remember, it's Opal."

"Oh, right, it's Opal," she said as the sarcasm oozed. "The stupid one. The prejudiced one. The one that is the butt of the jokes."

"Enough! As the *alpha* female in this slutty band of Sluts I command that the sniping desist, and furthermore that Micah propose some sort of compromise. Yes, because it is Opal."

To which Opal sighed and rolled her eyes with great exaggeration.

"I can do this," Micah drawled. "Once upon a time, a *dear* friend accompanied me to a class reunion to *shield* me from those who might do me harm."

"To keep you from doing something to provoke said harm," I reminded him.

"Alright, yes, I have been known to behave inappropriately in certain social situations. That is neither here nor there, snookums, as this is not about me. It is about my sugar plum, and so I propose that I join you two on your adventure."

"Why?" Opal asked.

"To protect you, just as R.P. protected me. I shall protect you from dangers both real and imagined. I shall commiserate with you if the dykes do not find you attractive. I shall comfort you if you get lucky, only to find a dreaded gender-bent penis where you least expect it."

"I'm not a lesbian," Opal said again.

"Oh for god's sake he's kidding. And that is not even the point," I said. "The point is to have fun—and let Micah be your tour guide."

"Come on, sugar plum. We shall have quite the time."

"Please? For moi?"

Opal's glance went from one to the other. "Oh, all right. But it's still scary."

"You'll be over that by the end of the first day," Micah said.

And, indeed, she was. By the second day she had met enough thoroughly delightful, thoroughly non-threatening individuals to be most at ease. Which just proves how easily fear of a specific group can be overcome—by simply spending a little time with a few members of said group.

Still, I had no luck breaking into publishing on that particular foray. I thought I caught a glimpse of Mr. Scarpete, but it was fleeting and something like an LGBTQQ book festival seemed mightily unlikely as a venue in which he might be interested. I must admit he had been on my mind, though, which could have then tricked me into thinking I had seen him out of the corner of my eye. The mind is an amazing thing, capable of all kinds of conjuring.

Too, I had been struggling not to think of Scarpete as an opportunity missed, which would be woefully bittersweet, and could easily devolve into bitterness. That would be extremely counterproductive, and not in the least way healthily slutty. So I continued to be true to the **tenet**s and **cut** more **bait**.

"It seems like we're seeing the same people over and over," Diamond said in Memphis. "A lot of the same writers I've never heard of."

"So many books," I said, deflated. "So little time."

"This isn't the R.P. I know. Not this defeatist. Besides, what if, as you say, they don't ever read your work? Or read it after you are dead and gone? Would you let that change the way you have decided to live your life?"

"Bless you," I said, "for being the Slut you are."

For indeed, dear Diamond was correct. One should never let the response of others deter one from one's dream. It was a definite insight, although it, like anything worth learning, did not "take" right away (again, repetition). Therefore I continued to focus on what might be standing in my way, keeping me on the outside looking in on something that was not particularly encouraging. Did I really want to be one of the scores of authors sitting behind rows and rows of tables with stacks of books in front of them, hoping someone might wander up and look at their work, let alone *buy* it? Did I want to be that lone author sitting at a tiny table in a huge bookstore, while nine out of ten people took great pains not to make eye contact lest they have some unwanted book shoved into their unwilling hands? What had the world of publishing come to if not into the state of a soulless, overly saturated market that relies on networking and connections to find the Next Big Thing and make the Next Big Buck?

"Do they always talk so damn much about how hard it is to get published?" Emerald asked in Chicago, as my enthusiasm flagged further.

I sighed. "Like winning the lottery."

"Well, girl, you just keep throwing it out there. Somebody's going to come along and give you the right numbers."

"I don't know. It feels dirtier and dirtier all the time. The business, the self-promotion, the sycophants, everything."

Emerald sighed. "Yeah. But the saddest part is that so many of these authors nobody's heard of are brilliant. They should be getting attention."

"But they get lost in a sea of pulp and glitz and trash."

"You really feeling the filth?"

I nodded in assertion.

"Then don't do it."

"Quit writing? I could never do that."

"No, fool. Quit doing this."

This, meaning: quit debasing yourself, slinking about these groupings of the famous and wannabe famous, hoping for something like recognition and a shot at publication. It was so like Emerald to cut to the chase and lay out the simple truth. And there came upon me a heavenly insight, as the murky slime slid away and crystalline lucidity poured forth into the greening glade of my cragged and tormented mind. I had said it, out loud: "I could never do that," i.e., quit writing. It was not really about getting published, being recognized, etc. It was *absolutely* not about anything as filthy as money. It was simply and exquisitely about my life force. I could not *not* write, no matter what, and Emerald had put her beautifully manicured fingernail directly upon it.

I love my friends.

I have not gone to a conference or a fest or a symposium since.

Even though it must be reiterated that there has been an up-side of the down-side (the constant traveling and attendant debasement): the meeting of hordes of other authors who see the world in ways that are delicious or humorous or filled with irony or darkness, many of whom I have read and admire, some of whom, as Emerald noted, should be alongside the great ones, though that might well never happen as the publishing industry fails to nurture, even cuts off its support to so many. And with the delicious development of e-books comes the urge to say "fuck you" to the smarmy middle men pimps of the trade. These good folk (the authors) I shall dearly miss. (Of course, I have also met a small handful of arrogant ass-holes and embarrassingly transparent suck-ups, a couple of fairly famous ones; easy enough to bid *them* adieu.)

A dalliance or two found me out there on the road, and the potential for further trysts and such were ever present. Yet I continued to find that my initial attraction to that Scarpete character went on ripening in spite of his rather odd and rude behavior—and in spite of his absence, which really did seem to make my heart grow fonder. Consequently I took to reminding myself, as must we all, to be wary of past patterns in selecting those with whom to forge a bond of intimacy. As the Hand Job debacle illustriously illustrates, my propensity to crawl into the cranium of a complicated male has not served me well. Perhaps such an inclination to delve into the warped but **simple** reality of one Mr. Scarpete could be perceived as a turn for the better.

And the more I pondered it the more likely it seemed that it would come to pass.

And it did. In late ought-nine I got a phone call and soon found myself at a very shabby abode, where one Mr. Scarpete, who was apparently drawn to shabby abodes and who had aroused many prickles of curiosity within my bosom, in spite of those warts of his—the contrariness and the lack of polite posturings—welcomed me in for an afternoon drink. He was a bourbon man. It fit.

"It's the job. It takes me places," he said when I queried him.

"Prithee, where?"

"You never know. I'm all over the place."

"No specifics?"

"Confidential." He poured us each a shot in a pair of non-descript glasses.

"But you came back here."

"Yeah."

"Another job?"

"No. I just like it here." He said it with an endearing little squint. It'll be my base of operations."

I looked around. "*This* place?" It was bare and forlorn, a table and chairs where we sat, in a kitchen/living area, but no couch or television. I could see into a bedroom, where a radio sat on a bedside table. And there was, thankfully, a bed.

"It's got all I need. I'm pretty—"

"Simple," I said.

"Yeah," he lit a cigarette. Here was a vice we could enjoy together, so I, too, brought out a dreaded fag and leaned toward him. I have to say the atmosphere was quite sexually charged. Seven years of foreplay in the form of banter will do that. I cupped his hand when he lit my smoke, and let it linger there.

"Are you married, Mr. Scarpete? Is that your secret?"

"Already told you I'm simple."

"But smart at the same time," I added.

"Got to be."

"In order to?"

"Follow the clues. Keep it straight. Keep it honest, real."

"And what about *that*? What about our last little banter about reality?"

"What about it?"

"Are we going to play some more with Schrodinger's kitties?"

He laughed that half laugh of his. "Sure, if you want to."

"Why are you being so accommodating, when you were so contrary before?"

"It's simple. You weren't being so straight before, and I don't do games. But you seem like the real deal, too—you speak your mind, or really want to, honestly."

"Quite true."

"And as long as you're straight with me, this'll be simple. Honesty is a strength in a world full of bullshit."

"Such the pessimist."

"I come across a lot of liars in my line of work."

"I, for one, am quite decidedly done with liars."

He raised his glass, I clinked it with mine and took a drink, warm, taking a tingle to the tips of my fingers. What little inhibition I did have would be gone in no time.

"We've established that honesty is a strength of mine. And what is *your* strong suit, with women? With what upon your resume do you court moi?"

"Well," he smiled, very slowly, looking down at his drink. He took a sip, and, "I'm good at taking direction."

OMG! Is that not the *perfect* answer?!?

I put out the barely smoked fag, stood up, walked over to him, placed my palm next to his cheek and held it there for a few beats. "Let's see exactly how good you are," I said.

He picked up the bottle and led me to the bedroom.

How good was he at taking those oh, so very important directions?

Masterful.

Chapter 13: Re-formatting: Writing Our Own Stories

Over the course of a few weeks I spent several afternoons with this man who "gets" women probably better than any one man I have ever known. He has some kind of radar, a gift of a purity of logic that allows him to do that "taking direction" thing with a finesse that most men, unfortunately, lack. Therefore it is incumbent upon me to deliver a final decree unto you, **Tenet Number Twenty-Seven: When it comes to men, offer specific instructions about what you want and never fail to give direction.** Yes, this is yet another beautifully simple concept that too many women overlook, thereby sabotaging too many perfectly good relationships. Men in general tend to be very literal creatures and certainly cannot read your mind, so do not expect them to. Mind reading is actually a pretty damn tall order, having little to do with reality. I guarantee you, ladies, **Tenet Number Twenty-Seven** is tres effective, in all areas.

For example, in giving direction I have learned and continue to learn more about myself, for learning is lifelong, if one is living correctly. I have learned what my knee-jerk reactions are, and how they dissolve with candor. I have learned that it is lovely to be with a decent man and simply—*be*, drinking in the moments as if they are like unto fine, aged wine. In verbalizing, honestly, what I want, whether it be what to do of an evening, how to spend a sunny morning, or where a delicate touch might make a pleasant physical outcome, I find more and more how genuinely one can live one's waning years. Yes, it took over a half century for me to figure out what many already know, but the important thing is that it can be learned at any moment in a life, if one is willing.

And have you, dear reader, found parallels between my learning curve and your own? Is my formerly morose metaphor your morose metaphor? Is your personal life in a state of deception? Because I guarantee your societal life—the larger narrative of our collective lives and lies—has most certainly, most assuredly, been in such a lowly state. I do hope that I have given you some idea of how to crawl back from the emotional bankruptcy of tattered trust, as self-help was to be a sliver of this treatise. You can re-write your story. How, though, can our society be re-written—be saved from the same devastation, and, ultimately, best be served?

The first best answer, of course, is education. As stated previously, I know a thing or two about a thing or two about learning. The main thing I know about it is that it requires bountiful repetition. Mr. Scarpete was correct about asking the questions, over and over, in slightly varying ways, to solidify the cracking of the (nut) case—moi. In the realm of self-help, the most basic of the basic tools, such as the twelve steps of Alcoholics Anonymous, are, as any addict knows, intended to be repeated over and over and over again. I, too, have emphasized this approach in the writing of the sentences and the rewriting of the life. And here, in a reiterative fashion, I should like to look carefully at how we can perhaps revive the collective intellect, which is in grave need of said revival. Hallelujah!

After spending a couple of decades in a classroom I have witnessed a recently very rapid decline in high quality students who pass through the hallowed hallways and corridors of knowledge, and I am here to tell you the situation is, as earlier referenced, **g-r-i-m**. With the exception of a few spikes, I can safely say that each class rotating through the public school system is dumber than the one before; and, according to my former colleagues, with whom I have base-touched from time to time, things have been dumbed down ever more.

It is not enough that enabling parents have bitched, moaned, whined, and complained about grades so much that rampant inflation has resulted; not enough that the lack of literacy is so systemic that a number of teachers routinely mangle the English language and fail to thoroughly understand their own content areas—are, indeed, as dumb as some of their own students; but now we have the debacle of No Child Left Behind, which sealed the deal on the production of stupidity.

NCLB was premised on the faulty assumption, ignoring all manner of research on the many and varied kinds of intelligences that have nothing to do with the realm of the academic, that all students can learn "x" amount of book learnin'. Ludicrous. Just as there are different levels of "smart," there are also different levels of "dumb," and NCLB has snatched a myriad of "smart" down to the "less smart" or even "less dumb" level. Thank you, Mr. President for putting it to rest. Amen.

Perhaps it is the preponderance of video games and movies and hours in front of a flickering screen, or the lack of true childhood play and its inherent lessons in problem-solving, or the over-parenting of self-absorbed nimrods or the failing teacher training programs, or the maudlin media, or the rise of the shorthanded text messaging that is to blame. Any of these things could, in and of themselves, account for the retardating of the masses; put them all together and you have a perfect storm for stupidity.

Yes, the nation becomes more and more vapid with every tap of my tips on the laptop keys. It is no wonder that so many well-intentioned citizens lack the ability to reason and root out accurate truths. They have never been challenged to think, to ponder, to follow the bouncing ball linking one premise to another to another to another, leading to something like a—*gasp*!—logical conclusion; and it is to our shame that we allow this to continue to devolve into utter societal moronish doofushood.

Of course, when I write my expose of the public school system, I shall address these issues and more in astounding detail; for my purposes here it is best to keep it in the shell of a nut. Since that is the case, a simple "To Do" list seems to be in order.

Things To Do In an Attempt To Make Smarter People, Ergo a Smarter Populace:

• Do not reproduce if you and your spouse are both stupid. If even one of you is stupid, give it serious thought. If you are unable to eliminate childlessness, for the love of god, please consider the tasteful simplicity of having an only child. This is yet another echo of **Tenet Number One**.

• Require logic and debate and the recognition of propaganda and the study of much history and the study and commitment to memory of the U.S. Constitution before you even think about awarding a high school diploma (okay the truly slow-witted can receive a certificate of attendance). A stupid populace elects stupid leaders, adopts a herd mentality, and fails to feed its starving intellect.

• Put technical classes in the middle schools. And art. And music. And dance. And debate. This goes to **Tenet Number Five**, the voice of G(g)od. Address the fact that intelligence comes in many aptitudes. Pay for it by refusing to buy any more standardized tests, period.

- Make difficult classes more demanding. Make the little buggers work their asses off for those precious grades. Stop giving everybody and his/her cousin "A's".

- Don't be one of those parents who has gone to the schoolhouse to defend your child or quibble over a grade *even one time*. And if you do it once and then find yourself doing it a second or third time, then god help you for you are one of those I have been mightily bashing in these pages. And another thing: turn off the television, the computer, the video game, and the texter phone and read, read, read—yes you. Make reading a requirement of being a member of your family. Sell any children who fail to fall in line and donate the money to your local school. Readers gain the intellect to pull off **Tenet Number Nineteen**, the critically important banter.

- Put academics at the same level, and ultimately above the level, of importance and status given to athletics. Tell all the washed up former jocks who are living through their sons and daughters to just deal. And for god's sake, never put a coach in a history classroom unless (s)he has an actual degree in history.

- Do not hire teachers who are not readers, and pay them twice as much as you already do. Only hire secondary teachers who are not only degreed in education but also in their content area. Fire any teacher who does not allow dissenting points of views in class discussions (in the context of logic, of course). See **Tenet Number Two**.

We are raising a generation of pudgy little piggy children who make A's for being mediocre, who cannot express a critically thought out set of sentences, and whose mommies and daddies run behind them cleaning up all the musses and fusses in their porcine little lives. We allow the profiteering pharmaceutical companies to offer free samples of soma via television commercials and medicate ourselves and our offspring into lobotomized oblivion. Could it be that the powers that be have been digging on the whole zoned-out mess of it? After all, those zany, madcap Nazis of the 1930's knew well that supreme power depends upon keeping the folks scared and stupid; for the past decade or so we Americans have been scared and stupid. Could it be that we were witnessing the withering of the great democratic experiment?

Were we sliding, ever so subtly and not-so-subtly, toward a corporate fascist state? Could we ever find ourselves in that dark place again?

Or can we re-write that story? I, Ruby Pearl Saffire, she of the half-full glass, she of the optimistic worldview, choose to hope for a thorough revision of the societal manuscript so that it works for the good, no matter what kind of creepy foreshadowing has gone before. Mayhaps many of you reading this are becoming aware for the first time that you have been, quite frankly, snookered. Others, those who have been effectively brainwashed in such a way that the hard-wiring knows no logic will likely, even at this late point in my treatise, toss it into the waste basket. I care not. For those amongst us who fail to see what is situated right before our very eyes I have only one response: bite me. For the most of us, of any political or religious or philosophical persuasion, who are choosing light over dark, hope over fear, enlightenment over stupidity, can collectively decide to take our beloved nation to a new and uplifting place, where we can reside upon the high moral ground in joy and peace forever unto eternity, amen and amen.

For verily I say unto you, I have rewritten my life. You can re-write yours. And together we can re-write ours.

Let's take a summarizing little look at one person's revision.

Once upon a time, when I was a braless teenybopper with a pretty face and just-capped pearly whites (before my insight about Doctoring the Image), I was more than "pretty." I actually lay claim to being quite a beauty in the day. I have not belabored this point thus far as I feared some might find it alienating, boastful, or superficial. But being a *former* beauty is a part of the arc of my life story. Unfortunately, it did not necessarily affect me in a positive way, in this beauty-obsessed culture of ours. Yes, I have benefited from my looks, just as I have benefited from this white skin in which I so conveniently walk the earth. I have found myself on the favored end of the prejudice against all that is the opposite of me, physically (not counting the rampant sexism we have not yet fully exorcised from society). At the same time, however, I have, in prior years, been seen *only* as a "pretty thing," on a very superficial level, unable to find appreciation for anything like, oh, intellect or wit. And I allowed myself to be perceived as such for much of my youth, content to slide along on the free ride offered unto me. And then I discovered the writer within my lovely bosom; unfortunately, I discovered Hand Job quickly thereafter and refocused my lens on him, oblivious to the fact that we all bring familial psychodramas into relationships, familiar as such little plays are. And the bulk of parental toxicity comes from their expectations being at odds with the reality of what a child in fact becomes, therefore instilling in that child a constant sense of failure and insecurity. My daddy called me a "jewel," society confirmed it, as did the mirror. Perceptions and expectations. A true double whammy.

I, like so many of you, dear bibliophiles, have allowed myself to be poisoned by the perceptions and expectations of others by attempting to live up to same; as opposed to—not *finding* myself (as Mr. Scarpete so errantly insists upon doing)—but *deciding* who I was/am/shall be. And look at the primary sources of those hopes in moi: a thoroughly insane mother, a mostly passively clueless alcoholic father, and a narcissistic sister bent on sabotage. Is it any wonder I had to spend a few decades working through that psychological morass by attempting to replicate it? First by marrying, for no cogent reason, a couple of passive alcoholic types; later by putting the whole package together (insanity *and* addiction) as manifested in Hand Job. One of my many therapists posited that, while most women have "daddy issues" to work through, I, in my marriage to Hand Job, was primarily working on "mommy issues," such as attempting to understand insanity in order to get to the real expectations beneath the insanity. Another shrinker of the head insisted that my aim was to "cure" Hand Job, thereby "curing" both my father and my mother, who are, to this day, oblivious to the real me. Yet another picker of the brain says I deserve to be a little loopy, given the path I have traveled. Who's right? Probably all of them, but I rather like the latter, which, translated, these days, says to me: Who cares? What difference does it make? What really matters right now?

What matters less and less to me is the aforementioned beauty I so casually possessed in years gone by. For there is nothing more pathetic than an aging beauty—as opposed to the beauty of aging naturally, and I do look forward to the day I wean myself from Miss Clairol, put away the self-consciousness of cosmetics, and simply be the totally real deal. Remember: No "work". Plastic surgery gives one the look of death, for it is death one is attempting to escape. Not only won't the escape be made, but all those procedures are going to make for a very grotesque and hideous corpse. I highly recommend a closed casket if you have had more than a little "work" done. But better yet, refuse to participate in the denial of death. Have a die-in. Start another political party—the Old Outlaw Party. *Something.* We are the Boomers— come on! We made everything that ever became cool, cool. Can we not make growing old the coolest? Why, certainly we can. Together, we can decide anything.

But alone, well, we can still decide anything. Who knew?

So celebrate the tell-tale signs of growing elder. I, like you, walk around in my shell each day, perceiving myself as having the appearance of my twenty-something self. Then the mirror reminds me that it is forever gone. One could decide to forfeit mirrors, but there are too many other surfaces of a reflective nature that would interfere with that huge bit of denial. And so I have begun my sentence-writing strategy in a commitment to re-programming the old gray matter to refrain from degrading its vessel, my physical container. It truly is proving to be tres effective, and I recommend it with oodles of thumbs-up enthusiasm.

As per previous instructions, the phrasings that will surely render one impervious to degrading designations will be unique to whatever individual shell is telling the tale, whether it is merely being revised or wholly rewritten. I only offer the examples below, culled from my scores of notebooks, to point you in what I trust to be a healthy direction:

- The greening veins that map my thighs are vestiges of delicious adventures and elegant escapades.
- The wrinkles framing my lovely eyes give form to the fact that I continue to see so much that is beautiful.
- The bountiful flaccidity of my lounging breasts attests to the singing admiration of suitors past and present.
- The browning spots upon the backs of my hands are the autumn leaves of my ever-evolving flesh.
- My feet with their patrician ankles are as lovely as they ever were, decorated now with lacey blood lines.

- I have a youthful spirit, and humor and laughter breathe new life into it every single day.
- One day soon I shall cast off the color and go supremely, glimmeringly gray, turning heads in admiration as I go.

Again, you get the idea.

I say all of this to get to the bottom-line, true-life, slut-ism that is this: I refuse to let my story write me; I shall write my own story. It won't be perfectly told—not at all. As I peruse and re-peruse this tome of poetry, social commentary, and self-help of mine, I stumble upon linguistical flaw after stylistical flaw. In several places the writing is uneven, even awkward—yea, on the edge of "bad." One editor says my metaphors seem to have been tossed into a Cuisinart and set on high, mixed as they are. Another fusses that I break rules of grammar and invent my own spellings of words to my detriment. I care not. I want my words to be as original as I am—and I am certainly nothing if not "mixed." Are not we all? For in other places in this manifesto for the postmenopausal set I find the verbal rhythm, symbolic coherence and wonderful wordsmithing which combine to signify more that a few visionary visitations to that sacred place to which the tennis players of the 1980's fondly referred, their eyes going dreamy with the perfection of this kinetic kingdom, as "the zone." It is the convergence of all things not only right, but supremely sublime. It is the hand of some god or another buffeting one's way through one's chosen calling. It is, simply, for one who writes, nothing shy of Nirvana.

Do a little exercise if you are a half century or older—or even younger. Take an appraising look back over your life thus far (for every life begs to be examined), and you will see the same things seen by yours truly—rough patches, smooth patches, horrible patches, and supreme patches—all quilted in random and jagged swaths, or falling into a clean-edged diamonded pattern, or, most likely, a bit of both. If you have had no adversity (i.e., jagged pieces) I would maintain that you can have no real understanding, of yourself, of others—certainly a dearth of empathy, which is the apex of emotional and social intelligence. Admittedly some have had more hardships and tragedies than others; unfortunately for the rest of us, some seem to enjoy their hardships and tragedies more than others ("misery addicts," I call them), as they make a point of wallowing in regret and "what if?" Some of the readers of my rather un-somber little confessional might advise me to do a bit of wallowing, but I long ago decided that a good Slut does not believe in regret. Sluts celebrate adversity by acknowledging it, having a cry, kicking its ass, and moving on, all the better, all the stronger, for having experienced it, awful as it initially felt.

And so, as the author of my own story, I say life has been rich and gets richer by the moment. Yes, I was authored by others for many, many years. And, having been the main character(s) in my life I have identified as several folks who were not me: a disappointing daughter; a persecuted sister; an intellectually insecure beauty queen; thrice a shallow, selfish ghost of a wife; for twenty years a waylaid wife of a crazy ghost; a token teacher; a self-loathing real estate salesperson; to name but a few.

Who am I, really?

I know this answer.

I am a friend, first of all. Friends matter more than anything; if chosen well, good ones last longer than any husband(s) and come with none of the baggage of family. I feel fortunate in that I have chosen well.

I am also a writer. I am a writer who did not migrate to New York but stayed in my beloved Southeast and found an independent publisher (I do so love the notion of "independence") who "gets it" more thoroughly than many women of an age, having lived it, as have I.

And, of course, I am a woman of an age. I have many more luxuries than twenty- and thirty-somethings. I do whatever the hell I want to do. If I want to spend the weekend in my pajamas, tapping away on the laptop, and take not a single bath or shower for those three days, then that is what I do. If I want a decadent dalliance on a summer's afternoon, I eat that peach. If I want a thick piece of strawberry cheesecake, I eat that as well—and I will add chocolate syrup and whipped cream, thank you very much. Witness said attitude in verse:

Of an Age

Let the mindless diet freaks run shrieking from this fright
Confections, icings, glazes, fillings give their flat feet flight
Let them pinch their waists and choose to pass when offered cake
Let them self-deny, turn down, miss out, and not partake
Of choco-drizzled candies, stiff-creamed dreams, all buttered, battered things
Frapped freezes, sweet fruit squeezes, and key lime a la king
I am of an age whose days are moving into a sunset
When sensual sugars are certain to be a celestial vignette
An age whose body image suffers not with ten pounds or two
Whose earthly pleasures sparkle sweet with divinity's déjà vu

Yes, with age comes more and more freedom. And if I want to spend time with the occasional single male, even keep him around after the aforementioned dalliance for several days, weeks, months, or beyond, that is what I shall do.

That current single man continues to be Mr. Scarpete, with whom I have, aside from some spirited banter, quite a calming relationship free of drama and brimming with rather steamy sex. I can feel some of you doubters squirming, thinking I should mind my earlier thoughts about heeding the old caution light at the intersection of Playing It Safe and Throwing Caution to the Wind Street. Tsk-tsk-tsk—wouldn't that be a black and white choice? Have you learned nothing?

No, never fear, dear, dear, peruser of my words. I am only going out to play, not making a play for anything, gasp, serious. I am having a banter, a tiny tour, a blush of wine, a vignette of an adventure, an exquisitely palate-pleasing nibble of another divine moment in life, for verily, life shall come to an end one day. And, if this man is indeed my soul mate, then he shall be there at the end, unless, of course, he reaches the jumping off place ahead of moi.

No, death I fear not, as Sluts do not fear (unless they possess a trifle of the agoraphobic bent as do I). In fact, if things go as planned, I shall die a good death in my great-grandmother's spool bed, situated in the sun room of my homey home, so that I can watch the birds play at the jasmine vines. I shall bid my dear best friends, those who are meant to survive me, farewell.

There is to be no deadened and morose funeral with dirges and long-winded prayers. Instead, my friends shall host a party here on the Waterhole Branch of Fish River, with music by Grayson Capps and the Lost Cause Minstrels, toast upon toast upon toast of whatever libations are desired. Micah will bring his jewel-collared cock, Cogburn, and walk him about the attendees before delivering, along with one Reverend Dr. T.L. Butts, a bawdy eulogy over my ashes (coffins are an utter waste of money; cemeteries are not eco-friendly whatsoever, as land will become more and more scarce with the Malthusian bumps in the human population).

Finally, the guests, with colorful Dixie cups, will scoop my ashes from a large, Tupperware bucket (up until that moment sealed and burped to keep in the freshness), then scatter them about the Branch—in the water, along the bank, beneath the elegant oaks dripping the Spanish moss that laces every breeze, within the sound of the scores of wind chimes that tinkle and gong and clatter and clink in swells of the chatter of creativity. And, as befits any good, well-done Slut after living clean (enough) and honest, I shall mingle with the heavens, with the celestial circle of life, in sensual, spiritual ecstasy, waltzing on some nether plane with Jesus, Elvis, and Lao Tzu.

Conclusion

I fear a conclusion might weaken the potency of the last sentence of Chapter 13, a sentence my editor utterly *adored*.

Afterword

You will note how drastically my attitude toward the "bibliophilic accessories" has changed from the front to the back of this tome.

And the change goes on.

Post Script

I love you.

Future offerings from Ruby Pearl Saffire:

The Unauthorized Biography of Ruby Pearl Saffire, by Ruby Pearl Saffire, as Told to Herself: A Memoir

Stews, Soups, Sauces, Dips, Drinks, and Decadence: A Slut's Guide to Good Eating

Parenting: If You Insist Upon Having the Little Monsters, Well, At Least Raise Them Like This

Exposed: The Public School System /NCLB: No Child Learning Bumpkis

The Fall of the Nixon Administration: A Comic Novel (I hope to co-write this one, with Suzanne Hudson and her late friend Catherine Caffey Gardner)

Shoe Burnin' Season: A Womanifesto . . .

(the tenets of which, are in bold-face type, for those aiming for a bold-face type of life)

AND that, as they say, was that . . . until I began submitting, angling for feedback, acceptance, and, please god, a contract. After all, there was now a completed manuscript for *Second Sluthood*, a treatise I was convinced that, with the appropriate advertising and salesmanship, might be a nice little financial whoopee cushion, as I rambled into retirement. And lo, the desired acceptance came. It came in the form of one Bohemia Burgmeier—yes, *that* Bohemia—she of the fancy-schmancy publishing world, who, right off the bat, actively sought me out, threw herself into my world, and proclaimed that she was altruistically dedicated to making me famous. It was the autumn of 2007 . . . on the eve of Shoe Burnin' Season . . .

Alright, so I *invited* her into RPS world, as she was the only real, albeit exasperating, connection I had made. I sent her, via snail mail, the completed *Second Sluthood*, here between these covers, and a copy of a manuscript in progress, a novel, *The Fall of the Nixon Administration*, which is not, again, by the way, about politics but is my aforementioned and as promised recounting of the savagery of my relationship with my monster—um, mother (and is actually based on a short story by Suzanne Hudson, who has agreed to co-author with me, along with the late Catherine Caffey Gardner, from the spirit world). A mere three weeks later I answered a knock upon my door.

"It's brilliant," she declared, in a most flattering change of tune. "And I will handle *everything*: agenting, publicity, management. Trust me. I know the biz. You're a mere babe in the woods. Clueless." She flipped her long, straight, New-York frosted blonde hair and tapped the toe of a red-soled stiletto. "What do you say? Never mind—just let me say it: You're welcome! Yep—I'm a stinkin' genius. Enjoy."

Business has never been my forte, so I agreed, in spite of her rather jarring boastfulness. She took up residence in an out-building on The Branch, a place where I often scribbled my words onto legal pads, a place my friends and I referred to as "The Writers' Shack." Bohemia immediately dubbed it "The Carriage House," and announced that she would "pretty it up."

"Enough with 'shacks' and overtly gothic southern references. We're creating a certain look, a certain image here," she said by way of explanation. "More genteel, you know. I'm prepping for investors and press, and I know what I'm doing. We have to dress to impress, that's all there is to it. Money attracts money. Don't you worry about a thing. I've got this."

"But Southern is what I am, and kind of gothic. That is, I was simmered in a roux that can't be denied."

"Let me worry about how you're presented in public," she ordered, flipping her from-a-bottle mane again. "I'll create the brand that *is* Ruby Pearl Saffire. Deal?"

Not knowing balls about brands, I heard myself say, "Deal."

It was only the beginning of my subverting my instincts and my principles, throwing them under the Bohemia bus of flattery, self-importance, and derision.

Yes, dear reader, it *was* a sudden change of the ether, Bohemia's out-of-the-blue and intense interest in my scribblings, my willingness to submit to her supposed and self-espoused expertise. I figured I had tried everything else I knew to try, so my openness to a new tack should not be altogether surprising. After all, I was already retired, prior to her . . . invasion, and I was ready to get back into literary world with a vengeance, having abundant time on my hands to write *and* promote. Plus, I could use a bit of rental income from her, which soon vaporized into a "bartering" system under which she proclaimed that *she* was the prolific giver.

"I do everything, all of this, for you, RP, because your work should be known in the world. And I'm making that my mission. You are a great southern writer."

New tenet: Flattery will get you everywhere, it seems. But it absolutely should NOT.

"Flattery bullshit," Marble opined. "This bitch is a con with a capital 'C'." Hmm, perhaps Marble,

314

who had dug some gold her own self, could recognize a fellow digger of said ore.

By this time, Bohemia had been a fixture for close to a month, spending the days yammering on her cell phone to potential publishers, currying favor with possible backers, brainstorming marketing schemes, obsessively engaging in Facebook world, proclaiming that social media was the be-all end-all of putting it out there. In short, she was doing all the things I found so distasteful. It was a relief to have someone who was willing to roll in the mud on my behalf, a sentiment about which my dear set of peeps had mixed opinions. Yes, my reliable and rock-solid band of merry sluts, The Dirty Half Dozen, had now become . . . The *Baker's* Dirty Half Dozen, thanks to Bohemia. But, thanks to the same, they were not particularly merry about it.

"Pushy, bossy, loud—those are the nicest adjectives I can come up with to describe her," Marble would fume.

"Not a subtle or a classy bone in that body," Diamond added. "Am I the only one who thinks she just makes things up as she goes along?"

Opal, who had, early on, befriended "Bo," as she preferred to be called, would jump into defense mode. "It's like my late husband always said, 'you need some cutthroat either in you, or around you,' and now you've got it! And thank goodness for Bo is all I can say. She even named me one of her 'grave diggers'. It's all about loyalty."

315

Bohemia's "grave diggers" was a small band of blessed-by-Bohemia, likely cowed by Bohemia, absolutist devotees of Bohemia, upon whom she could reportedly count if she ever did a for-real murder, proclaiming that "Those are the true friends, the loyal ones who'll help you hide the body."

I must go on the record here, to say that while I found her talk of grave diggers somewhat humorous at first, over time I began to take it in a darker vein, as in the workings of a criminal mind. My own true friends, in the hypothetical instance of my committing murder, would rally round me for an intervention, insisting that I confess, own up, turn myself in, do the time, repent, rehabilitate myself, all that good juju which is the real and true and honest measure of friendship. Bohemia was deeply damaged, at best; demonic, at worst. Too bad it took so long for me to see the light. But, regret be gone!

Regarding grave diggers, Micah would concur. "Those 'grave diggers' are just a bunch of stupid sycophants whose job it is to suck up to the succubus. They are Queen Bee's hive of female drones, whose purpose in life is to make the hive cozy. I swear, that woman has the most narcissistic need for control I believe I've ever seen. Not many women—or men, for that matter—ever make it to the 'cunt' category in my estimation, but that thing is the epitome of every coarse word for 'vagina' that ever was. She's a veritable Roget's entry."

"Tell us how you really feel, Micah," Emerald said, having withheld her own judgment, as per her training.

Bo, at the same time, had no qualms about trashing my friends to me, referring to Micah as "a bitchy little queen" and Marble as "gold digger Barbie." When I attempted to defend them, she was overpowering in her pronouncements. "You are so naïve, R.P., and I've been around the block repeatedly. They are simply horrible people, especially those two—and they say horrible things about you. You just don't understand them like I do."

On some level I recognized the bait I was being tossed, so I refused to take it and simply changed the subject, learning the lesson well: one can't make a logical argument with an emotional bitch who is never wrong about, well, anything. But she was *my* bitch, and she was motivated to handle *my* career. Give a little, get a little, I thought.

By the three-month mark, Diamond was giving, all right—giving more voice to her reservations, but in the form of questions put unto me. "Are you really comfortable with her being so involved in your life? I mean, aside from the career."

"Sure I am. Do you know how much it would cost to hire someone to do all that she's doing?"

"I know, but—there seem to be some issues, with boundaries, in so many ways."

"You're getting a mite judgy, aren't you?"

She retreated, for the time being. Unlike Bo, my posse was loathe to be bossy.

My, that was a nice little rhyme.

I sought an opinion from Scarpete, who, unsurprisingly, was neutral about Bohemia, as in all things: "It is what it is. She is who she is. It will all come to be what it will be."

"Que sera, sera," I remarked. "Profound."

Scarpete made a smirk face.

"Well, I like her," Opal insisted, at yet another meeting of the "let's evaluate Bo" club. "She's a smart woman—and sophisticated—and looking out for your interests. I'm thinking of investing some of my own money into this publishing venture."

"Well, I turned her down," Marble offered. "I smell a snake."

Opal was unfazed. "Snakes smell?"

"Poisonous ones do," Marble snapped. "And she was all over me, in the beginning, once she figured out how much cash I can access—and when that didn't pan out, she moved on to you, Opal. Do not be scammed!"

"Oh, for goodness sake, she's not a scammer! She's helping R.P. get a book deal. It's wonderful!"

"I'll tell you what she's not," Micah pronounced. "She's not NYC. That's what I have a nose for—an NYC wannabe. Manhattan's crawling with them, with hair that color and designer pumps. Guaranteed, she's some kind of a bullshit artist."

"But without the art," Emerald chimed in.

"Okay, enough," Diamond sighed. "I surrender, because this is sick territory we're into."

"Meaning what?"

Another sigh, a very heavy one. "It's just that—well, she walked straight off the page of the DSM-V—well several pages, I'm thinking."

"Prithee, tell more," I queried.

"Can't. Not ethical."

Which gave me some pause . . .

"I'll tell you what *I* think," Emerald announced. "I think this calls for a private eye. You know anybody like that? A detective of some kind?"

Leave it to Emerald to put her finger right on the most obvious, most common-sensical, solution.

My man. My own private dick.

Speaking of such, Scarpete had been and was a perfect fit for me, blowing into and out of my life like a whisper. I had my freedom much of the time, then, a few times a year, for a few weeks at a time, I had as much attention to those much beloved "directions" as any man I'd known (biblically) could provide. It was a love affair to be sure, but neither of us had any intention of making it a burden, as in, the shackling of the wedding vows. At our respective ages, now bending toward seventy—my lord, seventy!—an easy companionship and a delicious sex life hit just the right sweet spot—or g spot.

However, after being around Miss Bo a couple more times, his rigid neutrality fell away a bit. "That is one bossy broad," was his sole remark, offered in his own, sort of, nonjudgmental kind of way.

I asked him to take it on, the case of Bo B., take it on in the professional sense, operating on facts alone. Scarpete loves himself some hard facts. "Sure, I'll do some digging," he said, devoid of drama, as usual, although he threw in a slightly caustic, "Grave digging."

Drama was getting to be more and more routine on The Branch, just as a stealthy feeling of unease had settled into my stomach-pit. The "I'm doing so much for you" had gradually become "You don't appreciate me" which then became "I can't deal with all of this stress" which occasionally devolved into abject martyrdom. Which had me mightily puzzled. Was Diamond right about Bohemia's state of mind? Was Opal's gut on the mark? Was I being conned?

It's a funny, funny thing—not. **Next new tenet: When you relinquish too much control of your life, you end up losing much of yourself along with it.** That is a kind of emotional law, or should be. The control of all things business and promotional had gradually seeped into most aspects of my day to day living, with Bo as omnipresent as a deity. She would burst through my front door, no thought of knocking, bellowing, "RP!" at the top of her Yankee voice, followed by, "What were you thinking!?" Which might be in reference to an off-hand remark made in one of the few interviews she had lined up for me. "You shouldn't have said that! If you say you're looking for a small publisher, then the big ones won't bite. My god, I don't know why I think I can trust you to put it out there the way it should be."

And, lo, the way in which it was put "out there" more and more featured Ms. Bo, herself, as the genius behind the scenes, her extraordinary eye for talent, her declaration that we on the Branch were "family," destined for artistic elevation the likes of which could not be rivalled. When she managed to get us in front of a book club or a civic group or a library meet and greet, she took to making rambling speeches about the sanctity of the talent she nurtured so gratefully, the stewardship of her calling, the honor of being the bearer of the next Faulkner or Tennessee or Flannery. She likened herself to a farmer who nourished the crops of talent residing within her client, me. She dutifully, lo, gladly subverted her own self-interests, sacrificing her own needs and desires, laying any selfish inclinations upon the altar of all things literary. Her descriptions were simmered in such sappy sentimentality that Micah also took to carrying around a barf bag. And the tears came so often and with such ease that Micah would declare, "What a crock! As in crocodile. She's as faux weepy as an overzealous drag queen."

I do hate emotional manipulation, and I dared to say such out loud to "Bo."

"How dare you!?! I got you placed in one of the most widely circulated magazines in the southeast! I put your name in front of more potential publishers than you've ever imagined. You're goddamned welcome!"

Whereupon the reptilian tears would ensue.

And such moments merged with more and more aspects of my life and choices. For example, I voiced the desire to adopt a shelter dog.

"Oh, no—don't do that; you never know what you're getting. A trash dog, maybe. I know people who show dogs. Rich people. I used to work for them. I can get you a retired show dog. A smart dog."

"That sounds good. I'd like a little lap dog who'll cuddle with me."

"I'm picturing a German Shepherd. Or maybe a Border Collie."

"Small dog?"

"Let me think about it and make some calls."

Of course, silly, rebellious me—I wandered into an animal shelter, locked eyes with a little Yorkie looking creature, and love was fallen into, on the spot. I named him Will Luckie, after a character in my *Nixon* novel.

Bohemia did not speak to me for a full week, striding about the property, summoning a carpenter to screen in one of the porches on the Writer's Shack—I mean, Carriage House. She kicked off her stilettos and painted it with an obsessive determination and fervor.

She then named the entire property and hung out a hand-painted sign: "Musings on the Branch," with live oaks stenciled on, Spanish moss flowing from their branches,

"Because certain people name their properties," she said.

"It's a mark of class," Micah drawled later, "if you're a Kennedy. I'm sorry, but she ekes the faint aroma of rubbish."

I approached her with caution. "You know, Bohemia, this isn't Tara," I tried, thinking her "Musings" name a mite pretentious.

"You just don't get that we're working on a *brand* here," she said, attempting to explain her prior snit. "It *matters* what the property is named. It *matters* what kind of a dog you have," she said, batting at Will Luckie, who earnestly attempted to lick her hand. "He has no discipline, and you could have had a show dog!" She swatted his nose.

Will Luckie yelped in pain.

"Do NOT hit my dog," I seethed, one of the few times I exercised my spine with her. She strode off and sulked the rest of the day.

But, she ultimately revived. She demanded that we have "strategy sessions" every other Thursday, unless she switched the meeting to a random Monday or a random any day. Basically, I was at her beck and call. It was at one of these sessions that she dropped her biggest bombshell. "I'm not feeling the 'Sluthood' thing. I know it's commercial and all, but *The Fall of the Nixon Administration* is good, solid, serious, literary writing." She flipped her flagrant locks. "If you want to be taken seriously, focus on *Nixon*. Forget about the other— or use a pseudonym."

"You think I can be a serious author?" Surf's up: I had just caught another huge swell of validation. **Absolute tenet: Hear me now and hear me plain:**

323

the ego is your vile and dedicated enemy; when it is stirred, you will go down a horrid path of self-degradation and ultimate humiliation.

"Of course you can. I'll take you there, guide you through it. *Everybody* needs to read your work."

My ego preened like the proverbial peacock, all the silken-feathered, rich-hued male plumage fanning out from my inner creative light. I was the bomb. I was spinning out a spectrum of talent that flickered like the NBC creature of my childhood.

Of course, it did not hurt that, by then, she had found a small publisher, Sand Bar Books, and they were interested in both manuscripts, to be published under my true name, as a two book deal, *Sluthood* in 2009 and *Nixon* in 2010, giving me a real reason to work ever harder on that second manuscript. Of course, big money was not an option, but just to be published . . . I was over the moon. And I wouldn't risk losing the chance by refusing to attach my name to both books.

"You are all just so wrong, wrong, wrong!" Bohemia pounded her fist on the table at the publishing office in New Orleans. "R.P.'s name cannot be attached to both books. They're too different. It'll fuck up the brand."

"Brand?" Banksy Benedict, the owner of the house, raised his brows. "What brand?"

He was a direct, no-nonsense, to-the-point kind of a guy, with very little inclination toward social niceties. Bohemia had networked him at some conference or another, claiming she could barely stand him until she realized he had a shit-ton of money invested in an independent publishing house. Then she was on him like the proverbial white upon the rice, wooing him and flattering him, and passing his obsequious little "loyalty tests" as she called them. "He calls them 'bread crumbs'," she confided one evening. "When you have that much money, you *have* to put those loyalty tests in place, to be sure who's trustworthy and who might be playing you."

I did not get up on my soap box about how petty and childish I find such games to be, having come to the conclusion that the vast majority of folks truly are good and decent and well-meaning. I don't take loyalty tests, and never have I administered them. If you live in a paranoid world of laying traps and drizzling bread crumbs, your soul is damaged, at best; you have none, at worst.

"R.P. *has* to have an advance," was the demand Bohemia opened up the next meeting with. "She is worth it. She'll sell books. You've simply got to cough up a pittance, $5,000."

"We're small," Benedict countered. "We could only do, say, $1,500."

"2,500 at least," she snapped.

I despise dickering and haggling and talk of the giving and getting of money; it feels beyond nasty to me. I felt my face blush with the heat of a Sahara. "Oh, no, really, I'm just happy to be—"

"Don't talk," Bohemia commanded. "Do. Not. Speak."

I clammed up. And she did manage to get me my unwanted and unnecessary advance, just like the big boys (only their advances are infinitely larger, with lots and lots of zeroes). Which brought us back around, yet again, to "the brand."

"I'm creating an image," Bohemia declared, "and I know exactly what it's supposed to look like. Nobody else has to know any more detail than that. I can manage this. But it will be ruined-- absolutely RUINED if you publish that Slutty book under her real name!"

"Kind of over the top, isn't it?" Diamond observed, lending the perspective of a psychologist. "Obsessive, controlling. Did you see 'Misery'? The Kathy Bates character?"

"Sure—Annie Wilkes, the number one fan."

"Not for long a fan. Because obsession is a double-sided coin, with devotion on one side and destruction on the other."

"Oh, come on, there's no danger of physical harm, here."

"Not until she takes a sledge hammer to your legs."

"Aren't you being unethical?"

"No. I have a duty to warn, all that—I have moved on and now stand on *those* ethics. You've got to kick her to the curb. Seriously."

"No, Diamond, I can't. I really do need her. I think she just takes things a little too seriously. The brand and all. She's a business person, after all."

"I love you, R.P., but, honey-girl," Micah drawled, "you aren't anywhere near big enough to be a 'brand'. And she's a dirty bird."

"Well, of course I have no 'brand'. Not now, but—"

"Sorry, R.P., you're dealing with a sick-o," Diamond insisted. "And she knows she doesn't have my vote because I've made no secret of it. Are you aware that she tried to tell me that you can't stand me?"

"What?"

"Don't worry about it. I didn't believe her for a second. She's straight out of the textbook, very easy to read. She wants to get in between you and anyone in your life who would challenge her. Classic abusive behavior. Triangulation worthy of an elementary schooler."

This gave me pause. Truthfully, I was not one to be managed and controlled. And I resented the attempt to alienate an old friend. I was not that person, to go along with such negativity. And yet, I had some pretty dysfunctional baggage, as do we all. And at its core was that primal need for approval, a happy dance of love for my wordsmithing.

Banksy Benedict won the battle of wills, of course, and I signed a contract for the two books, under my very own name. Bohemia sulked for a couple of weeks before declaring, "We'll just have to make the best of it. I've managed bigger crises than this. If I know how to do anything, it's how to be a 'fixer'."

"That's a goddamned gangster word," Micah said later. "The self-importance!"

"She did get me $2,500," I bleated.

"Chump change," he harrumphed.

"Speaking of money, I've loaned her five thousand dollars," Opal said. "Well, *donated*, really, not loaned. I don't need it back. It's for advertising your novel, to get the word out."

"My lord," Diamond exhaled, "how shamelessly exploitative can one person be."

"But it's not even published yet." I was mortified by Bohemia's tasteless ability to request money. I felt the immediate need for a whore-bath.

"Oh, let's see what she can do, RP. She's the expert around here. You're my friend and you're worth it. Besides," Opal went on, "it's not like I don't have a big ol' pile of it. Money, I mean."

"Well, Bo has a big ol' pile of something," Micah remarked, "and it's steaming."

"R.P.'s my—our—friend," Opal repeated. "And I want to help!"

I relented and dared not berate Bohemia, for fear of what was becoming her more and more frequent histrionic hissy-fits, wherein she slung her Jesus cross upon her back and made monumental declarations of martyrdom: "No one, absolutely NO ONE appreciates all that I do for this effort, this cause, for YOU, R.P. Least of all you!"

"Of course we appreciate you," I attempted. "And I try not to do things that upset your vision of all of this."

I know. It was all-around pathetic on my part.

The fan once again caught the shit when I, independently of Bohemia, got a super short and pixie-ish haircut. By this time, I had become conditioned enough to fear Bohemia's negative reaction.

"My god, RP, this has to stop," Diamond insisted again. "You're not a shrinking violet! Besides, have you not seen her own hair? She must be going on sixty, and that Shank of blonde Cher hair comes across as downright delusional."

"Delusional hair?"

"I'm telling you the looney bins are full of ladies with clownish makeup and dyed, straightened teenager hair who seriously believe they look beautiful."

"You really think she's that mentally unstable?"

"You know I can't diagnose in this way; you make the call."

Bohemia made the call instead. "It's too short! It's too short!" she yelled, squawked, really. "How could you?"

"Jesus, it'll grow back," I said in a feeble attempt to placate. Yes, I had fallen full-on back into dysfunction.

"You are such an idiot about business. It's the brand, stupid! My god, you are so goddamn clueless!"

And with each berating of my incompetent self, there withered a bit of my spirit. Looking back, I can say with certainty that Diamond was right; it was like being in an abusive relationship. Adored at one moment and admonished at another. **Big fat tenet: As an invincible, epically wise little old lady, verily I say unto you: the chipping of the spirit, when done in teeny-tiny taps, is an insidious**

stealth assault, and when carried out by a Machiavellian narcissist, one can be certain the motives are always fed by self-interest.

And that, my beloved bibliophiles, is exactly what my disheveled dick discovered.

But first . . .

Just now, as I tapped out the "Machiavellian narcissist" descriptor there came a wave of insight. And what a fool I am for having missed the obvious parallels between my dealings with Bohemia and our current Bully in Chief, our own Dear Leader. For just as Bohemia's lingering chokehold on my doings was coming a-loose, albeit a full seven years after the trauma, and I was on the brink of penning this *Womanifesto*, the political season of 2016 was raining down upon us.

I was appalled, of course, that a sub-human with the vocabulary of a third grader, the maturity of a fifth grader, and a frat-boy attitude toward women was a serious contender for Commander in Chief. Even Opal was conflicted about it.

"Do you think he could do it? I mean, he'll get really good, smart people to help him, right?" Her eyes were actually pooling political tears.

"He'll get the smartest people," Micah spat out.

On the other hand, and somewhat surprisingly, Marble's conservative bent had shifted to dictatorial certainty, and to such an extent that she even sported a "Make America Great Again" cap. "I like it—he's a businessman and a gazillionaire—not a politician. It's about time we made a change. A big one."

"Oh, it'll be 'bigly'," Micah deadpanned.

Emerald and Diamond merely glared. For the first time, ever, I feared for the cohesiveness of our tight little girlie-gayly group. Our political discussions had always been lively and playful, but there was some kind of a dark undercurrent here, not unlike that of Rip Tide Bohemia. I tried to smooth away the tension.

"Come on, Chickies, I'm the rabid one here— well, rabid liberal. Marble, you're not allowed to be rabid. I swear, reality is turned all inside out and upside down."

But Emerald was not having it. "I don't see how any friends of mine can honestly call themselves comfortable on the same team as white supremacists and Klan members and the nuttiest conspiracy folks in the whole damn fruit basket!"

"Not to mention pussy-grabbing," Diamond chimed in.

Not that I disagreed with them, at all. But there were solid, long-term friendships sending out "at stake" signals here. Was it worth it? Politics? Really?

"As I've said repeatedly, I know this seems unethical," Diamond posited, "but I'm with that group of mental health professionals who have diagnosed him with Narcissistic personality disorder. And I'd throw in some sociopathic behavior, borderline personality, and who knows what else. A veritable gumbo of mental illnesses and disorders."

"Whatever," Marble spat out. "As long as it isn't Crooked Hillary. She's pure evil."

Yes, Marble parroted the "Crooked Hillary" moniker, just as Ye Olde Brainwasher intended. I could not hold back. "And probably one of the most investigated politicians ever—and with a stellar resume—and, hello? A woman."

"RP, you know a vote based on gender alone is shallow," Marble replied.

"Oh, did I mention the stellar resume?"

"He's just not . . . *dignified*," Opal sighed, awash in her southern sensibility. After all, one should never, ever, be—gasp—rude. "I mean, the crude language, the name-calling—I—I just don't know if I can *do* this. He's so lacking in—class. I can't."

"Well you have to," Marble insisted. "We have to get the country back."

"From whom?" Emerald demanded.

"From all the brown people," Diamond said, "because soon they will control things. You really think you can take it back?"

"No, honey," Micah jabbed, "that slave ship has sailed."

"Cheap!" Marble hissed. "That is so damn cheap!"

"I don't see color!" Opal declared, as she is wont to do, retreating into the all too familiar defensive crouch that unaware racists employ.

"Apparently you don't, sweetie, because that scarf and that skirt just do not *go*," Micah drawled, making enough laughter time for me to swoop in, as the Queen of Slutdom, and decree that politics was to be banned for the foreseeable future and that furthermore, there was to be no gloating or editorial commentary, post-election. Until further notice. Hear ye, hear ye.

Of course, as tip-top keyboard tapper, I am free to editorialize into the next decade. Such is the life of a writer. On election eve, I slept with one ear on the television, and, upon hearing the winner declared in the wee hours, proceeded to uncork a bottle of chardonnay and, in sheer shock, swilled wine into the next afternoon. Denial soon set in, and it was long past the inauguration, replete with manufactured crowd sizes, dicey body language between the Pussy-Grabber in Chief and Melano—I mean, Melania, and the staffing of the White House in Orwellian "up is down and down is up" fashion, before I truly felt the shock and awe of what happens when our citizenry abdicates its responsibility and chooses an entitled, petulant, impulsive, lying, bullying nimrod as leader of the free world.

And from day to day a new low is achieved, whilst left-leaning, lo, center-holding folks wonder: What if?

What if Obama boasted about grabbing women by the ass?

--now change that to "by the pussy"

--screwed and paid off a porn star?

--and a Playboy bunny?

--insulted war heroes? Mexicans? The disabled? Etc.?

333

--SEPARATED CHILDREN FROM THEIR PARENTS?

--kissed the asses of dictators and the likes of Putin?

--incited violence?

--incited racism?

--claimed he could do murder and still be beloved by his "base"?

--and on and on and on and on and . . . there's bound to be a paid for abortion or two out there, in a forest of sexual conquests and golden showers . . . and while I don't care about one's personal life on the one hand, well . . . it's the hypocrisy, stupid!

Shame. Shame is always the primary/initial emotion of one who has been conned. You were conned, America (well, a minority of you were). Now wear that shame—especially you, Fundamentalist Christian people—shame especially and exquisitely upon you, for you are the epitome of a hypocrite and a bastardized follower of the Jesus. In fact, you wouldn't recognize The Christ if he bled all over your ass.

And speaking of . . . right now, in my redneck of the woods, there is a delusional "preacher" man who is babbling in tongues, fretting over how the "witches" and their "witchcraft" are out to crucify Dear Leader!?! And what sub-human dots were connected to produce such a fiction? Did the dumb as dirt preacher-guy simply make a loose association between our so-called "president's" daily protests about the "witch hunt" and the Dark,

Satanic arts that are behind, oh, let's say, Halloween and that chip-porn-producing-in-a-pizza-parlor-basement (only there was no basement, let alone the absurd child porn ring) Jezebel called Hillary?

So my own personal Crazy Town was later paralleled by that of our nation, which had been finessed, grifted, deceived, played, hosed—yes, CONNED.

But I get it. I see how it can happen, this "con" thing. You're flattered, told how great you are—how great you could be—if only you will let some wonderful Somebody take care of things for you. Someone who knows all the answers, is the greatest, who never makes mistakes or gets things wrong, who certainly never needs forgiveness, not even from God. Bohemia, indeed, conned me, just as The Donald conned a segment of this country.

Meanwhile, going back in time, Scarpete's digging into the life of the psycho known as "Bohemia" turned into quite the eye-opener.

"Yeah, this broad's a piece of work, I'm telling you. Get this: her real name is Mindy Minchew."

"More alliteration. That's good, I suppose."

"Born in Heartland, Ohio. Raised by parents until they divorced, when the subject was eight. Mom never, ever abandoned her. There *was* an Auntie Em, but she did none of the child-rearing. She doted, though, singing the praises of upward mobility."

"The American Dream."

"The American Goddamn Dream."

"Took myself a little trip to Heartland, population 3,228, where everybody knows everybody's private business."

"The American Nightmare."

"By all accounts Miss Mindy's mom is a delightful person, not at all the horrible beast described by her daughter. Interesting factoid: Mom routinely warns folks not to befriend Mindy, characterizes her own daughter as 'a pathological liar'."

"Whoa," Diamond exhaled. "That is some harsh shit. But mother knows best, I suppose."

Scarpete continued, "Mom remarried five years later, which pissed the subject to high heaven, because it's all about her, according to her hometown acquaintances. So, when mom re-married, Miss Mindy was furious, let it be known that she did not approve, never accepted her stepfather. Our gal wanted out, and married right out of high school, knocked up, to a high school sweetheart from a well-heeled family; his family disapproved and held back on the trust fund, so it didn't take long for the subject to drive that poor guy into bankruptcy. Left the girl baby with the dad and hit the road."

"Nice," Diamond murmured. "That's a nifty bit of projection: claim your mother abandoned you when in actuality you abandoned your own daughter. Classic."

"Next marriage was to a wealthy architect in Chicago," Scarpete went on. "One Brooks Smelty. Divorced him three years later, claiming physical and mental abuse. By all accounts, though, she was the abusive one, prone to hysterics and some physical shoving. Mr. Smelty had a restraining order against her. She apparently stalked him and his money, made out like a bandit in the divorce proceedings. Paid cash for a house on the Atlantic Ocean and lived off the money for a decade or so, then went into the dog grooming business."

"Hard to picture that," I said, thinking of how she had "disciplined" my Will Luckie.

"Didn't do well at all. That's when she plugged into the literary circuit. Became assistant to a series of authors, never held a job for more than a year. Difficult to work with."

"No shit."

"Still she managed to impress enough Big Cheeses that she was invited to certain conferences and such around the country, coming up with gimmicky productions authors could plug into—for a fee, of course, to the publishers or to themselves. It's been about ten years ago that she started presenting herself as a New York editor and agent. Musta made thousands fleecing would-be authors for her, let's say, untutored advice."

"What, no college degree?"

"None."

"Junior college?"

"That's a negative."

"Not even a business school certificate in marketing or some such?"

"Nada."

"Come on. A two-week workshop?"

"Ix-nay."

"This is fucked up."

"Yeah," Scarpete conceded, "but there have been unschooled cons who have practiced medicine, under the radar, so it's not new."

"And nobody notices?"

"Oh, they notice, all right. I interviewed a dozen people or so who worked with her, knew her, etc. Here are some quotes: 'massively insecure,' 'often plays the victim,' 'erratic,' 'emotionally immature,' 'manipulative,' 'controlling,' it goes on. She does have a hard core group of devotees, not as solid as the 'grave diggers' but loyal in the face of hard evidence of the flaws."

"Not unlike a certain autocrat in the White House and his very base, crude, rude, and disgusting base."

"Right. But the toadies do tend to peel away over time, then she gets a new batch of suck-ups. Loves to think of herself as a Big Shot. A legend in her own mind. But definitely on the move more often than the average bear."

"Any other marriages?"

"Not as far as I could tell. There have been a series of men, though. She mostly goes for real estate guys, the kind with lots of commissions, especially when she moves to a new place, which happens fairly often. A few of them have actually offered homes for her to live in."

"What's in it for them?"

"Good question. At least one of them evicted her when she took up with a musician, some guy she hit the road with for a time. She typically stays in a place long enough to sniff out the cash, make wealthy alliances, come up with schemes to promote herself, mainly, helping along a core group of loyalists, then, once she's 'found out' for the fraud she is, she moves on, runs away."

"What is going to become of my book, then, if that happens?"

"It'll be fine," Marble said. "The contract is signed; it's coming out within weeks."

"But don't I need her help?" Clearly my Stockholm Syndrome was dug in.

"Sure," Scarpete said, "if you believe her phony press releases."

"She hasn't done anything," Diamond declared, "that any one of us couldn't do, even better. For one thing, you kinda need those all-important 'people skills' if you're in a line of work *that deals with the public*."

Micah laughed, "I bet that bitch's report card had 'does not play well with others' marked on it starting on day one of nursery school. That thing is a bad seed."

And so it was that I screwed up my courage. Not a fan of confrontation, I was nonetheless going to have to confront. I had barely gotten the first few words out: "I can't continue to—"

"I knew it! I knew you'd turn on me, just like everyone does. I've done all this work, gone out of my way, and all for you. You don't appreciate a goddamn thing!"

"Of course I do but—"

"I know what you think of me. And I'm not crazy! I've never eavesdropped on you and your friends! I'm not a liar! I'm not a thief!"

And I pondered: WTF? Diamond was always talking about projection, that anytime fingers were pointed and judgment rendered in an emotional state, it was very likely that self-revelation was on display. Had this woman stolen from me? She certainly had not repaid any "loans" of living space or of my friends' money. Had she literally stolen any possessions of mine?

There ensued an hour-long rant followed by a crowbar taken to the screen porch she had built, dismantling it completely and setting the pile of lumber on fire.

My peeps and I watched from the within the confines of my home.

"Call the police," Marble urged. "She can't destroy your property like this. Press charges."

"Shhh, Marble! R.P., I get what you're doing, completely," Diamond said.

"What is she doing?" Opal said.

"She's gauging the crazy," Diamond said. "She's seeing how far this person—this Mindy—will go for the sake of vindictiveness. And I've got to say, this is on the high end of the crazy gauge."

That was the moment that Micah dubbed Mindy/Bo the "psycho-cunt," a moniker that stuck "like cum on a pube." Micah would declare. That classy queen certainly has a way with words.

"Bohemia's" dramatic departure concluded with her mysteriously digging in the flower bed by my front door, followed by the loading of a rented SUV. We watched from behind the window curtains as she carried out a sentimental keepsake of mine, a small card catalogue from our school library, requested by me once the library went digital. It was a very personal reminder of the Age of Books, not to mention a meaningful token of my career, taken by someone who could barely hold down the occasional job, let alone have an entire career. I quite nearly confronted her about it, quickly deciding that it would only feed into her narrative of drama and hysteria. It was only an object, albeit sentimental. If she was ugly or sick enough to take it, then she could have it. Ashes to ashes. Cunt to cunt.

A great cloud lifted as she drove away. My friends and I burned incense and sage and chanted away the evil spirits that might be lingering, the fetid dark energy that might be thrumming among the tears of Spanish moss, the acrid toxicity of that succubus-like soul, all things dank and disheartening . . .

I did not think things could get worse, and yet . . . an unexpected phone call, just two weeks later, from Banksy Benedict at Sand Bar Books became the blow of all blows. "I'm really sorry this happened," he began, and my stomach pit dropped. Mindy, in the persona of one Bohemia Burgmeier, had made certain that an earlier, unedited version of my manuscript was sent to the printer, and the print run of 1,500 books was to remain in warehouse until they could be destroyed, so as not to sully the publisher's solid reputation. The book was chock-full of errors. It was a big financial loss for them, but surely I did not want a sloppy, unedited book out in the world, did I? Well, of course not. Insult heaped onto injury was the fact that they elected to release my rights for both books back to me, as they could not presently afford to do an entirely new print run on a thoroughly and better-edited manuscript. I should shop it around and maybe come back to them next year, or perhaps the year after that, once they bounced back.

It was devastating. My dream had been snatched away by a creature fueled by spite, the like of which I had never seen in an adult human either before or since. I was broken, crushed, mangled, knotted up, torn down, decimated, etc. And that is the stew in which I simmered for going on a decade, until approximately 2016, post-election. It's not that I totally shut down, crippled by depression or anything as serious as that, but my writing spirit was in crisis—paralyzed. Both manuscripts gathered dust on the bookshelf of life while I managed to have a pretty good time, roaming the back roads with my buds, reading, movie-going, participating all the joys of retirement, save one.

And then . . . there was . . . The Donald.

And my long-simmering, barely perceptible pain and anger rose up mightily in my soul, demanding to be purged via *A Womanifesto* that would settle old scores, force the truth into the Light, and squash a toxic bitch like the stinkbug that she was. The ironical fact that it took a person of her ilk, Donald Trump, to click the hair-triggers of my PTSD was not lost upon me. They were birds of a feather, two peas in a pod, a pot and someone calling the kettle black. So many parallels in this currently parallel universe!

Yes, like any other patriot, anyone else with a fierce love for country—or cuntry—I had to do *something*. Once again, ONE MORE TIME, my ashes found their Phoenix. I absolutely DO know how to do this—this coming-back-from-the-dead-a-la-Lazarus thing. Hallelujah!

A few months after Bohemia's histrionic and hissy-fitty departure back in 2009, Emerald noticed an unusual plant shooting up in my flower bed, right where Mindy/Bo had been rooting around. "I've never seen a plant like that around here," Emerald said, drawing on her gardening hobby.

But Micah knew right away what it was. "It's a corpse plant," he drawled. "Because it gives off the stench of rotting flesh as it blooms. That's why people don't plant them near their homes, because the flesh-rot smell inundates everything. The blooms are glorious, though. They bloom every few years in Central Park. Also called a 'voodoo lily'. Well, shut mah mouth, but I do believe the psycho-cunt is attemptin' to hex you. Bippety-bobbity!"

"She had to order the bulbs," Diamond said. "She prepped for this long before y'all officially fell out. Wow, she went to quite a bit of trouble and preparation to throw you some vindictiveness. Makes me wonder what else she's capable of."

"Well, if anything happens to me, you all know where to look for the murderer. I put it on the record, right here and now," I said. "And my steel-trap brained Scarpete knows exactly who the grave diggers will be."

"I'm not worried," Marble said. "All bullies and abusers are pure cowards when you get right down to it."

"Truly," Diamond agreed. "But in her case, it's a bit more demented. I think it was never about R.P. or her books or anything other than control and attention—that was the most pathologically controlling person I've ever observed, and I've seen some dandies. And the narcissism is epic. Shameless."

We dug up the voodoo bulb and transplanted to the back of the property. Over the seasons it has sprouted out pups in marvelous multiplication, mini-plants that my friends and I dig up, pot, and sell for twenty dollars each to raise money for one of Marble's charities. Our corpse plants are very much in demand around these parts. Good truly does come out of rot, if one puts in the appropriate energy.

Whenever we speak of it/her/"Bo" today, I resist the urge to connect the dots to our nanny-nanny-boo-boo, self-absorbed president. Instead, I draw upon the #metoo movement, a force of energy that I do so admire, the taking of the female spirit back unto the female soul, demanding justice.

344

Poetic justice is nice, too. I put my head together with Micah's queer eye to design a lovely t-shirt to commemorate this updated version of my *Womanifesto*. The front cover image—that of a male peacock, just because (and maybe a bit of a nod to Flannery) along with the title, on the front of said t-shirt; on the back, well, of course, the image of a glass of red wine—and a quote, plus three more lines:

"I survived Bohemia Burgmeier."
R.P. Saffire
#youtoo?

It is amazing the hordes of the wronged who have come from the woodwork, to bring their unbosomings to moi, to validate my experiences, and to sing in my vast chorus. It seems that Ms. Burgmeier really got around, like the skanky ho that she is.

As I have noted throughout this treatise, learning takes much repetition for most of us. And yet again, I had to recover from the muffling of my creative spirit, this time via the embrace of my writing self. **Ultimate tenet: And lo, I say unto you: you really, *really* don't want to piss off a writer. Writers will eviscerate you on the page at every turn. You will see yourself stripped naked of clothing, then stripped of flesh, then the meat will be scraped from the bone, leaving the skeletal remains of your former self to represent the worst of your lack of character.** Hand Job found that out. "Bohemia," too, will discover it. And I truly believe that this traitor of a president—he who embraces dictators and enemies, who fears and therefore excoriates the free press (that "fourth estate" so essential to democracy), and who lacks the character that god gave a cockroach—will "come to meet" the Jesus he is due to confront, and it won't be pretty, but it will end well for America. I am always and forever the Sunny Optimist.

Of course, I don't know if any of these bad actors will actually *learn* from their errors. I have the feeling that Hand Job is the only one with any hope of redemption, as he is capable of insight whereas the other two are not. I had hoped I had learned from my own mistakes, yet here I am, revisiting toxicity as I approached the age of seventy. Oh well. Cut bait. Fish. All that.

A few further updates:

The Dirty Half-Dozen, peacefully restored to its purest number, continues to abide, mostly in peace and harmony, but not without the occasional good-natured verbal sparring. After playing the field a bit, Micah has been seeing a delightful man for a couple of years now, and they are making it their mission to see that gay marriage becomes legal in the altered state of Alabama. The rest of us are skeptical but supportive—even Opal has come around a tiny bit, as have many, outside the south. Diamond, too, has been dating—a woman. It seems her lack of engagement with the hubby was a bit more complex than it seemed at first blush. It's called "sexual fluidity."

"Why are there suddenly homosexuals everywhere?" Opal sighed, one late afternoon. "On the TV, in my group of friends, everywhere?"

Like I said, she has come around a *bit*.

"Dear, the two places you named are hardly 'everywhere.' I assure you there are no more homosexuals now than at any other time in history. It seems we have evolved."

"Evolved into what?"

"Into more self-aware and accepting creatures. You love and accept both Micah and Diamond, correct?"

"Of course. But I just don't see why it has to be *everywhere*, like it's normal or something."

"Fuck normal," I said. "Normal is an arcane little 20th century notion."

Opal still has trouble from time to time, making some crucial intellectual leaps. For example, back when the long-ago election of 2012 drew near, she salivated and panted, not unlike an anxious dog, over her man Mitt, while Marble saw the Morman gazillionaire as one who would surely lead her people—the wealthy—out of bondage, glory hallelujah. But we continued to love them both.

Diamond and Micah were in full-panic mode at the thought of a Romney regime. "My *god*," Micah moaned, literally wringing his hands, "if that silver-haired *spawn* of his forbears' polygamist *sect* sneaks his gold-plated ass, all shrouded in his magic underpants, into the White House, what's to become of us? It'll be gay-mageddon!"

Imagine how he feels about a potential Pence presidency . . .

Emerald and I contended it was a win-win situation for us liberals. If Obama won, he won; and if he lost, one H. Clinton would win, and **big**, in four years. Surely the slow learning curve of the populace would have moved past repeating the same mistakes within the four ideologically mish-mashed years of a somewhat Romney term. But then, it might be a moot concern if the ice caps had fully melted and we were immersed in the apocalypse by then. Seems we were right. Until now.

How I long for Dubya!

Speaking of climate change, remember how panicked Opal was after Katrina? She has doubled down ever since, because, unlike too many of the mouth-breathing masses, she knows about the science supported climate change. In other words, she "believes in" global warming, as does anyone with half a brain (dear Opal *was* able to make this intellectual leap; she clearly has at least three-quarters of a brain). So, she plans to not only survive the tide of brown people amassing on the fringes of her world, she plans to also survive the tidal surge that will surely come with the melting of massive amounts of ice. I try to explain that it is most likely not going to befall her in this lifetime, but if it were, and if she really wanted to prepare, she should simply buy some property inland, as our little bit of coastline will surely be submerged—in a hundred years, give or take.

As I look back over these pages, I find a few ironies, not least among them the fact that I, who ran screaming from internetical world and all things bloggy, am now tapping out the final words of an e-book. Another striking irony is how much the publishing biz has changed in a relatively short time. **The bad-assest tenet: Agent? I don't need no stinkin' agent! And the same for traditional publishers, publicists, the whole lot of the vultures who feed off of the arts. Fuck 'em. Yo, "Bo," I am NOT "clueless," "incompetent," "useless," "naïve," or "sucky" at any of the business-related tasks at hand. You see, I actually know how to get along with folks, how to "play well with others." So fuck YOU, "Bo." I am Ruby, hear me roar.**

Also ironical is the teensy shift in the fashion biz I so excoriated in this (earlier) work. As we gluttons in America balloon into Obese Nation, I do declare I see plumper models on the runway and in the mags—occasionally, anyway. It gives one pause. And a bit of hope, for, as we descend into the poverty that will likely be with us the next couple of decades, we might find ourselves losing a pound or two. Let the people of China blow up into the fatties of the world, eh?

It just feels to me, about now, like a seminal evolutionary shift, a movement of the collective consciousness into a heightened state of empathy and goodness, in spite of The Donald (and Boris and Natasha). Perhaps we needed the "You're Fired!" guy to energize a final, decisive push into the future. Sure, there are still crazies and terrorists and goddamn reality shows on the tube that want to drag us all down, but it feels like, under the surface of it all, the human race is getting to a deeper level of understanding. The 20th century is truly gone, done, over with, and the 21st could be grand. Could be. Should be. If we get up off our fat asses and evolve, already. Women, by the way, included—yea, at the forefront, even.

Scarpete is much more cynical. He boils it down to three little words: "God's gotta go."

By which he means, religion is, along with money, the root cause of evil-doing in the world, wars included.

"Come on, sugar-spy," I argue, spiritually adventurous being that I am. "There's a big difference between mainline religion and the crazies who strap bombs on themselves."

"Not really."

"Pray tell, how can you say that with a straight face?"

"Maybe I should put it this way: No better."

Yes, dear reader, even today, I continue to have the occasional monogamous fun with this mysterious but uncomplicated man.

"What do you mean, no better?"

"The mainliners are no better than the crazies. One religion is no better than another. They're all a crock."

"Even if they are, which I would beg to differ with, they do get folks through life—or several thousand lives—or through the night."

"We know too much to believe that shit."

"Well sure, there is no way to take it *literally*. I mean, they've found the goddamned god particle. Hello. And DNA tells us we did not all descend from the same two humans. That is just a fact, but—"

"So no Garden of Eden, no Adam and Eve. No Adam and Eve, no original sin. No original sin, no need for Jesus. The whole thing is blown out of the water."

I want to make some kind of clever remark about walking on water, but I plow on. "Like I said, you can't take it literally. People who do are being willfully stupid. But spirituality is overarching. It's the collective mind. It's—"

"God's gotta go. Without the mainliners to enable the literalists, the world would be a better place."

"Yes, I would love for every stripe of religious terrorist to fall dead right this second, but let people have whatever warm fuzzy they need in the belief department."

"Enablers."

I sigh. "I do admit to having little respect for obviously made up, huckster-type religions, like scientology—and Mormonism, the obvious cultish ones."

"Which ones aren't cults?"

"Traditional ones. As in, thousands of years."

"They're just older cults." Here he chuckles. "And since when are you traditional?"

He does make me laugh. And that is really the essence of life, is it not? We all see those flat-affected faces of the down, the depressed, the humorless, the hopeless, the nay-sayers . . . the laugh-less. They are the undead, the zombies who do not care to or do not understand how to really live a life. Having stumbled into my fifties, revived, only to flag in my sixties, BUT now skipping toward my seventies, my little trek through this particular life is growing ever shorter. Spiritually bathed in the beauty of a peacock's plumage, though, is how I make ready for the next realm, the leaping into the lilt of love and humor. **Thus, the truest tenet for me: The essence of my soul (regardless of what one Scarpete atheist says) is growing ever brighter. Its light is laughter—multi-colored, full throated, delight-filled, from deep in the belly, laughter. It is that which is merely the voice of god.**

And I hope, truly, that these words, within this, my *Womanifesto*, bring out some of the laughter that sustains you. May you be blessed with good humor, good friends, gratitude . . . and grit. May the rich colors of a peacock's fine feathers fan your spirit with a light extraordinaire, a purpose unique to you, couched in years of sublime living, a divinity of the soul. And love.

Acknowledgments

I would like to thank all the "little people" who . . .

I kid.

I adore Jim Davis, of LA Book Fest fame, a clever wordsmith he. I thank you, Jim, for you know what . . .

Of course I always have line-editor-genius Jay Qualey (departed this earth, for now: here's to you, with a cold glass of cheap sweet red wine) read my work, and he was kind enough to make a list of all those edits that slid under the radar and into the paperback, via Bohemia—a to do list for this, my e-book and *Womanifesto*.

My artiste extraordinaire-cum-illustrious illustrator, Nancy Raia, did lovely work for the sabotaged book. Thank you, Nancy. Sadly, e-book readers will miss out on the artwork. You must Google Nancy Raia, dear readers.

My front cover artist, Linda Perry Ledet/Fidelis, is a genius and deserves heaps of gratitude. And back-cover artist Kevin D'Amico, though he is not fond of this particular work, will surely forgive my mentioning his talented butt.

And speaking of forgiveness, having bestowed as much on Bohemia Burgmeier as is possible, my heart is at ease, even with such residual vestiges of anger as befits one who has been wronged by a sociopath with no capacity for insight or the ability to apologize. Forgiveness is much more accessible when an apology, however hollow it is, is in the mix.

But I do thank her, for making me a much better writer. Cheers, Bo!

Oddly enough, I thank Hand Job. I thought it only fair that I share with him my intention of writing this book. I cannot say that he was tickled, but he did, rather begrudgingly, acknowledge that I must do whatever it is I must do in order to purge his betrayal from my poisoned system. Good on, Hand Job!

As for one Mr. Scarpete, I do not want to jinx our relationship by fawning over him in these lines. Besides, he would find it obsequious. Not that I give a good goddamn, but . . .

I thank my family (in passing), but it is the Dirty Half Dozen, they who hold me aloft, to whom I am most grateful. Friends, as noted within the pages of my little diatribe, are what really count, and my core crowd is impeccably and genuinely superb and superior to any friends who have gone before or come and gone.

Finally, thank you to all the aging sluts—ahem, *women*— out there, particularly the ones who have stood up as good, patriotic, red-blooded Americans and **bought this book**. God bless you, and God bless America!

God bless us, every one.

Addendum to the Acknowledgements

How in the world of literary prize winners could I forget to mention my magnificent mentor, Suzanne Hudson, she of the singing linguistical meanderings? Mea culpa, Suz! Of course, I am a fan. To say "number one fan" would be creepacious, though, as Ms. Hudson has had her own disturbing doings with a stalker or two. At any rate, I decided to request some impressions from my own posse and will let The Dirty Half Dozen join me here in speaking for themselves.

"Hudson is merely the baddest ass of all badasses. And, trust me, I know asses. You *must* go out and buy her deliciously wicked stories, collected in *Opposable Thumbs* and the more recent *All the Way to Memphis*."

Micah (Lang)

"As a woman of color I can honestly say that Hudson 'gets it.' She writes about race with the kind of truth-telling that I frankly don't often see when white folks attempt, say, to write black characters. Hell, my 'African-American' daughter especially loved Hudson's *In the Dark of the Moon*. She said there wasn't anything cute or contrived about the kind of 'revenge of the help' in this big fat book, a family saga that intersects the lives of generations in 20th Century southwest Georgia. Nope, it ain't cute and it ain't contrived. It's goddamned real—maybe too real for some folks, who'll NEVER 'get it'."

Emerald Gray

"*In the Dark of the Moon* is Suzanne Hudson's tour de force. It should be required reading; you should be required to squirm. If you don't, then you have no heart or soul."

Diamond Jones

"It's all great—her novel *In a Temple of Trees,* my personal favorite, is a compelling literary mystery shrouded in the secrets of intertwined families, with the intersection of the races simmered in the hunting culture of southwest Alabama, where, even today you can find pockets of the past in the backwoods. It was inspired by a real murder back in 1966, which led to a sure-enough investigation, which led to the prize-winning true crime book, *Murder Creek*, by Joe Formichella. How cool is that?"

Marble Gotrocks

"I squirmed, okay, Diamond? Yes some of it is really, really hard to digest, but in the end you're glad you did. Whatever violence or darkness or disturbing content there is, it really does lead to redemption, to salvation—and I'm all about getting saved. Praise the Lord. Peace."

Opal White

"Suzanne Hudson? She's likeable enough. Just not sure how I feel about fiction."

Scarpete

"She's a horrible person but a great writer."
Bohemia Burgmeier

THE END
(TRULY)